Tooth Decay With A Side of Fae

The Tooth Fairy Chronicles

Book One

Victoria Rocus

Serenade Publishing

For Victor...my Mo Shiorghra...my one and only... my now and always

GLOSSARY AND PRONUNCIATION OF ANCIENT OTHERWORLD GAELIC

Athair - (ă-hair) - "father" - when capitalized, used as a formal title

Bod - (bŭd) - "penis, dick" - slang word

Cac - (cock) - "shit" – slang word

Danu - (dă-new) - "Mother goddess" - ancient Celtic goddess of fertility

Duana - (dō-a-na) "dark and swarthy" - Duncan Fitzpatrick's secret code name

Gancanagh - (ghan-kan-ah) - "love talker" - Celtic incubus

Iasc Dearg - (yesk dearg) - "Red Fish"- a sport fish found in the streams of the Otherworld

I Idir - (ē ēdar) "In Between"- the Fae kingdom in the Otherworld ruled byThe Morrigan, Queen Maeve, as its monarch.

Leannain Siorai - (Yee- ann Shir-ee) - "Eternal Lovers"

Mac- (mc)- "son of"- a title given to an eldest son and heir of a Ruling House

Mag Turied - (măd twired) - "Plains of the Pillar" - a mythical battle in which King *Nuada* lost his arm and had it replaced with a silver one

Mathair - (mǎ-hair) - "mother" - when capitalized, used as a formal title.

Mo Chailin - (mō ha-lean) - "My Girl"

Mo Mhuirnin - (a whar-hean) - "my darlin" or "my sweetheart" - the name of Declan's horse in the Beltane *Stiopal* competition

Mo Shiorghra - (mō hear-gra) - "My Eternal Love" - a soulmate in magical Fae tradition

Nasctha - (nǒs-ka) - "bonded"- refers to "fated mates" in magical Fae tradition

Nuada - (new-a-da) - the name of an ancient Celtic king who possessed a silver arm; a major House from that bloodline within *I Idir's* Ruling Council

Ridre Dubh - (rid-ada dōv) - "Black Knight" - the "Hand of Justice in *I Idir"* and The Morrigan's right-hand counsel; a position currently held by the 27th Merlin, Theodore H. Beckett (Myrdynn)

Sidhe - (Shē) - the term used for the Fae race in Celtic mythology, as well as the forts and mounds they once lived in during ancient times.

Siobhan - (Shiv-awn) - a Celtic female name meaning "gracious gift"

Stiopal - (Stē-ōval) - "Steeple" - a equestrian race of skill held in *I Idir* during Beltane

Tir na Fathach - (tear na fa-ha) - "Land of the Giants" - mountainous property on the border between the Otherworld kingdoms of *I Idir* and Avalon, and currently under the care of House *Nuada*

Tuatha de Danann - (two-ha de dan-an) "The Shining

Ones"- a race of ancient, magically gifted Fae with royal bloodlines. They currently compose *I Idir's* ruling council under the Monarchy of The Morrigan, Queen Maeve

Ysbaddaden - (yes-badaden) - "Chief of the Giants"- a foreboding giant character from ancient Celtic mythology

TOOTH 1

MR. SNUGGLES

IT WAS ALL the cat's fault. Mr. Snuggles was the reason I found myself hiding under the plastic canopy bed in a Calico Critter's Country Cottage while that tabby demon swatted at me with scratching post sharpened claws. Nowhere in my orders was there even a mention that the house at 1628 Hollyhock Lane was under the protection of a Felis Catus. Assignments with this type of hazard were always assigned to Extractors at Molar level or higher. I was still a mere Deciduous Cadet, a snatch and grab kind of Extractor. Taking on a sneaky, evil feline was not part of my job description. Worst of all, despite a thorough examination of every nook and cranny under the kid's pillow, there was no sign of any baby tooth.

Mr. Snuggles had managed to push the tiny bed away from the wall and was now batting it back and forth across the vinyl floor, obviously trying to knock it over and retrieve the meaty fairy nugget hanging on underneath it for dear life. I was at the point of having no other choice but to push the panic button on my locket. It would mean yet another write-up, but in the whole scheme of things, it was still better than ending up as a Fairy Fancy Feast.

Seconds later, a laser pointer light appeared in the far corner of the child's bedroom. Mr. Snuggles was on it in an instant, leaving me free to crawl out from under the bed. Erik Ashton, Molar Extractor Extraordinaire, joined me in the Calico Critter Cottage. Just peachy. It would have to be Erik on call this evening.

"Again, Parker?" Erik moved the laser around the room, keeping Mr. Snuggles far away from the two of us. "Isn't this like the third time this month?"

Just about every female in the Corps, and several males as well, lusted after Erik, and he had slept with most of them. In his Mundane life, he was a social media influencer, a pretty internet face with all the right words and the ability to start trends on a whim. Yet, there was no denying his skill within the Corps. Ashton was willing to go anywhere, handle any situation, no matter how hazardous, to retrieve that precious baby tooth. He was a legend, and in my opinion, the meanest sonofabitch I'd ever met.

He looked at me, the usual disgust noticeable in his sneer. "I'm getting tired of rescuing your fat ass, Parker. You know I gotta write you up again. I hope you at least retrieved the tooth before you started playing dollhouse?"

"Yeah, about that...I checked everywhere under that pillow, Erik. There's no tooth."

He tisked and waved the laser pointer around in circles, making Mr. Snuggles run around until he began to trip and stumble, obviously dizzy. I was starting to feel sorry for the damn cat. I knew firsthand how it felt to be under Erik's thumb.

"God damn it, Parker. Can't you do anything right? Now I'll have to look for myself." The cat had collapsed in an exhausted heap, allowing Erik easy access to the child's pillow. He slithered under it without the slightest notice from the sleeping occupant but was back in less than a minute, scowling.

"Let me see your orders, Parker." He pulled out a tiny flashlight from the pocket of his leather pants. I let myself gloat for a mere instant. It wasn't my fault. Someone at dispatch had screwed up this time.

I watched as he pointed the flashlight at the paper then held it up with the flashlight behind it. "What's the address here?" he snarled.

"1628 Hollyhock Lane. Just like it says, Erik." I tried to sound innocent but wasn't working too hard to keep the sarcasm out of my voice.

"Well, it appears you're both a slob and a moron, Parker! That's a 3, not an 8. You're supposed to be at 1623. There's some kind of stain on this paper, right over the address. Looks like coffee. Do you always use your Corps Orders as a coaster?" He shoved the paper and the flashlight at me, but I didn't take them from him. I didn't need to look for myself. I knew he probably was right. I remembered putting my mug down on a stack of papers.

"Sorry, Erik. I'll head over to 1623 and handle the extraction."

"Do it pronto, Cadet. Daylight is in less than an hour. This better be the last time I have to save your sorry ass, otherwise you'll be polishing bicuspids from now until you're ninety." He turned to leave but then added, "And Parker...see about requesting a bigger uniform. You look like a sausage in that one."

On that pleasant note he was gone. I gathered up my tools and prepared to leave before Mr. Snuggles got a second wind. Erik was right about me needing to move my ass. I had less than forty minutes to get to 1623 and retrieve the tooth. My ability to move magically in the Mundane World as a member of the Tooth Fairy Corps disappears with the rising of the sun. I'd have a hard time explaining why Rosalinda Parker, D.D.S. was found standing in a strange kid's bedroom wearing too tight black leather pants and a pink satin shirt with a giant tooth on the back. No excuse would ever cover that. Not in Salem, Massachusetts, where residents already are touchy about anything odd or supernatural.

I'd never asked for this job. It's supposed to go to the eldest child of a current Extractor, but when testing showed that my older sister Claire didn't possess one iota of Fae DNA, a one in a million genetic role of the dice, the responsibility shifted entirely to me. Even then, I thought I had years before I had to worry about it. My Mother, Wisdom Extractor #4762, wasn't due to retire for at least another seventy years. That was before the cancer took her. It was common Fae knowledge that cancer diagnoses, especially blood cancers, were not all that uncommon among preternaturals who traveled frequently between the dimensions. Studies on the subject had picked up speed in the last five years, thanks in no small way to researchers like Dr. Robyn Brannigan, but not in enough time to help my mom. So I'm Deciduous Cadet #4763, whether I wanted the position or not.

I didn't need this Tooth Fairy shit. I was plenty happy in my Mundane job. Happy to be just Dr. Rosie to my pint-sized patients. My practice had grown so much in the past three years that I had to hire two new hygienists and even needed to knock out a side wall to enlarge my waiting room. If my practice left me with little time for the social niceties other women my age enjoyed, it was worth the price. I loved working in pediatric dentistry. What I didn't like was the expectation that I should feel privileged to help the common good of the Fae Other-world as one of thousands of low level *Sidhe* destined to carry out the work of the tooth fairy.

I blinked over to the house at 1623, retrieved the tooth without any issues, and slipped it into my satin bag. Once I got back home, I planned to deposit it with the others in my home safe. I knew that I really needed to take a few days off and make time for a deposit drop in *I Idir*, my Otherworld hometown. My safe at home held double the number of teeth that regulations suggest we store in the Mundane World.

Normal people have the wrong idea about the whole tooth fairy legend. Parents in the Mundane World regard it as a cute little folk tale created to encourage good dental hygiene, but it's a hell of a lot more complex than that. Since the beginning of time, teeth have been a greatly desired commodity in the Fae Otherworld, a necessary ingredient for a whole list of dark arts and magical spells. Lately, something more sinister has become a huge problematic issue.

The root of the tooth contains a decent amount of DNA, some of it magical in mixed blood children. Certain agencies in the Mundane World are experimenting with this DNA in an effort to extract components that would make it possible for non-preternaturals to cross over into the Otherworld dimension without the immediate physical side effects they usually suffer. The crisis this would cause by the Mundanes in the Fae Otherworld makes me shudder. The Morrigan and her special Corps of assets have been doing what they can to keep this from happening, but for how long they can prevent it is the real question.

Gathering up the tooth bag, I close my eyes and wish myself home. I open one eye and then the other. Yup. I'm in the right place. Normal sized and safe and sound at home, the smell of those overripe bananas I keep forgetting to throw away an olfactory reminder I made it back safely. I use Fae magic so infrequently that I'm still nervous it won't work like it is supposed to. I peel off the sweaty uniform and throw it into a corner. Erik was right. I need the next size up, but requesting leather pants in size 2x turns my stomach. Two cows would have to sacrifice themselves for trousers that size.

That thought should have sent me straight for the Low Fat-High Protein Kale Smoothie I promised myself I'd have for breakfast. It didn't. My screw-up and Erik's nasty comments called for something yummy to fill the dark empty spot that's now wormed its way inside of me. I break two eggs in a bowl, add some vanilla and a half cup of heavy cream and whip it all together. Ten minutes later, I sit down, alone, to brioche French toast with fresh strawberries, a Cafe Au Lait, heavy on the milk, and a side chaser of insecure discontent.

TOOTH 2

BLOWING OUT A MATCH

Thursday is my "late day." I normally don't start seeing patients until 1:00 PM, which makes for a late evening but keeps me off the Extraction Schedule for that particular day. The Tooth Fairy Corps normally frowns upon life in the Mundane World taking precedence over Extraction duties, but my professional life in dentistry, especially in pediatrics, gives me easy access to lost teeth that otherwise might wind up in the wrong hands, so I'm allowed a bit more leeway than your average Cadet. It also leaves my mornings free for the hobby that is the true passion in my life.

I have been fascinated by tiny things for as long as I can remember. My mother always was convinced it was due to my Fae DNA, my soul's longing to live in the Otherworld where my size wouldn't matter. What she really meant was that I secretly wished I wasn't the chubby little Fatso the world saw me as. Although my sister hadn't inherited any of my Mom's Tooth Fairy DNA, she was blessed by the Universe with her lithe, willowy build. Mom was able to wear junior brand clothes in size 4 well into her fifties, even after two babies and a long-celebrated career as Salem's most sought-after pastry chef. My sister, Claire, obviously was cut from the same cloth, minus the Fae shit. She just gave birth to fully human twins, my nephews, Daniel and Jamison, a little over five weeks ago and she already is able to wear all of her super chic and tiny pre-pregnancy attire. It's more than a little annoying. The least she could do is to have a little bit of muffin top hanging over the waistband of her skinniest jeans.

Except for my handful of nuisance preternatural genes, I apparently take after my dad in the DNA Wheel of Fortune. Dad, along with every person in his family, is as round as he is tall, the progeny of hearty peasant stock from eastern Europe with appetites better suited for heavy labor, not the sedate desk jobs most currently have. I'm pretty sure I was born fat, two weeks past my due date and a whopping nine pounds. Every photo from my childhood shows me chubby-cheeked and standing on thick ankles. Not much has changed over the years, except that now I regularly get to wear a white lab coat that gives me an all-over "Stay-Puff Marshmallow" look.

So maybe Ma was right after all. I'm obsessed with these dollhouse miniatures because they are little and cute, something I definitely am not. In my mind though, I reason that it's more about creating a story, a back-history, for every room I make. All my houses have imaginary characters living in them, and I plan, build and decorate according to the stories I've invented in my head. It lets me be creative on a level that my real life, with its schedules, rules and routines, doesn't allow. My dollhouse world is a perfect world that I can control with a touch of paint or a carefully placed chair, and it belongs to me and me alone.

Thursday mornings are devoted entirely to my hobby. Today, my plans include staining shingles for my newest addition, a bungalow cottage I've imagined is located somewhere on Cape Cod's shoreline, and then prepping the walls in the foyer of my three-story Victorian for a coat of buttermilk colored paint I hope to put on later this evening. Being able to shrink down on command from sunset to sunrise is my secret weapon to achieve near perfection with my houses. Using full-sized, human hands makes it nearly impossible to get into those tight spaces around corners and windows but when you yourself are in 1/12 scale, it's a piece of cake to get a more professional look. Most evenings when I'm on Extraction duty I come home either too late or too exhausted to stay small and work inside my dollhouses. But on those occasional nights when I can squeeze in an hour or two of puttering around, I like to have stuff ready so I can take full advantage of that opportunity.

This is why I ignore the first text from Mel. And then the second. My hands are full of "Mocha" wood stain, and if I don't pull these shingles out fast enough, they'll end up much darker than weathered shingles should look. I love Mel. She's the best personal assistant any dentist could have. She's also a really good friend. But seriously, she's a chronic, over-the-top worrier. Everything is a priority for her, even if it's really not. Don't get me wrong. I'm pretty sure that without Mel my practice wouldn't have grown like it has. She keeps the place running smoothly, does the hiring, orders the supplies, and generally keeps me somewhat on a schedule. Plus, she's my shoulder to cry on and the ear I vent to when things get crazy. Mel is also *Sidhe*, so she understands my conflicted feelings on the subject. We met at a festival in the Otherworld's Kingdom of *I Idir*, from where our Fae families hail. Since that first weekend, we've been fast friends and top-notch co-workers. I just wish she'd ease up a little on her need to get me "organized." I do just fine. And if my office is a bit "cluttered" or I'm a little behind on paperwork, the world surely will not stop spinning on its axis... in either of its dimensions.

After the third unanswered text Mel actually calls me. I think about ignoring the call, but she'll take it as a personal snub and everyone in the office will spend the rest of the day suffering under her bitchy mood. It isn't worth it. When Mel isn't happy, no one at the practice has a good day. I wipe my hands on a rag and answer on the fourth ring. "Hey, Mel, what's up?"

The voice on the other end is high-pitched and annoyed. "Rosie, I've been trying to reach you for over an hour. Why the hell haven't you been answering?"

"Sorry, Mel. I had my hands in stain, and it's hard to stop in the middle of a project. What's so important?"

"Buttons to banjos, Rosie!" This is as close to cussing as Mel gets. Being Fae, she understands the power of words and is extremely careful in their use. "I know you love those dollhouses, Girlfriend, but you're a grown woman, a professional one at that! It's high time you consider getting a real social life, either here or in *I Idir*. I just happen to know a few single mermen from my aqua aerobics class. Nice fellows and not too hard on the eyes, if you can get over the whole fishtail thing. You should come to class with me so I can introduce you. At least they would understand about the whole tooth fairy gig."

I hold back a snort. I know Mel means well, but the thought of me squeezing my fat ass into a swimsuit to meet some bug-eyed, merman leaves me queasy. She's right about it being easier to stick to preternatural guys, though. No secrets to keep, no lies to tell. Unfortunately, I take after my mom in that sense. She freely admitted to being attracted only to fully human guys, like my dad, who aren't into the lying and cheating so common among the Fae male population. I'm the same way. Maybe we're drawn to the novelty of someone having zero magic. It's like they're some kind of magical virgin. Or maybe it has something to do with the "naughtiness" of mingling with the "other kind." I'm not sure of the how and why of my human kink, and it's not a conversation I'm ready to have with Mel, even if she's the closest thing I have to a BFF. "Thanks for the offer, Mel, but you know I'm not much of a water person. I can't even swim. It doesn't make sense for me to start thinking about dating someone with gills."

Mel produces the snort I previously had held back out of politeness. "Well, you darn well need to start thinking about dating someone, Rosalinda. You don't want to end up an old maid. Maybe you should consider a Match-maker in *I Idir*. I've heard Madame Tisma has the best handfast numbers. You should look her up the next time you're in *I Idir*."

I see the can of stain thickening up and developing a film over its open top; I need to get back to my project, and this stupid conversation is keeping me from it. "Did you have some other reason for calling me besides a dose of matchmaking?"

A full minute of silence ensues. I obviously have offended her, and now everyone's day is screwed. The voice on the phone is clipped. "Well, excuse me for caring about the welfare of my good friend. From now on, I'll keep my social invitations off the table, Dr. Parker. I'm just calling to remind you that you have a 4:00 appointment with the tax accountant and that you need to bring your paperwork with you to the office today."

Fuck. I'd forgotten all about that. I haven't even begun to look for those papers. "Oh. Is that today?"

"Yes, Dr. Parker," Mel answers. "Today is June 7th. You made this appointment over three weeks ago. Mr. Fitzpatrick is the best enrolled tax agent in all of Salem, and Cockles to Clarinets, Rose, you need the absolute best to help you get out of the huge mess you've created for yourself."

"It's just some back taxes, Mel," I counter. "It'll all be fine. You'll see."

"Five years of non-payment is not 'just some back taxes,' Dr. Parker! People can go to jail for not filing and paying their personal and business taxes," my friend scolds. "Everyone in this town knows you're the most remarkable kid's dentist ever to practice here. Your patients and their parents love you to pieces, and you have a freakin' waiting list a mile long of kids wanting to see, of all things, the dentist! But Rosie, outside of the office, you're a hot mess."

It is my turn to have hurt feelings. "Thanks so much for that, Mel. It's just what I want to hear from a good friend."

Mel's voice has a tremble in it when she answers. "It's precisely because I'm such a good friend, Rosie, that I can say it. You're 33 years old and a medical professional. You're also Fae, whether you like it or not. It's time to get your shit together. You need to stop living in your make-believe dollhouse world and join us in the real one."

TOOTH 3

MR. TAX MAN

HOLY HELL. I'm late for my "late day." Again. This time around, I'd gotten involved with my roof staining project and completely lost track of time, leaving myself only 40 minutes to shower, dress and drive to the office before my first appointment at 1:00 PM. My practice is on the first level of the Witch City Mall, located on Church Street next to the Peabody Essex Museum. I realized when I first decided to rent there that I would take an abundance of grief over my "participation in the commercialization of Salem's sordid history," but the rent was controlled and remarkably low for a premium spot in that pricey section of town, and I was promised that if the travel agency next door ever moved-out I'd be able to expand into their space, which I've recently been able to do.

The fact that so many "know-it-all" types ignore the magical history of Salem proves just how little Mundane World knows about its preternatural neighbors.

An ancient ley line runs directly through Salem and nearby Swampscott, Massachusetts, making this a visitor hot-spot for a variety of Otherworldly guests and probably also is the reason the area has received its infamous reputation. Historically, whenever unaware humans and Otherworldly types mixed it up, the outcome generally was not positive.

Still, I have been living comfortably here all my life, and I've never thought much about the advantages of the magical power boost the ley lines provide. Except for my work with the Tooth Corps and the advantage my tiny size lends to my hobby, magic prowess is just something I have learned to live with, like psoriasis or IBS. It's there in my life and I've learned to cope.

Now it's early June and tourist season is in high gear. Traffic is a snarled mess per usual this time of year, so I get to the office with only minutes to spare before my first patient is set to arrive. The moment I see Mel scowling at me from the front desk, I realize that despite her reminder phone call earlier this morning she sees that I forgot to bring my tax paperwork. If she knew I hadn't even bothered to gather it up, I would be facing far worse than a dirty look.

I swing through my office's front door, tote bag and purse in one hand, car keys and overly full Dunkin' Doughnuts iced tea in the other. Without an extra set of hands, I push the heavy glass door open with my right hip, apparently misjudging the necessary force required to keep it open long enough to pass through. It swings back quickly, banging the arm holding the squishy cup. The lid pops off instantly, tea sloshing out all over my hand and down the front of my light gray pants, soaking me to my unmentionables. "Uhmmm…a little help here, if you please," I cry out to anyone within hearing distance.

Nancy, my newest hygienist, rushes from behind the reception counter to take my tote bag and half-empty teacup from my hands. "Would you like me to put these in your office, Dr. Parker? I can see if there's an extra pair of scrubs in the back if you'd like to change your wet pants?"

I hand my things to her. "That would be great, Nancy. If you find a pair you think will work for me, will you leave a pair in my office as well? Thank you." As she scurries off to handle my request, I walk toward the reception area where my personal assistant is working on perfecting one of her infamous, long-suffering poses. I put my hand up to stop her before she even begins to scold me. "I don't want to hear it, Mel. The day is already off to a horrible start, and I'm not in the mood for a lecture."

She sniffs and hands me a patient file. "Your impacted molar extraction will be here…" Mel pauses and looks up at the large wall clock behind her, "I expect in the next five minutes. Gretchen has you all set up in Exam Room # 4. I scheduled the usual forty-five minutes for that procedure. After that you have three regular check-ups and two patients needing fillings. Your meeting with Mr. Fitzpatrick is scheduled between those at 4:00 PM."

What I'm thinking isn't pretty, and I cowardly wonder whether I can just send Mel a text from the safety of my office. She won't be happy I *forgot* the paperwork. "Yeah… about that, Mel. Stuff came up at home and I completely forgot about bringing the paperwork with me to work.

You're gonna need to give that guy a call and cancel for today. Maybe set up another appointment for some time later this month, after the summer vacation rush. I'll have more time then." I turn and start walking toward my office, but Mel follows me in and shuts the door behind her.

"Rosie…we've been friends for a long time. I love my job here, and I'd like to keep it. Unfortunately, you're starting to make that seem impossible. I'm doing my very best to keep you as professionally organized as I can, but your determination to undermine that goal every chance you get is becoming too much of a hassle. You and I both know this IRS thing could be really bad, not just for you, but for everyone here. We rely on our jobs to pay the bills. If the IRS shuts you down, even for a few weeks, it affects us all. And what about your patients? They depend on you as well! Trust you with their dental health! How is it going to look if they find out you committed tax fraud, even if it was done unwittingly? I think it's incredibly selfish and irresponsible of you to take this as frivolously as you have been, Dr. Rosalinda Ann Parker."

When Mel uses a person's whole name, they know they're in deep shit. I don't want to lose her friendship or the important position she holds in my practice, so I swallow my pretend pride and do my best to grovel. "You're right, Mel. One hundred percent correct. And I promise…I'll try to get better organized. I really will."

She folds her arms in front of her chest, not so easily swayed. "You say that all the time, Rosie, but then you don't bother to do anything about it. Do you realize how much trouble I went through to set up this meeting with

Mr. Fitzpatrick? Normal people go to HIS office, Rosie. The fact that he's coming to yours instead is a big favor. There's no way I'm calling him this late in the day to cancel. At least meet with him and see what he has to say. Find out if you're in as much trouble as I think you are. You can always set up a future meeting for a later date to go over your paperwork. If he's even willing to take you on as a client. He may meet with you and decide you've messed things up so much, he's not even interested in helping you dig yourself out from under it."

I resent that my friend thinks I won't be able to charm the mighty Declan Fitzpatrick. I may not be the most organized dentist around, but hot damn, people like me. One doesn't have a waiting list of wanna-be-patients two pages long without being personable. I plan on giving old Mr. Tax Guy my best 'Dr. Rosie, the Pied Piper of Teeth' spiel. He'll be begging to take my cheerful self on as his client. "I'm going to work really hard at convincing Fitzi the Tax guy to like me, Mel. This is all gonna work out. You'll see."

My PA doesn't look too convinced but shrugs her shoulders and says, "I hope you're right, Rose. There's a lot riding on this tax problem getting fixed."

We're interrupted by Nancy, who has returned with some scrub pants for me to change in to. She hands me a purple pair printed with tiny images of winged tooth fairies, which, all things considered, is ridiculous irony. How the hell the Mundane World came up with the ridiculous notion that all Fae have wings is beyond me. It's so species insensitive. Nancy is apologetic. "This is the best of the choices, Dr. Parker. I hope it's okay?"

What Nancy means is that this is the largest pair of scrubs we have on hand. I usually wear my regular clothes to work, with my lab coat over them, so no one has ever bothered to purchase pants in a size big enough to fit my ass. I have no choice now but to wear these, no matter how tight they're going to be or how ridiculous they'll look. The tea stain on my current pants makes it looks like I peed myself, so purple tooth fairy scrubs it is.

The rest of the afternoon proceeds like any other typical Thursday. The extraction patient is a nine-year-old boy who, even on his best day, normally isn't willing to go along with the program. Today however, he gags on the bite block and vomits his entire lunch. My lab coat bears the brunt of the eruption, but some of it leaks through to my blouse; even with a fresh lab coat and a good sponging off of my own clothes, I spend the rest of the day sporting the aroma of Eau De Puke. The regular check-ups are a breeze - sweet little kids happy to chat with Dr. Rosie about soccer, the Boston Red Sox, and the benefits of French braids; but by the time the last child and parent leaves, I'm running a good twenty minutes behind schedule. Mel comes to hurry me along, with the admonishment that my "pressing 4:00 PM appointment is waiting impatiently in my office."

I have a preconceived notion of what a tax accountant should look like, especially one with this guy's long and star-studded reputation. I assume he'll be well-seasoned, old, and balding, with scrunched up shoulders and a wrinkled forehead from years of scowling down at numbers; so, when I pull down my face mask to my chin and swing into my office with a cheerful, "I'm so sorry to keep you waiting..." the rest of the words stick in my throat at my first eyeful of D.P. Fitzpatrick.

First off, he's younger than I'd expected. A lot younger. How does one get to be an expert in their field in their early thirties? He stands up as I enter the room, all 6 foot 4 of him, suited out in what must be Brooks Brothers, his shoes so shiny I can see my double chin in them. He's a ginger, like myself, and for a second I wonder whether he's Fae but shake that thought off as nonsense. Most Fae are redheads, or strawberry blondes, but not every redhead in the Mundane World is Fae, although I have learned that there are a lot more of them than anyone knows. Yes, indeed. Mr. Declan P. Fitzpatrick is the whole damn, sexy, hot package, but it's the eyes behind his tortoise shell glasses that have me mesmerized. They are the most unusual shade of green I've ever seen. Not the pale celery green one mostly sees, but a lush, mossy shade that brings to mind Spring mornings.

Holy shit! Did I just actually think up that crazy notion? What the hell do I know about Spring mornings anyway? Better get your mind off your hootch, Rosie, and back to business. I stick my hand out to shake his but then let it conspicuously fall to my side when he doesn't reciprocate. Tax Guy must sense my confusion. He stares at me and says, "People have given up hand shaking since the onset of Covid. It's a social nicety that I'm happy to see banished, Dr. Parker. As a medical professional, I'm surprised you're still holding on to such an unnecessary and unsanitary gesture."

I don't know how to respond to this statement. It's not like what he's saying isn't true; it's that his clipped, condescending tone, which seems to carry with it the very slightest bit of Old Country brogue, rubs me the wrong way. It sounds rude to my ears, and whatever initial impression I'd had about his good looks evaporates instantly. I match his tone. "As you wish, Mr. Fitzpatrick," I say, as I coolly point to the chair on the other side of my desk and motion for him to have a seat. I see that Mel already tried to placate him with a cup of coffee, which sits untouched and probably cold on the corner of the desk. I have already made up my mind not to hire him. There's something about him I instantly dislike, and the sooner we have our discussion the sooner Mel can show him the exit.

My personal office is not much larger than any one of my standard exam rooms. With the file cabinets, the bookcase, and one of my completed dollhouses fighting for space along with my desk and chairs, maneuvering around in here is a tight squeeze. I edge my way around the desk, twisting as I wiggle through the tight spot, hoping not to crush the tiny landscaped bushes surrounding the miniature building with my right hip. True to form, I avoid smashing the mini landscaping, but my left hip bumps into the desk corner, knocking over the coffee cup and spilling its entire contents directly in the lap of D.P. Fitzpatrick, E.A.

TOOTH 4

HOT PANTS DOES A DANCE

Apparently, the coffee that spilled on Mr. Tax Man wasn't quite as cold as I had thought it to be, if his hopping jig is any indication. He jumps from his chair as if there is a spring under his ass, grabbing his crotch and swearing in what I recognize as Gaelic, thus proving me correct regarding his heritage. I grab some paper towels from behind my desk and move to help wipe the liquid from his pants, but when I see where the bulk of it has landed, I stop dead in my tracks, pretty sure I don't want to get that up close and personal with this stranger's genitalia. I'm not at all sure what to do next, so I stick my head out the door and call to Mel to bring some ice. Mr. Fitzpatrick is doing his best to pull his pants' fabric away from his skin, but wet wool doesn't have much give to it, so it sticks like glue to…uhmm…every nook and cranny.

Knowing that it was my fat ass that had knocked over the cup in the first place, and realizing that the man had a

front row view of me doing it, is mortifying. I try to apologize, but my voice registers as a squeak, sounding several
octaves higher than normal and far more breathy. "Mr.
Fitzpatrick, I am so very sorry. I absolutely did not intend
to cause you any bod…harm." My breath catches at the
exact moment I'm trying to say the word 'bodily' with the
'ily' part becoming lost in the high-pitched sound; it
emerges as 'bod' instead. Tax Man looks at me as if I've
lost my mind, and his cheeks flush bright pink. It takes me
a couple of seconds to remember that the slang word 'bod'
means 'dick' in Gaelic, and even though the mistake I'd
just made had been entirely unintentional, my realization
of it causes me to look down at the aforementioned
appendage just before I turn around and clamp a hand
over my mouth to reign in a nervous barrage of teenage
giggles.

Thank all of the goddesses in the Otherworld that Mel
chooses this moment to walk in carrying a bag of ice and
several clean cloth towels. She is polite and professional,
whereas I quickly retreat to the ladies' room, unable to
control my silly giggling. By the time I pull myself
together, splash some cold water on my face, and exit the
bathroom Declan Fitzpatrick is on his way out of my
office wearing a pair of light blue scrubs, carrying his
damp suit pants over his arm. He walks past me without a
word and marches straight through the front door. I
know I should have tried to say something to him before
he left, but I was completely distracted by the way the
borrowed scrubs hugged his ass. My naughty girl self
wonders whether the coffee soaked all the way through to
his boxers and thus whether he currently is going 'com-

mando'. This is not a good thought to have, as it makes me start giggling all over again.

Throughout the rest of the afternoon, I'm grateful that my patients continue to bring me back to my usual professional happy place, and the rest of my day passes without incident, though Mel is not speaking to me. We usually take our dinner break at the same time and eat together in my office on Thursday evenings, but today she chooses to settle herself in the staff lounge to eat with the hygienists. It's a sure-fire sign I've screwed up royally.

I feel badly, but I don't feel guilty. It's not as though I spilled the coffee on purpose. I think a normal person would have stopped to let me apologize, even allowing me to pay for their dry cleaning so that bygones could be bygones. A mature adult doesn't storm away like an angry bull. Still, I feel as though I've embarrassed Mel, especially since I left her to clean up my mess. Literally. She thought she had done me a tremendous favor by snagging the best tax accountant in the county, and I treated the result of her efforts like it was a joke. It doesn't matter that I think Declan Fitzpatrick is a pompous horse's ass. I must try to make things right, if only for Mel's sake and to ensure peace in the workplace.

I consider going to Declan's office to apologize in person. Better yet, experience has taught me that when planning to 'eat crow', it's best to bring along something the recently wronged will find far more delicious. I have, unfortunately, eaten enough crow in my lifetime to be picking feathers from my teeth constantly. I contemplate the entire mess while I pack my things at the end of the day. It's unusually quiet, and I notice I'm the last one here.

Mel went home without so much as a goodbye. Whatever peace offering I ultimately decide to take with me to humble myself in front of Mr. Brooks Brothers better be top notch. I mentally run through a list of my favorite recipes and decide on blueberry lemon scones. It's pretty clear that the lad is from the Old Sod, and no proper Irishman can resist a delicious scone with his morning Barry's Breakfast Tea. I have the best recipe ever, created by my pastry chef Mom for Salem's Wenham Tea Room. It produces scones that are extraordinarily flaky, with a rich butter flavor and just the right touch of lemon tartness. I mentally double dare Mr. Hot Pants to be able to resist them along with my sincerest apology.

TOOTH 5

OF SCONES AND SCORN

MORNINGS ARE my favorite time to bake. The temperature in the house is cooler, the humidity is lower, and today the quiet solitude of the sunrise is providing a calming and reflective balm to my unusually anxious self. For all of my bravado, it actually bothers me that Mel is angry with me and that Fitzie the Tax Man thinks I'm an unprofessional, sex-craved, ding-dong. *Speaking of ding-dongs, I wonder whether Fitzie's suffered any lasting scars from yesterday's events? What a crazy frickin' thing to think about while I'm baking.* My dual social personalities have always been a quandary. Within the confines of my practice, my professional relationship skills are easy and natural for me, and I never lack self-confidence. One-on-one communication between me and my kids, or even me and their parents, doesn't fill me with the same dread as it does trying to hold conversations with other adults in social encounters. The breezy chit chat that comes bubbling forth from my lips when I am *Dr. Rosie* seems to dry up the moment I step out of my office. This is why I've decided to bring scones with me to my apology session with the Tax Man. I will them to deflect attention away from me while placing it squarely on the fragrant triangles of deliciousness… where it belongs.

I stopped on my way home last night to pick up everything I might need for this morning's bake-a-thon: plump fresh blueberries, Kerrygold Irish butter, and a few juicy Meyer lemons. It's these few, special ingredients that turn my scones from being 'just good' to 'utterly spectacular'. I already had plenty of regular American butter in my fridge at home. I buy it in bulk from Costco. When I choose to use the more expensive Irish butter in a recipe, you can bet your bippity boppity boo that I am aiming to mix up something particularly special. Unlike its US cousin, Irish butter contains 82% butterfat and a lot less water, so it creates a finished product with a flakier texture and a more intense buttery flavor. Meyer lemons are a serious no-brainer for all of my cooking. Because they are a cross between a citron and a mandarin, they are far sweeter than their counterparts, and their bright, pebbled peel makes the best zest. At the last minute I decided to double up on the ingredients and make a second batch for Mel and the staff; it certainly couldn't hurt to go back to the office bearing gifts.

With Alexa playing my favorite baking playlist in the background, I cream, beat, and whip all the baking magic together. *Jeez, Rosie...that just sounded like a sentence from a kinky, naughty book. Where is your mind lately?* I make each batch separately so the butter can stay icy cold; that's the true secret to making flaky scones. When I pull the batches from the oven, I'm pretty damn proud of myself. They are as perfect as perfect can be, with their golden-brown tops and deep purple blueberries peeking through layers of tender pastry. While they cool, I shower and get ready for the day.

The Tax Man's website says his office hours are from 9:00 AM to 4:00 PM on Fridays, so I plan to stop by and drop off my gift with apology before heading to my own office. I search my closet for something reasonably attractive, although anything would be better than what he saw me wearing yesterday: my gigantic ass squeezed into hideous purple fairy scrubs. I settle on a linen shift in sage green that Mel says looks great on me and a pair of matching flats. I wear my hair up and even add a touch of blush and lip gloss. This is the dressiest I've been in a month, and after a quick last check in the mirror, my confidence level grows a tiny bit. Maybe.

I pack the scones for Mr. Fitzpatrick in a wicker basket and add a large chintz bow to the handle. Okay, maybe it is a bit over the top, but I really screwed up yesterday. The least I can do is make my 'I'm terribly sorry I scalded your manly bits' gift the best it can be. I tuck a little note and my business card inside the basket along with a request for another appointment with my fingers crossed that all this hoopla will make the necessary amends. It's times like these I wish my magical skills were better. I'm pretty sure there are Fae Glamour spells designed specifically for such moments, but I have never taken the time nor the energy to explore the extent of my magical talent. For my entire life, I've limited my magical self to my duties within Corps assignments, a few trips back and forth to the Otherworld, and, of course, the size adjustment I use for my dollhouse work. For the most part, this has suited me just fine, though I sometimes wonder whether a spell or two wouldn't make my life easier.

The office of D. P. Fitzpatrick, EA, is less than a mile from my own, in a row of Tudor front buildings made to look like old Salem. I already am aware that the D stands for Declan but am now curious as to the meaning of the P. I conjure up all types of options until I remember the abbreviation DP from a smutty romance novel Mel insisted I would love. Love? Hell...I didn't even know what half the stuff they described was! I had to look it all up on Google, and now, recalling the urban slang meaning of DP, I giggle a little about seeing DP Fitz-patrick again. I tell myself to knock it off with all of the inappropriate thoughts I've been having about the Tax Man and how I need to put a stop to the constant giggles I've been having regarding anything concerning this guy.

DP's office is small but tastefully decorated with very masculine objects. It reminds me more of a smoking room in a private club, with its horse prints and leather club chairs, than an office. To the right, I spy a hostess set up, which includes individually wrapped granola bars and a selection of different K-cup coffees, but, thankfully, there's not a single blueberry lemon scone in sight. Mine will stand out. The receptionist sits behind a heavy wooden desk, with a door behind her that I assume is Tax Man's personal space. Usually, I try hard not to judge people by their appearance. I certainly wouldn't want anyone judging me. But everything about the receptionist, whose name, Eleanor Pitch, is printed on the plastic placard on the desk, screams total bitch, which, by the way, rhymes perfectly with her last name as if the Universe knew in advance how she'd turn out.

The Eleanor part isn't right, though. This woman looks more like a Tiffany or an Ashley, all willowy thin, blonde, and doe-eyed. She also is wearing a linen shift, but hers is perfectly tailored, and I'm certain it was not on the same rack as mine at the local T. J. Maxx store. She looks up and smiles at me with her perfect, little, white teeth. "Can I help you?" she asks.

"Good morning. I was wondering if I might have a few minutes with Mr. Fitzpatrick." I raise the basket up to reveal its contents. "I wanted to stop by and bring him some homemade scones." When she doesn't reply, I add, "He and I met yesterday afternoon. I'm Rosie Parker."

Her eyes widen, and her fake smile sort of slides off her lips. "The dentist?" she now asks.

I get the feeling she's heard the whole, sordid story and already disapproves of me. "Yes. I'm Dr. Rosalinda Parker. I'm hoping Mr. Fitzpatrick will take me on as a client."

Ms. Pitch the Bitch sits straight up in her chair and folds her hands in front of her. "I'm sorry, Dr. Parker. Mr. Fitzpatrick is in with another client right now. In fact, his Friday schedule is absolutely full. Perhaps another day?"

I know a brush off when I hear one. I give it another shot. "I really don't think this will take very long, Ms… Pitch, and I really do need to see him. Do you think maybe I can wait just a bit and see whether the other client leaves soon, and then maybe I can just slide in for a few minutes before his next appointment?"

Blondie shakes her head to signal a no go. "I'm afraid that would be impossible, Dr. Parker. Mr. Fitzpatrick is a stickler about his appointments. If you don't have one, he won't see you. Period."

I'm frustrated and, frankly, more than just a little disappointed. I was mentally set to do this today, and the scones won't get any fresher by Monday. I settle on my only remaining option, which truly is a last resort. Plopping the basket on the desk, I smile as sweetly as I can. "Well, if he's that busy, I understand. I have days like that myself. If you could just see that Mr. Fitzpatrick gets this basket of scones and my note, I'd be most grateful."

Witchy Bitchy looks at my basket like I'm offering her a rattlesnake instead of baked goods. She sighs and pulls my gift towards her, then places it on the floor behind her desk. "I will see that he gets this, Doctor, but you should know that Mr. Fitzpatrick is very health conscious. He's an advocate for a diet free of gluten, processed sugar, and animal by-products." She looks down at the basket behind her desk. "I don't suppose these were made with organic flour, either?"

I hold back a sarcastic retort about the fake, non-organic tits plastered to her chest. There's no sense in having the Gatekeeper hate me as well. "No," I answer. "Just the regular, everyday kind of flour."

She sighs again, this time with additional drama. "As I said, Dr. Parker, I will see that he gets them, but in all honesty, I sincerely doubt he'll want to eat them."

Okay. I admit it. I feel disrespected, and my confidence

level, so banner-waving high this morning, sinks to a depressing new low. I feel my face getting hot and have no doubt that a red flush is rising from my neck upward. I force the next words out of my mouth. "Whatever, Ms. Pitch. Perhaps your clients might enjoy them rather than those stale, tasteless granola bars sitting on your coffee bar." Then I turn around and walk out the door.

The ensuing ride to my office provides me the alternating challenge between trying hard not to scream and trying hard not to cry. Once again, my best laid plans have turned to complete shit. Instead of dwelling on my failure, I turn the radio up high and sing my heart out along with Willie Nelson, who, if you ask me, really nails the human condition. By the time I reach the Witch City Mall, I feel ready to tackle Mel. I can, in good conscience, tell her that I tried my very best to make amends for what happened yesterday.

When I hit the door, scones in hand, I immediately sense that something bad is afoot. The hygienists are standing around the reception desk with Mel, and no one looks happy. "What's wrong?" I ask.

"Mrs. Scoville called this morning," Mel explains. "Sammy has norovirus. Apparently, it's making the rounds through all of Salem's day camps and little league teams. Four other parents have already called to cancel today because their kids are sick."

Sick kids are not unusual in my line of work, but the word norovirus strikes terror among my office staff: it's just a more technical name for stomach flu, that wretched 36-hour marathon of nausea, vomiting, and diarrhea. The horrific news now is that Sammy Scoville is the kid who puked on me yesterday afternoon, apparently not from the bite block as we originally had thought, but rather from the virus that was brewing in his pint-sized gastronomical tract.

Since Covid, we spend our days masked and gloved. We sanitize everything after every patient, and constant hand washing is part of our routine. However, norovirus is a persistent little bugger with an uncanny ability to seek new hosts in the same easy fashion as the pandemic virus. One touch of an infected surface, a saliva spray established while talking, or any type of shared food, and the virus is transferred easily. It's quite possible none of us has contracted it. It's also just as possible that we all are biding our time until the first symptoms hit. Children are usually the biggest victims of this virus, so if my hygienists have picked it up, their symptoms will be uncomfortable but short-lived in nature. That's not the case for Mel and me.

Because of the slight differences in Fae DNA, we don't seem to contract the same viruses or illnesses that humans do. We usually are immune to respiratory illnesses, like the common cold or even Covid, which haven't affected either of us. We Fae have our own medical issues that correlate to the magical energy in our make-up, but some of the nastier Mundane bugs can and do cross between Fae and humans, and when they do, all hell tends to break loose. We can end up sick like no nobody's business.

I make my decision quickly and easily. "I think it would be most prudent for us to close the practice today through Monday. I'll have our sanitizing crew come in and do a whole sweep. By next week, maybe this thing will have run its course."

There is unanimous agreement, and Mel promises to call all our remaining patients scheduled for today, Saturday, and Monday to give them the news. I see by the faces of my staff that everyone is hoping they haven't carried the bug home to their families. A whole house full of puking family members is not a pretty scenario. As I lock up and head back to my car, I tell myself that I'm only imagining that my stomach is unsettled, and I don't give Mr. Tax Man another thought.

TOOTH 6

FOLLOWED

DURING THE ENTIRE drive home from my office, I try convincing myself I'm not on my way to having the full-blown stomach flu, but even with *Barry Manilow's Greatest Hits* playing in the background, I can't ignore the churning, gurgling sensation starting somewhere near my appendix and working its way across my entire belly. I'm so intent on matching my waves of nausea to the beat of *Copacabana* I almost miss the dark gray Honda Civic that seems to have become my shadow.

I know. It sounds crazy. I'm not usually one of those jumpy-type people who fear everything about living in the urban jungle. However, like most of the Fae population, I also don't much believe in coincidences. The Universe is more in control and connected than any of the Mundanes want to accept, and I'm nearly sure that it absolutely is not a random quirk in time that the occupants of said gray Honda need to stop at the same gas station at Essex and Webb to use the restroom and then again at the Shell on Mason and Franklin…just like me.

Hoping to disprove my unsettling theory, I linger in the Shell's Quick Mart, picking up ginger ale and saltines for what I expect will be my only sustenance for the next few days. I spend time browsing the magazine rack, allowing several minutes to pass and willing the damn car to drive away so I can laugh at my ridiculous notion that anyone would follow Rosalinda Parker, D.D.S. covertly home. After nearly fifteen minutes of staring at the same eight magazines, the guy at the counter is eyeballing my stalling technique, and I'm starting to feel altogether shitty. I pay for my purchases and head back to my car. I pointedly look directly at the Honda to let the driver know he's been made.

Apparently, bad guys do not react much to getting the stink-eye. The gray car pulls out shortly after I do, and I see in my rearview mirror that it stays discreetly two cars behind me. I break out in a cold sweat, though I can't tell whether it's from fear or the nasty virus; it could be both, so I am relieved when I finally turn down my street. Then it dawns on me that maybe leading them to my house is not the best plan for subterfuge. I consider calling 911 but hesitate. Several of Salem's finest have children who are my patients, and I do not wish to become a funny story at the next neighborhood barbeque if I'm overreacting.

Before I can make a decision, the Honda drives past without a glance from its driver, continues down Newcastle Road, turns down Walsh Street, and I lose sight of it. I make a run for my door, locking it behind me, and double checking, then triple checking, that I have rearmed my security system. I am shaking from the experience. Or maybe from the flu. Hard to tell at this moment. All I know is I need my jammies and my bed, and perhaps a nearby, handy bucket.

When I finally wake from my flu nap, the sun is bright in the west window of my bedroom signaling that it is late afternoon. According to my Safe House system, no one has attempted to breach my parameters. I shuffle to the kitchen and pour myself a short glass of ginger ale and bring it back to bed; then I pull the covers up around me despite an outside temperature of 84 degrees. I put on the television and alternately doze, worry, and run to the bathroom for the next several hours. The room is dark and Pat and Vanna are spinning and spelling when my front doorbell rings. The noise gives me a start, and I shake myself out of a half-awake stupor. With shaky hands I check the image from the front door camera on my cell phone.

The man at my door is tall and wearing a dark suit. I can't see his face, but I recognize the wicker basket with the big chintz bow as the one I left with Eleanor Bitch this morning. The man looks up towards the camera, and now my hands are sweaty as well as shaky. The one and only D. P. Fitzpatrick, E.A. is at my frickin' front door.

TOOTH 7

HERE... HOLD MY BUCKET

MAYBE IT'S THE FEVER, or possibly dehydration settling in, but for the life of me I can't imagine why the Tax Man would be standing outside my door on a Friday night. I do the only sensible thing in a situation like this. I turn out the bedroom light, pull the covers over my head, and hope he goes away. A minute later the doorbell rings again with three short blasts. I swear I can feel his annoyance seething out from every one of his quick stabs at that little white button. I bring up the camera link on my cell phone again and take another peek. He now apparently has noticed the camera above the door frame and lifts up the scone basket, pantomiming his explanation for being on my front porch. I want to tell him to just leave it and go, but my security system doesn't have audio, and I curse myself for trying to save $23 on a lesser model.

I feel I have no choice but to pull on my tatty, leopard

spotted robe and trudge downstairs to answer the door. I consider just yelling at him through the closed door, but that seems incredibly impolite after he's made the effort to return the damn basket. I make a mental note to use only disposable containers for any future 'sorry I burned your balls' apology gifts. I pull together the best neutral expression I can muster and open the door. "Mr. Fitzpatrick…what a pleasant surprise. What brings you to my door on this balmy Friday night?"

The next words out of his mouth are far from swoon worthy. Or even polite. "You look like hell, Dr. Parker."

I figured him for an asshole the moment we met, but this is a whole new level of rude. "I'm afraid you caught me in bed for the night. Is there anything special you wanted?"

D. P. looks at the expensive watch on his wrist, and I wonder who the hell even bothers with watches these days. "It's only 6:40. On a Friday night," he pronounces. "That's rather early…even for a dentist, Dr. Parker."

Alrighty then! The Tax Man has gone above and beyond the norms of any standard asshole definition, maligning my honorable profession in such a derogatory fashion. I decide from now on that the D. P. in his name will stand for Declan, the Pretentious Prick, which somehow seems worse in my mind than my original DP thought. The tension I feel in this situation causes my stomach to do the old heave ho, and I realize that I have not thrown up in quite some time. I'm probably due for a whopper of an episode. I need to make D.P. go away. And soon. "As much as I'm enjoying your delightful wit, Mr.

Fitzpatrick, I really need to lie down. As I asked before, why are you here?"

Declan the Pretentious Prick shoves the basket toward me, and my tummy situation gets more precarious. "I needed to return your basket, Dr. Parker, and I thought it would be best if I did it as quickly as possible. I wouldn't want you to think I'm the kind of person who keeps someone else's borrowed property."

Beads of sweat are building up across my hairline, and bile washes up my throat. For the life of me, I can't figure out why he's being such a stubborn bastard when it's obvious I am...unwell.

"It was a gift," I say. "You were expected to just keep the basket."

He leans against my door frame and folds his arms across his chest, causing me to take an involuntary step back. I don't want him closer. It's a sure thing that I have a bad case of vomit breath. Not to mention that I'm probably contagious as hell, though it would serve him right to wake up tomorrow morning puking his guts out. "Most people would have put their gift of baked goods in a disposable container, Dr. Parker," he says in a tone that even in my deathly ill stage I can tell is condescending. "The fact that you used this expensive basket is a sure-fire indication that you wished to have me personally return it to you."

What the Pretentious Prick is implying is enough to make me want to punch him in the gut. And I would have done just that except that I felt a wave of stomach garbage rush up my throat in that exact moment. Instead of confronting the Tax Man, I clamp a hand over my mouth and run for the guest bathroom down the hall. I'm barely able to close the door before being violently ill.

For the next several minutes I can do nothing but wish I were dead. I hate throwing up, and in my misery, I usually turn into a mountain of self-pity; so, when I hear a knock on the bathroom door, I have no patience or politeness. "Why are you still here, Tax Man?" I yell this with my head still hanging over the toilet bowl. "Do you not have one shred of common decency? Just go away! Please!"

He speaks to the crack in the door. "Are you alright in there?"

"Does it sound like I'm frickin' alright? I have the flu, so please just let yourself out," I moan.

I can still hear him on the other side of the door. "Do you want me to call an ambulance?" he asks.

"NO! Like I said, it's just the flu. Norovirus from one of my patients."

The Prick stays put. "Do you want me to call a friend or something?"

"No. That isn't necessary," I answer.

He's silent for a few moments, then adds sort of questioningly, "I could stay until I'm sure you're going to be okay?"

Holy shit! Is the man that dense? Like I would ever want him, of all people, on the other side of the door when I come out all sweaty, teary-eyed, and reeking of puke. Yeah. Thanks, but no thanks. I don't want to give him any more fodder for future put-downs. "I'm a grown woman, Mr. Fitzpatrick. I'll be fine in a few days when the virus runs its course. I just need you to go now."

I don't hear anything for a minute or two, and then he says, "As you wish, Dr. Parker. I hope you feel better soon." Then, I hear footsteps down the hall and the front door closing. I lay down on the cold bathroom tile with a rolled-up towel for a pillow and have myself a really good cry.

TOOTH 8

YOU'VE GOT MAIL

I AM miserable all night long, my norovirus symptoms being only half the reason. I'm beyond mortified by what occurred the previous evening with D.P. Fitzpatrick; it was bad enough that he believed my apology basket was merely a school-girl's attempt to see him again, but to have him stand outside the bathroom door, listening to me retch non-stop for ten minutes, was the ultimate humiliation. It also meant he'd walked through my living room to get to said bathroom door and undoubtedly had seen my assorted, unfinished craft projects, stacks and stacks of unopened mail, dirty plates, and basket of unwashed laundry with my bras sitting directly on top, scattered throughout the room.

At this point, I may just have to accept that THE Tax Man won't be MY Tax Man. There must be another enrolled agent somewhere within reasonable proximity I can hire instead. Mel simply will have to understand I did everything I could to try and make this work. I wonder how much I should tell her about what's happened within the past 24 hours.

My dismal experience with Fitzi initially took precedence over yesterday's concern regarding the Gray Honda, but in the light of a new day, I find it worrisome again. I can't fathom why anyone would follow me, but I decide I need to let someone know about the scary gray Honda. Just in case.

I text Mel to check how she's feeling and receive an "Ugh" and several green vomit emojis in return. Not wishing to carry on an emoji war, I end our communication and drag my laptop into bed with me to read my emails. There are plenty of offers from salespeople regarding things I might need for my office, a swarm of dating ads, and an email from a Nigerian prince offering me a million dollars, but nothing else. I am so in need of human communication, I contemplate answering the prince just for some fun, but decide it's probably a good way to get my computer hacked.

The next idea comes to me like a sharp jolt to my brain. I decide to contact the Tax Man and let him know that I truly am sorry about the way things worked out, explaining about all the misunderstandings and accidents, as well as to inform him that I intend to find someone else to handle my IRS problems. I even will be the bigger person and ask him if he possibly could suggest someone else who might be a better fit for me. I am sure the phone number on his business card is for his office, and being that it's Saturday, I doubt anyone would be in. Besides, all things considered, I don't feel confident enough actually to speak to the man, and texting is something I feel belongs strictly between friends, which we are so very not. Thus, I resolve to send him an email, fingers crossed that Eleanor the Bitch doesn't handle his digital mail for him.

To: D.P.FitzpatrickE.A.@hotmail.com
From: SmilesDocParker@gmail.com
Subject: Tax problems
Dear Mr. Fitzpatrick,
Thank you for returning my basket. I am sorry I did not see you out properly yesterday. As you might have noticed, I was rather indisposed. In addition, I also wish to apologize for the coffee incident on Thursday and for all of the misunderstandings that followed.
In light of these, I think it best we part ways. I respect your expertise in your field, but I doubt at this point we can put aside our differences and work together.
However, I would appreciate your personal recommendation of someone else whom I might use to handle my IRS issues.
Thank you for your patience and understanding,
Rosalinda Parker, D.D.S.

I pause a moment but hit the send button before I can change my mind. This is the mature and adult thing to do. I lay the computer next to me and wonder whether I will get a response. I don't wait long for my answer. My laptop dings immediately with an email notification.

To: SmilesDocParker@gmail.com
From: D.P.FitzpatrickEA@hotmail.com
Subject: Re: Tax problems
Dear Dr. Parker,
An apology of this sort is unnecessary, though I suppose I
should, in return, thank you for poisoning me with your baked
goods. I find myself indisposed as well.
As for your tax problems, I have no idea what they involve, as
we haven't yet been able to discuss them. It is impossible for me
to recommend someone else without knowing what your
account entails.
D. P. Fitzpatrick

   I read his email twice, just to be sure I really saw what
I just saw. The Pretentious Prick is beyond belief! There is
no way I'm going to take this lying down, even if I actually
am typing my response while lying down. I put the P in
his name in bold face type so I can snicker to myself while
I do it.

To: D.P.FitzpatrickEA@hotmail.com
From: SmilesDocParker@gmail.com
Subject: Re: Tax problems
Dear D. **P.** Fitzpatrick
You are an extremely rude man as well as a ridiculously
silly one. How could my scones possibly have poisoned
you, as your delightful Ms. Pitch informed me that you
would never in this lifetime eat non-organic, gluten-filled,
sugar and butter loaded baked goods such as mine?
Either she is a liar or you are! Unless, of course, you are
admitting that you actually eat normal food? Or, possibly,

that you are over-exaggerating just how ill you really are? Oh…the very shame of it!
R. Parker

I don't even bother moving the computer from my lap this time. I bet the Pretentious Prick comes up with a snotty response pronto. Sure enough, his next email arrives in my box within a minute.

To: SmilesDocParker@gmail.com
From   D.P.Fitzpatrick@hotmail.com
Subject: Re: Tax Problems
Dear Dr. Parker,
I assure you that I feel truly wretched. I am sure you are rubbing your hands together over the idea that you have caused me additional discomfort. Apparently, trying to burn me wasn't enough. And, as a general practice, I don't eat unhealthy, processed junk food. As you claimed your scones were home-made, I thought I would take my chances. In hindsight, it obviously was a bad decision.
D.P. Fitzpatrick

Grrrr. This asshole is insufferable. I answer back.

To: D.P.Fitzpatrick@hotmail.com
From: SmilesDocParker@gmail.com
Subject: Re: Tax Problems
Dear D. **P.** Fitzpatrick
My scones absolutely were 100% homemade! You weren't poisoned. You have norovirus. I'm sure you are shocked that a super human like yourself could catch a lowly flu

bug. It happens. Get over yourself.
Parker

I have no doubt that this will engender an even quicker response. I am not wrong.

To: SmilesDocParker@gmail.com
From: D.P.Fitzpatrick@hotmail.com
Subject: Re: Tax problems
Dear Parker
Let's not forget the most likely source for passing this hideous virus to me. That's what I get for trying to make sure you were okay yesterday. No good deed goes unpunished, as they say. Btw...what is up with the silly bold-facing of the P in my name. I hope it is not some derogatory stab at my middle name?
D. Fitzpatrick

Okay, Mister. If it's the truth you want, it's the truth you'll get.

To: D.P.FitzpatrickEA@hotmail.com
From: SmilesDocParker@gmail.com
Subject: Re: Tax problems
Dear D. **P**.,
Based on our last several emails I have surmised that the **P** in D. **P**. Fitzpatrick stands for any one of the following: prick, pecker, peter or putz. Possibly, perhaps, even pretentious, pathetic, or the ever-popular pain in the ass. As it is quite obvious you have no interest in handling my

case, I suggest we cease and desist all further communication.

R. Parker

I hit the send button with every ounce of indignation burning in my gut along with the virus. I don't expect any response, so this time I am more than a little surprised when my laptop signals receipt of another email.

To: SmilesDocParker@gmail.com
From: D.P.FitzpatrickEA@hotmail.com
Subject: Re: Tax problems
Dear Dr. Parker,
You seem to have an unusually high amount of interest in my genitalia. I'm not sure if I should be offended or flattered. However, I never said I wasn't interested in taking your case. I am now exceptionally curious to learn just how much of a debacle your IRS issues are in light of how hard you've worked to garnish my interest.
Once I no longer feel the need to lie down and die, I will contact you to set up a future appointment to discuss the debacle further.
Declan

My stomach does a flip flop. He signed this last one Declan. Oh my.

TOOTH 9

HOLDING ON LINE 3

I AM NOT WELL ENOUGH to return to my dental practice until Tuesday, and even then I need to forgo my usual morning coffee and croissant in favor of a cup of weak tea and unbuttered toast. My staff and patients are much more sympathetic and forgiving about my bout with the flu than the higher-ups at the Tooth Fairy Corps. I have already received two sternly worded raven-grams reminding me to check-in for Corps duty as soon as I physically am able to handle the magic. Illness of any kind, Fae or human, wreaks havoc on a person's energy force, thus limiting their magical abilities.

I let my superiors know that I have returned to my dentist position but will have to delay my return to active Corps duty until Friday at the very earliest. I also let them know that I have four extractions scheduled for this week, so I will have four more baby teeth to add to my weekly quota. This buys me a little extra consideration.

I haven't heard from Declan since Saturday morning. I smile when I think about his name and even giggle secretly when I say it out loud to myself. Which is silly, of course. I am a grown woman. I am not supposed to giggle over the names of men whom I hardly know, particularly over one who most likely thinks I'm certifiably, bat-shit crazy.

I assume the Tax Man will contact me next via email since that was our last form of communication, so I'm startled when Mel comes into an exam room while I'm with a patient to tell me that Mr. Fitzpatrick is holding on line 3. She asks me if I have time to take his call or whether she should ask him to call me back at a later time. She is grinning like the Cheshire Cat. I have told her only bits and pieces of what transpired between Declan and me, but she is Fae, so it's easy enough for her to read my general thoughts and emotions. I suppose I could shield them from her, but it takes so much energy that normally I don't bother.

There is no way in hell I want to miss this call from him. In the back of my mind a fear lingers that maybe the Tax Man will not bother to call back again. "Tell Mr. Fitz-patrick I will be with him shortly," I say to Mel. "Please let him know that I'm just finishing up with a patient."

It's highly possible I may have cut short my usual end-of-visit-chit-chat with Penny Morganstein and her mother. In return, I let her select an extra token from my treasure chest, which she seems to enjoy more than our usual conversation. We say our good-byes and I head toward my office, and if anyone asks me, I will deny that I have sweaty palms. I pass Mel on the way and she grins manically at me while giving me an enthusiastic thumbs up.

Closing the door behind me, I slide into my desk chair, wipe my sweaty hands on my lab coat, and pick up the receiver. "Good morning, Mr. Fitzpatrick. What can I do for you?" I'm using a voice that I hope sounds like a cheerful, confident professional would use, but to my ear it ends up sounding more like a kindergarten teacher on speed. I jump when I hear Mel's voice on the other end.

"Wrong line, Dr. Parker. Mr. Fitzpatrick is holding on line 3."

"Sorry, Mel." I hang up, hit the button for line 3, and try again. "Good morning, Mr. Fitzpatrick. What can I do for you?" All my words tumble out in one long breath, like I've been running a marathon.

"Good morning, Dr. Parker." There's a slight roll to the r in the way he says my last name, and the a in Parker sounds more like ay. It's the same slight accent I heard when we first met, and I wonder how long he's been away from Ireland, which, of course, is none of my business. "I hope I haven't caught you at a bad time?" he asks.

"Not at all. I...I uhm..." I stop only because I forget what I want to say, so focused am I on his accent. "I was just finishing up with a patient. I have a few minutes before my next one." There's a pause on his end, and the silence makes me nervous, so I jump in with the first thing I can think of: "Are you calling about my tax case?"

Another long pause. "Of course, Dr. Parker. As I am a tax specialist, that is the most logical assumption. I'd like us to meet so I can look over the communications you've received from the IRS. That will give me an idea of what their major issues are, and then we can plan your case going forward. I was hoping we both might be free at the same time today. Perhaps for about an hour or so?"

I pull out my cell phone to check the schedule Mel sends to me every morning. It appears my only free time today is between 1:50 and 3:10. "According to my patient schedule, Mr. Fitzpatrick, the only time I have available is between 2:00 and 3:00. I'm afraid I'll be booked solid until after 7:00." The notion of meeting the Tax Man for dinner makes my heart race, but he squelches that little fantasy pronto.

"I'm busy this evening, but I think I can make the afternoon time block work," he says. "As this is just an introductory meeting, it shouldn't require us to spend a great deal of time together."

Wow. The Tax Man really knows how to charm a lady. I'm glad this is not a video chat or a Zoom meeting. My face is red and hot. I try to keep the hurt feelings out of my voice. I don't know why my mind jumped so quickly to dinner dates anyway. D.P. Fitzpatrick is just the hired help. Nothing more. "That will be great. Do you want to meet at my office or yours?" I hope he doesn't say his office. It's a twenty-five-minute drive from my office to his during afternoon traffic, and I'm doubtful I can squeeze that into my schedule and still remain on time. Something tells me the Tax Man has no patience for tardiness. Plus, I have no desire to see Eleanor Bitch again, all things considered. This turns out not to be a problem.

"I'd prefer to stay clear of your office and its germ issues, Dr. Parker. Will it work for you to meet at that ridiculous coffee shop in your Mall? The witch themed one on the second level?"

I know which one he means. It's called the Cup and Cauldron and caters strictly to the tourist trade featuring overpriced coffee drinks with names like The Broom's Brew and Familiar's Frappe. I find it rather taste-less and derogatory toward practitioners of magic, but I keep my opinions to myself. Fortunately, it's at least easy for me to get there on time. "That will be fine, Mr. Fitz-patrick. I will see you at 2:00 pm, then?"

"Agreed," he confirms. "Please bring with you any correspondence you've received from the IRS." Then he promptly hangs up without even so much as a polite good-bye.

TOOTH 10

THE BLOUSE WITH A VIEW

I THANK ALL the Otherworld goddesses I can remember that I actually paid attention to how I dressed this morning. After lying around in a tattered bathrobe and my jammies for the past four days, I decided to wear something that would make me look better than I feel. Normally, I don't wear anything that's low cut, as I'm what people might call a curvy girl, which really means I'm extra stacked on top so that anything past an open first button reveals far too much cleavage. The particular blouse I'm wearing today doesn't have buttons, but its sweetheart neckline acts like a pair of stage curtains open just wide enough to put my girls in full view, front and center. Because it is brand new and has such a lovely rose and moss green pattern I decided to wear it, figuring that my lab coat would cover up my décolletage. I ponder whether I would have chosen this same blouse if I had known in advance that I would be meeting with the Tax Man today, but I can't come up with a definitive answer.

For the rest of the morning and the early afternoon, I try not to think about my upcoming meeting at the coffee shop, but this is a losing battle. Of course, I have no clue where the letters the IRS sent me might be. Thankfully, Mel had taken charge of them and neatly organized them by date, placing them in a manilla business folder labeled IRS Communications. I would like to say I have read them and fully understand what my problems with the US Internal Revenue Service entail, but I'd be lying. My Dad had always taken care of my taxes, but since his stroke six years ago and his subsequent placement in a nursing care facility, I let things like this slide. My attention has been focused entirely on building up my practice, with the rest of my time filled with my Corps duties and, of course, my little hobby. It isn't like I wanted these things to get away from me. It just sort of happened.

At 1:45 Mel hustles me out of the office, insisting I leave my lab coat behind. I think this is absolutely ridiculous since I am a dentist and a lab coat is perfectly acceptable clothing, even in public. My PA grins at me like she's just swallowed a canary and pushes me towards the door while ticking off an entire list of things I am not supposed to say or do during my meeting with Mr. Fitzpatrick. She is annoyed because I won't touch up my lipstick before I go, so I remind her that this is strictly a business meeting and nothing more, but when I get to the escalator, I second guess myself and wonder whether I should have added a fresh swipe of Blushing Berry to my lips.

I'm not really sure about the protocol for meetings

that occur outside of the office. Should I go straight to the table first or stop and purchase something before proceeding? I would feel a bit rude taking up a seat without buying a drink. I easily spot the Tax Man. He's the only one in the shop wearing a wool suit while it's ninety degrees outside. Plus, he's a hottie, no doubt about it. He's sitting at a small table near a large cardboard cutout of an ugly hag on a broom, and I try not to let the insulting image distract me from my purpose. I quickly notice that the Tax Man has a cup in front of him, signaling that I also should purchase a beverage before making my way to meet him. Stepping in line, I turn around and note that he definitely has seen me. I wave my hand slightly, but he doesn't return my wave, so I let my hand drop self-consciously back down to my side, recon-firming my belief that when it comes to normal social graces, D.P. Fitzpatrick is about the rudest man I've ever met.

Ordering one of the stereotypical witch concoctions is out of the question, so I settle for herbal peppermint tea, which is the least offensive choice both to my heritage and my still-wonky tummy. I am grateful not to be wearing high, wobbly heels, as the damn barista has filled my tiny little cup to the very brim, and I worry about sloshing most of the tea out of the cup before I get to the table.

Okay. I'll admit it. I'm nervous, and I don't think the fluttering in my gut has anything to do with lingering flu symptoms. The Tax Man politely stands when I arrive and pulls out a chair for me, so now I feel guilty for thinking of him as the rudest man I've ever met. That is until he takes the cup from my hand and puts it on the table next to us. "I hope you don't mind, Dr. Parker, but that cup is much too full, and I haven't fully recovered from your last accident with a hot beverage."

My face feels hot and I am sure I am blushing from embarrassment, but then he smiles just the tiniest of smiles and puts the cup back in front of me. "Just teasing, Dr. Parker, though I wish you could have seen your face." He takes a sip from his cup and makes a face of his own. "Of course, I didn't do you any favors returning that swill to you. If this is what passes as tea, no wonder Americans have no civility."

My tongue feels as if it's grown six times larger, and no words seem able to escape my lipstick-free mouth. Part of me is annoyed that the jerk embarrassed me like he did, but another part would do it all over again for another chance to see his hint of a smile. Plus, for some inexplicable reason, his slight brogue continues to throw me completely off my game, and I want to slap myself out of it, whatever it is. The best I can muster is a simple "Hmmmm." Then I take a sip of my tea and grimace. D.P. Fitzpatrick is right. The tea is astoundingly bad, a cross between furniture polish and minty fresh toothpaste. Plus, it's so hot it burns my tongue.

That half smile makes an appearance again, and I'm almost tempted to take an extra sip for a chance to see another. Until, of course, he opens his mouth to speak. "As I somehow expected, Dr. Parker, you appear to be the type of person who never takes good advice when it's freely handed to you. I do hope that if I take your case, that won't be a problem. Did you bring the IRS letters as I instructed?"

What is it with this impossible man? One minute he's holding out my chair like a gentleman and the next he's teasing and insulting me! At this point, I again am ready to forget the whole damn thing; I'd rather go to jail for tax evasion than work with such a pompous ass. On the other hand, I'm no shrinking violet either. My honor is at stake! If Declan, the Prick, Fitzpatrick thinks he can scare me off that easily, then he's in for a rude awakening. I settle myself squarely in the chair. "Of course I've brought the letters. Do you think I have time in my busy schedule for sitting around and drinking bad tea with someone who likes to throw up my past mistakes?" I realize my poor choice of words immediately after I say them.

He smirks. "Please, Dr. Parker. We've both had enough of 'throwing up,' don't you agree?"

"Ugh! You are impossible to like, Mr. Fitzpatrick," I mutter under my breath while leaning down to pick up the tote containing the tax file at my feet. As I move upright, I see his face; there's absolutely no doubt in my mind that the Tax Man is staring straight down my blouse and catching himself a grand view of the Twin Peaks.

I sit up quickly and hand him the folder. If he's embarrassed by the fact I've just caught him looking at my boobs he doesn't show it, and though I feel I should say something snarky, the moment has passed. Truth be told, I'm rather happy I chose this blouse today and that the Tax Man apparently appreciates the view. So shoot me. It's a confidence boost on a day I can use some extra confidence.

Letters in hand, the Tax Man now is all business. If his grunting, dismal expressions and head shaking are any indication, my IRS news is not good. He looks up and asks, "Do you have a drug addiction I'm not aware of, Dr. Parker?"

I give him a look of pure, incredulous shock. "No! I'm a medical professional! Of course I don't have a drug problem. Why would you ask such a silly question?"

He answers my question with another of his own. "A gambling addiction then?"

"Another ridiculous question! Absolutely not! What are you getting at, Mr. Fitzpatrick?"

Tax Man slides the letters back into the folder but keeps them. "Dr. Parker, I have to be honest. You appear to be an intelligent person. You have a thriving dental practice. For the life of me, I cannot fathom why you would ignore paying your taxes if there isn't an outlying problem."

The words stick in my throat. I don't have a logical explanation for why things got as bad as they did. It just happened. One year turned into two and two into three and so on. Plus, I certainly can't tell this Mundane how I spend my evenings. Instead, I just mumble. "I've had a lot of…family difficulties. I'd rather not discuss them if you don't mind."

D. P. Fitzpatrick tisks loudly at me. "Please tell me you at least have proper paperwork…business receipts, W2s, bank statements…those sorts of things?"

I know I have the types of paperwork he's talking about. Somewhere at home. Stuffed in assorted boxes and bags. None of it properly filed. None of it organized. I don't tell him that part. "I'm not an idiot, you know. Yes… I have those things," I say.

"At your office or your home?" he asks.

"At my home," I lie. That statement might not be entirely true. I think there possibly could be a box of papers somewhere in my office but I would need to locate it. "I can transfer it all to my office," I volunteer.

The Tax Man takes the folder from the table and stands up. "That won't be necessary, Dr. Parker. We'll just go through them all at your home. That way you won't misplace anything in the transfer." He looks at his watch and says, "I'm afraid I need to cut our meeting short. I have a 3:00 appointment, and the traffic back is abominable. I know I'm busy the rest of the week, and I'm sure you have a backlog of patients after your illness. Is it possible to meet on Saturday afternoon? Let's say around noon?"

This catches me off guard, and I can't think of an excuse quickly enough. At least not with him looking at me. I end up agreeing, though how I possibly will be ready to have D. P. Fitzpatrick as a guest in my home by Saturday eludes me at the moment. "Uh…sure. No problem. Noon is fine. Do you need the address?" I ask.

"No need, Dr. Parker. I already know it," he replies, a tad too smugly for my taste. D.P. removes his suit jacket and throws it over his arm, ready to brave the June heat waiting outside the mall. I try not to notice the way his dress shirt tightly hugs his forearms, then change my mind. If the Tax Man can grab a look down my blouse, then I have every right to ogle his biceps. And as he walks away, I decide to ogle his ass as well.

TOOTH 11

THE TAX MAN COMETH

I CAN'T IMAGINE why in the name of the Universe I ever acquiesced to the Tax Man's suggestion that we meet at my house. I must truly have lost my mind. More likely, my brain became paralyzed by an onslaught of nasty thoughts regarding toned biceps and one really lovely ass. Unfortunately, I also wasn't feeling totally back to normal health wise, and D.P. was correct in assuming that I had a backlog of patients to see in addition to the ones previously scheduled for this week. Making matters worse, the Corps absolutely refused to let me off the hook for my Friday night retrievals. I had been persona non grata for the entire week, forcing other cadets to pick up my baby teeth in addition to their own; therefore, as compensation, they gave me an extra heavy load to make up for this imposition.

The extra work kept me from returning home until just after 2:00 AM Saturday morning. I accomplished six retrievals from different homes scattered throughout Salem, and I am thoroughly exhausted. However, before I do anything else, I put my precious cargo into my secret, special hidey-hole. The compartment already is overflowing, requiring me to push the teeth around to make room for all of them to fit, which reminds me that I absolutely must make time ASAP for a quick trip to the Otherworld to drop them all off.

Since the summer night weather here in Salem is nearly as muggy as during the day, a shower and a complete change of clothes is necessary before I even can attempt to finish the chores that need to be done before my noon appointment with the Tax Man. As I mop the kitchen floor, I wonder whether I should whip up some goodies in case the Tax Man takes afternoon tea as I imagine he might.

I forgo the idea of scones, worried they might dredge up images of last Friday. I still have some Kerrygold butter and Meyer lemons in the fridge from my last baking adventure, so I decide on my perfected adaptation of the classic lemon bar, a dreamy concoction that strikes the perfect balance between sweet and tart. Between the baking and subsequent cleaning up, it's almost 10:00 AM before I finish. Then, I shower and change clothes again and plop myself on the sofa to relax a bit before D.P. Fitzpatrick arrives.

At some point, my relaxation turns into REM sleep, so that when the Ring Door Bell signals that there is an arrival at my front door, I am startled awake with drool on my chin and a crick in my neck. I wipe my chin with the back of my hand, pop a cinnamon Tic Tac in my mouth, *(Really, Rosie? A Tic Tac? Do you actually think you're going to get that close?)* and answer the door.

I almost expect the Tax Man to be wearing his usual tailored suit, but evidently even D.P. relaxes just a bit on Saturday. He's dressed in khaki slacks, a plain white polo shirt, and sockless Sperry Topsiders. He still has his heavy leather briefcase in his left hand, ready for detailed tax work…whatever that entails. "Good afternoon, Dr. Parker," he says. "I hope you're ready for what I expect to be a very long day?"

Why does everything out of this man's mouth have a touch of sarcasm to it? Or maybe it's just me personally that provokes it? Despite my misgivings, I am determined to kill him with kindness, though by the end of the day I hope I will not want to kill him literally. "A good afternoon to you as well, Mr. Fitzpatrick. Won't you come in? I've been so looking forward to working out my tax… issues today."

D.P. steps through my door. "I sincerely doubt everything will be settled today, Dr. Parker. You've let this dereliction go on far too long for any easy fix, but we'll tackle as much as possible today." He looks around my parlor and if he notices it's a lot neater than the last time he saw it, thankfully he doesn't comment. I don't respond to his dereliction remark either, but I literally have to bite my tongue in order not to. We've gotten this far, so I'm working diligently not to screw up this meeting. I want this whole tax mess cleared up and D.P. Fitzpatrick out of my life as quickly as possible. *(Sure, Rosie. That's what you keep saying to yourself, so why then did you make those lemon bars and why are you sucking on cinnamon Tic Tacs?)*

Originally, I had planned for us to work at the dining room table, but when I saw exactly how many bags and bins of paperwork were stored in my office suite upstairs, I changed my mind. Way too much heavy stuff to carry downstairs. The loft is home to both my hobby supplies and my home office. I've spent the better part of this week trying to put some sense of order to it, and by Saturday, I've made plenty of room for the Tax Man to do his work. This also means he will have a full view of all my doll-houses, and from what I know already of D.P.'s personality, I brace myself for whatever dismissive comments he will make about them. It's okay. I'm used to people not understanding. The general public thinks that my houses are simply silly children's toys; thus, I am more than surprised when the Tax Man seems impressed by my work. He carefully pulls out a dressed bed from my Victorian house and presses down on the mattress, commenting that "a wee person actually could sleep on this."

His statement makes me catch my breath. It's disconcerting because I have, in fact, slept on that very same mattress as a wee person...just for the fun of it. Obviously, I can't tell him that. I have no doubts that the Tax Man already has a less than stellar opinion regarding my sanity. Still, it's heartwarming to have D.P. compliment me on something that means the world to me.

The Tax Man grunts his approval over the space I've set up for him to work, but then tisks loudly upon seeing the multitude of unfiled and disorganized paperwork. Truthfully, it does look rather overwhelming. He grabs one of the largest boxes and pulls out a stack of receipts, invoices, and accounting statements from my practice. As he goes through them, he tasks me with arranging them in piles according to his instructions. He pulls a laptop from his case, creates a spreadsheet, and begins entering information. There is practically no interaction between us, except when he hands me papers to put in their rightful piles.

In all honesty, I admit that I'm strangely disappointed. I've always understood that D.P. was coming here strictly for business purposes, but I had hoped to glean a little personal information from him during some idle conversation. It appears this won't be possible since there's absolutely no conversing going on whatsoever. After enduring an hour of deafening silence, I ask whether he would mind if I put on some music. I receive a curt affirmative nod in response, but when Alexa starts belting out Barry Manilow's Greatest Hits, he looks up and frowns. "Can we find something a little less...karaoke, Dr. Parker?" he asks.

And so it seems that there is nothing Dr. Parker can do correctly to please this man. I regret agreeing to meet with him at my house; the Tax Man makes me feel inadequate in so many ways, and this fact bothers me more acutely here in my own home. I also regret going to so much trouble attempting to be a good hostess, and when 3:00 PM finally rolls around and I have had all I can take of sitting in agonizing, ignored silence, I decide it's time for tea. At least it will get me out of this room with him. I clear my throat to get his attention as his eyes are glued to the spreadsheet on his computer screen. "I could use some afternoon tea, Mr. Fitzpatrick. How about you?"

D.P. finally looks up at me. "That would be most appreciated, Dr. Parker. Thank you." Then he goes right back to his work.

I make my way down to the kitchen and boil water for tea. I put two china cups on a tray, along with two small plates and the lemon bars I made this morning. While the water boils, I realize I am hungrier than I thought, probably because I hadn't made time for breakfast. With this in mind, I take a few hard-boiled eggs from my fridge, add some mayo and fresh chives, and whip up a few tea sandwiches, with the crusts properly cut, of course, and add these to the tray. I didn't bother to ask the Tax Man his choice of tea. I choose Barry's Afternoon Blend, an Irish import I assume he's had before.

Making my way back upstairs with the loaded tray, I hear humming from the loft. It stops me in my tracks. D.P. is a hummer? I would never have guessed. And if I am shocked by the humming, I am frozen in place by what I hear next. There is a rustle of papers, and the Tax Man sighs deeply. Then he mumbles, "Ah, Sweet Rosie, whatever am I going to do with you, Lass?"

TOOTH 12

SWEET ROSIE LASS

MY FEET ARE FROZEN to the spot and suddenly I feel much too warm. Did D.P. really just call me Sweet Rosie? Oy! The way he says the word Lass, rolling off his tongue with the slight sound of Ireland layered on top. It does things to me. I feel a strong need to sneak back down to the kitchen and think about this for a moment, but the tray I'm holding is getting heavier the longer I stand here, and the tea isn't getting any hotter while my blush continues. I square my shoulders, take a deep breath, and march, smiling pleasantly, into my loft hoping the Tax Man doesn't realize I heard what I heard.

D.P. Fitzpatrick doesn't even look up from his work. I finally call out "Tea time!" before he bobs his head up, checks his watch, and begins to clear some space in front of him. I place the tray before him on the table and roll a chair directly across from him. The Tax Man doesn't ask; he autonomously takes a cup and saucer from the tray and adds one cube of sugar and a splash of milk before pouring in some Barry's Afternoon Blend, and then he slides the china cup towards me. This catches me off guard: initially because of the chivalrous gesture and secondarily because this is...well...exactly the way I take my tea. I can't help but blurt out, "Thank you, Mr. Fitzpatrick, but how did you happen to know how I like my tea?"

D.P. looks at me with the barest hint of a smile. "An easy deduction, Dr. Parker. From the looks of this tray, you obviously know what makes up a proper afternoon tea. I just assumed you would be of the type to want your own 'cuppa' in the same correct manner as well." To prove his point, he makes a second cup for himself in the exact same way, but I am sure that when we met at the coffee shop earlier in the week he'd drunk his tea plain. The Tax Man draws my attention away from the subject with an entirely different topic. "If you would be so kind as to enlighten me, Dr. Parker, about this fascinating hobby of yours. However do you get into all those tiny nooks and crannies? It must be quite difficult, is it not?"

I feel another rush of heat begin to build around my neckline. His question is similar to others I receive all the time, but his asking of it makes me nervous. If I told him how I get such expert paint coverage, he'd certainly run from my house immediately, fearing me a complete madwoman. Using his method, I turn the tables with a question of my own. "Oh, I have a whole list of... uhmm... special techniques, but before we get to that, I have a favor to ask of you."

He raises an eyebrow, but agrees. "Request away, Dr. Parker."

I smile as pleasantly as I can, hoping to appear as the Sweet Rosie, Lass he thinks I am. "Since it looks like we'll be spending quite a bit of time together, I was rather hoping we might dispense with the formal titles. Maybe you could just call me Rosie?"

His half smile appears again, though to my eye it seems a bit smirkier than before. Or maybe I'm just imagining it. He nods and replies, "As you wish...Rosie."

There's that rolling of the r again. I don't know why it gets to me...every...single...time. I wait for him to ask me to call him by his first name. He helps himself to another egg salad sandwich and adds a lemon bar to his plate. *So much for gluten free and organic. You're full of shit, Eleanor Bitch.* I get annoyed waiting for his expected response, so I jump in and ask him directly. "Would it be okay then if I call you Declan?"

His smile is genuine this time. He replies, "That would be fine. I can only imagine it will be an improvement over some of the other names you've called me."

Touche. I did call him several names beginning with the letter p that were less than polite. I ignore his comment, neither apologizing nor making a multitude of lame excuses. Instead, I launch into the whole history of my dollhouse collection. He munches while I talk and as I wander around the room pointing out the different houses and their finer points. Declan appears genuinely interested in my hobby, asking appropriate questions and commenting positively. It makes my heart happier than it has been for a very long time.

Eventually the tray is clear of treats, and the teapot is empty. The Tax Man looks at his watch again and says, "Time to get back to work. I had planned to get through at least three or four boxes today."

I am a little disappointed to end what's been a very pleasant hour. I have the tiniest spark of hope that perhaps my Tax Man is just as attracted to me as I am to him. It's become impossible for me to deny that I am more than a little fascinated by Declan Fitzpatrick. This proves my point that I simply am drawn to Mundane men. I want the necessity of us meeting regularly to last as long as possible, but then I worry that perhaps there is someone else special in the Tax Man's life. He's not wearing a wedding band, so I'm broadly guessing he isn't married. Is there a girlfriend? Maybe more than one? When you look like the Tax Man, you don't spend Saturday nights alone. What if he has a date after our meeting here? If that's the case, I really don't want to know about it. Besides, I have Corps orders for tonight. When Declan leaves, I'll leave shortly behind him.

The two of us settle back into our routine of earlier. He sorts and enters data into his computer then hands the paperwork to me to place in the appropriate piles. We are back to zero communication. I allow myself the luxury of staring at him while he is engrossed totally in my messed-up taxes. I note the slight cowlick near the top of his head, the scattering of freckles at his neckline where his polo shirt is unbuttoned, and the fact that he bites his lower lip when he studies numbers. It's crazy adorable. *Knock it off, Rosie! You're sitting here drooling over a man that has been, up until now, only mildly pleasant to you. You're making a big leap here girlfriend! Mundane men are notably casual about their relationships. Don't set yourself up for a big fall.* I tell my inner self to shut up and go away. If I want to dream about spending time horizontally with Declan Fitzpatrick, I am entitled to do so. If only for a little while.

But even my naughty daydreams don't stave off the boredom caused by hour after hour of unmitigated silence. I try to chat the Tax Man up, but he looks genuinely annoyed that I am keeping him from his work. At one point, I struggle to stay awake in my chair. I've been up for nearly 24 hours, and I still have night time Corps assignments to complete. To prevent myself from dozing, I pace the limited space, which wins me yet another disapproving look from Declan. Instead, I simply resign myself to putting up with complete boredom until my Tax Man decides he's had enough for the night. Before returning to my prison chair, I glance out the window and my heart jumps into my throat.

There's a gray Honda parked across the street from my house. It looks very much like the one that followed me home last week. Two men in hoodies exit the car and appear to head towards my front door. My Ring DoorBell chimes but then suddenly is silent. I turn to the Tax Man. "Uhhhmmm…Declan…I think someone just broke into my house."

Declan looks up and registers the panicked look on my face. I bring up the door's security camera feed on my phone, but there is no one at the front door. That's obviously because they already are inside. We both hear them banging around downstairs as well as the faintest sounds of male voices at the bottom of the stairs. I start to punch

911 into my phone, but the Tax Man grabs it out of my hand.

"We don't have time for that, Lass." Declan Fitzpatrick takes my hand in his, and before I can utter a single word, my Tax Man and I are wee sized and standing in the Master Suite of my largest Victorian dollhouse. There's one major problem with this scenario as I currently see it: it's not my magic that put us here.

TOOTH 13

THE FAE FACTS

I AM beyond shocked and more than a little upset. I look at mini-sized D.P. and open my mouth to give him a rousing piece of my mind. "What the fu…" My words are cut off. Mr. Tax Man clamps his hand over my mouth and drags me toward a French armoire that is the most expensive miniature in my collection. It was a custom order, handmade in Paris by a Master Craftsman, and it cost me more than I'll ever admit. He opens the door, and before shoving me in, signals for my silence with a finger to his lips. Declan listens for a second, then joins me in the tiny, cramped space. He pulls both doors shut, leaving his side open a tiny crack to see out into the room. I just hope the armoire can hold both of our weights without the bottom panel giving way.

At the same moment as D.P. closes his door, the two men enter my loft office space. I can see only a tiny sliver into the room through the crack D.P. left open. From his side, I'm guessing Declan probably can see more. The men are wearing dark hoodies and Gaiters covering their faces, leaving only their eyes showing. They have pistols in their hands, and the taller of the two points to a floral painting on my east wall. They remove it and toss it to the floor, obliterating what I believe to be my lovely lakeside cottage. I hear the painting hit the floor along with the sound of smashing, cracking wood causing me to shudder. The Tax Man puts his arms around me and pulls me even closer, which is disconcerting because my boobs already are smooshed against his chest, and I can feel D.P.'s breath on the top of my head. I hadn't noticed before, but this close I can tell he is wearing an aftershave or cologne of some sort, a woodsy, green scent. Or maybe it's just good ole' fashioned Irish Spring soap, which is kind of funny when you think about it. I am startled to hear his voice in my head. *"I know this is awful, Lass. Stay still. I expect they will leave soon, and we can fix anything they've damaged. It will be okay."*

Mental telepathy is universal among all types of Fae. I've become so lapsed regarding my magical side that I rarely give it any thought. Mel is the only other *Sidhe* I've been in daily contact with since my mom passed, and the two of us never communicate this way. Except for the tooth fairy gig, and my occasional hobby challenges, I live my life in Mundane style…the way I like it. However, now that I know D.P. has access to my head, I wonder what other thoughts to which he might have been privy. Apparently, he has access now, because he immediately answers my question. *"I've never accessed your thoughts. Not intentionally. Just stay still. We'll talk when they leave."*

I respond back, hoping I'm doing it right. It's been a long time, and I'm rusty. *"You better believe we're gonna talk, Mr. Fitzpatrick."*

"Ah...so I'm back to being Mr. Fitzpatrick again. As ya wish, Dr. Parker, though I do wish ya would stop wiggling against me. It's vera...distracting," the Tax Man responds.

I know I'm blushing, and I feel sweat beginning to build around my collar. I'm pretty sure it's not just from lack of air in the armoire. Outside the dollhouse, I hear a heavy thump as another one of my treasures hits the floor. One man speaks to the other. It's not English. If I had to guess, I would say it's some type of Eastern European language, possibly Russian. From my limited view, I see them look out the window, which is open. I know I didn't open it. Not with the AC on. There is no comment from the Tax Man.

Eventually, I hear the men leave the loft and thump down the stairs. They spend a few minutes downstairs and then I hear the front door open and close, followed by the sound of a car driving away. D.P. releases his hold on me, and in the blink of an eye, I find myself back to normal size and standing in my loft. I look around at the damage; all my lovely things, so much time and hard work, in pieces on the floor. The window is still open, and there is a fire safety ladder hanging from the sill. It wasn't me who put it there, but it's a great idea. The two men must have seen it and assumed we residents crawled out the window, down the ladder, and escaped before they made it to the loft. Before the jerks left the room, they made sure to tear the place apart completely, obviously looking for something. I feel tears burning at the corners of my eyes, and they're not only for the lost pieces of my collection. It's my fault for expecting too much. There are no fairy tales in real life, and D.P. Fitzpatrick is about as far from being Prince Charming as I am from being any kind of love story heroine. I can't tolerate being in this loft or within his presence any longer, so I head downstairs without a word to the Tax Man.

He doesn't directly follow me down. I plop myself on the sofa and try not to cry. I see that the two men broke the frame of my front door. It closes, but it doesn't lock. I realize that none of my security precautions have, in truth, kept me safe. The Tax Man eventually comes downstairs and sits on the sofa next to me. I am too angry to want him there, so I get up in dramatic fashion and move to the armchair across from the sofa. He sighs. "That's very childish, you know."

I don't answer for a full two minutes. I don't know where to begin or what to say to Declan Fitzpatrick, the man who turned out to be nothing I had imagined. Finally, my need to know wins over my plan to remain silent. "You better damn well spill it, Fitzpatrick. You're obviously Fae…Upper Realm *Sidhe*, I would guess."

He leans back into the sofa and puts his arms behind his head. Looking at him now, I wonder how I could have missed all the little tell-tale signs. The too high forehead, the fuller bottom lip, the pale skin, ginger hair and green eyes, not to mention the tall, lithe build and the long, thin fingers. If I went and lifted the hair off the sides of his face, I surely would find that his ears veered to the pointed side of shape. Worse yet, what does it say about my own lax abilities that I didn't sense it immediately? It's a reminder of how lazy I've gotten about my magical heritage.

The Tax Man answers my question. "You are correct. I am *Sidhe* on both my father and mother's side. House *Nuada.*"

This throws me for a loop, and I need to think about it for a moment before responding. I lean forward in my chair. "Shit! House *Nuada*? That means you're *Tuatha De Danaan*! That's like frickin' Fae royalty! You're just a few steps below *I Idir*'s throne. Why the hell are you pretending to be a damn tax accountant?"

D.P. makes a face like I've obviously somehow insulted him by stating the facts. "I am not 'pretending' to be a tax account," he complains. "I AM a licensed CPA, and an IRS Enrolled Agent. An excellent one at that, I may add." As is typical, he tries to get me off topic by asking a question of his own. "Dr. Parker, do you have any idea why those men would select your house to break into?"

"No, I haven't got an 'f-ing clue. They obviously were looking for something. But I don't have any real valuables, so they picked the wrong damn house to rob."

The Tax Man makes a face. I'm not sure whether it's because of my salty language or the fact that I seem clueless. Before I can determine which, there is a loud knock at my front door. My Ring camera no longer is operating, so I can't see who it might be. I'm not expecting anyone.

Apparently, D.P. is. He gets up from the sofa to answer the door, which is terribly rude since it's my house. "I called someone to help sort this all out," he explains.

I see a uniformed man at my door, and at first, I don't put it all together. It makes total sense to call the police, but the officer at the door looks vaguely familiar. He greets the Tax Man, and it's obvious they know each other. He turns to speak to me, and then it hits me like a bolt of lightening. The uniformed man at my door is none other than the Sheriff of Essex County, Ted Beckett, Merlin heir and Black Knight of *I Idir*.

TOOTH 14

OF HIDEY-HOLES AND HEISTS

HAVING the Black Knight of *I Idir* show up at my door pretty much guarantees that whatever is going on here is very bad news for me. This guy is the long arm of the law in my Fae Otherworld hometown, and if D.P. specifically called for Ted Beckett, I can't imagine it's regarding a routine, everyday style home invasion, even if he also happens to be the Sheriff of Essex County. Undoubtedly, if this were merely a Mundane criminal act, one of the Essex County Deputies would be standing here right now. Since it's not, and it's the damn Sheriff himself standing here, I definitely should be scared shitless. Our *Ridre Dubh* (Black Knight) has quite a no-nonsense reputation for the breaking of magical law. I don't think that I've broken any, but I don't really keep up with that shit, so who knows? Plus, the man is drop dead, movie-star gorgeous, and all I can do in the moment is stand here and gawk like a star-struck teenager.

Next to me, the Tax Man clears his throat, and I remember that magic protocol requires me to invite the Sheriff formally into my home. Technically, I don't bother with wards on my house so I can't see why it's necessary, but these Fae types are generally sticklers for rules, so I do as I am required. "Won't you come in, Sheriff Beckett?" Then I wonder whether I've already screwed up by using the wrong title. "I'm sorry. Would you prefer I call you Lord Merlin? Or perhaps Sir Knight?"

The Wonder Boy of *I Idir* smiles at me, and gracious good goddess, I want to fall down on my knees and bask in the glory of that smile forever. Okay...so maybe I'm exaggerating a little. But damn! He's got to be one of the most handsome men I've ever seen. Plus, I can tell my fawning annoys D.P., so there's that added bonus. The Black Knight laughs and says, "Sheriff is just fine, Dr. Parker. I have more titles than any one man needs."

I lead him to the sofa and gesture for him to sit, taking a place next to him and relegating the Tax Man to the armchair across from us. Once seated, I remember that I haven't performed my proper hostess duties, so I ask, "Would you care for something to drink, Sheriff? Some coffee or tea? A soft drink, perhaps?" I ignore my other guest, which might be rude, but that's too damn bad. He's currently on my shit list. If I were being honest with myself, I'd have to admit that I'm more disappointed that he's Fae rather than upset that he wasn't upfront about it. I had gotten my hopes up, and well...now any thoughts I had about pursuing a relationship other than business is off the table.

"Thank you, Dr. Parker. That's very kind of you, but

I'm fine." He leans forward and looks at me intently with his gorgeous baby blues. "Dr. Parker...do you have any idea why those men targeted your house?"

There's a blush slowly creeping up my neck, caused by the suspicion that, somehow, I'm in trouble and also because the Black Knight is looking directly at me. My words feel jumbled in my mouth. "I just assumed it was a common everyday B and E, Sheriff." I see the corner of his mouth curl up over the B and E part. He probably guesses I watch too many crime dramas.

The Sheriff throws a look toward D.P. and I become even more worried. His voice is pleasant and neutral sounding, but his questions are loaded. "Dr. Parker, I understand that you are sworn by oath to secrecy, but as the *Ridre Dubh* I'm fully aware that you're a Tooth Fairy Cadet. Perhaps this event is tied to your service to the Crown?"

My stomach drops to my feet. If the Sheriff knows I'm a tooth fairy, then D.P. probably knows as well, and he's probably known since the first moment we met. A huge sense of embarrassment overwhelms me. These two are among the creme de la creme of Fae magical skill hierarchy and social status. Tooth fairies, on the other hand, sit at the bottom of that same ladder. We almost all are born of mixed heritage, mostly Mundane, and live our lives mainly in the Mundane world, having only the slightest interaction with the Otherworld. Without even looking at him, I can feel the Tax Man's eyes on me from his armchair perch, and it's a pretty good guess he thinks I am a loser.

A voice pops into my head. *"I think no such thing, Dr.*

Parker. I resent you assuming that I'm the type of person who cares about other people's heritage or social standing. It's unfair and untrue."

I answer back, hoping the Black Night is not privy to this mental conversation. "Stay the hell out of my head, Declan Fitzpatrick! I don't want you there! It's a personal assault."

Out of the corner of my eye, I see his eyes flicker. Maybe assault is too harsh a word. He looks upset. "If you don't want your thoughts exposed, Dr. Parker, then practice some self-control and put up a damn shield. I know you are perfectly capable of doing so. Your thoughts are an open book for anyone with magical ability to read. Not shielding is both dangerous and stupid."

Next to me, the Sheriff coughs, and I realize he's waiting for me to stop arguing with the Tax Man and answer his question. I think about fabricating a story about why I have so many baby teeth stored in the Mundane World, but decide both of them probably can see right through any lies, so I opt for the truth.

"Well, Sir, it might be possible that if they are… uhmmm…of the sort that might understand the magical value of baby teeth, and they are also aware of my role in the Corps, they might have been looking for the teeth I store at home before I deposit them in I Idir."

D.P. and the Black Knight exchange pointed looks; then Beckett speaks directly to the Tax Man. "Your observations, Fitz?"

"There were two of them, standard weapons, using the usual modus operandi typical of the Russians," Fitzpatrick explains. "They only spoke a few words, but it was definitely Chechen. Based on my magical read of them, this was definitely meant to be a snatch and grab, both of the target and of the teeth. They came prepared with injectables and zip ties. I'm almost positive they were working on orders from higher ups, so I wasn't able to determine what they wanted with Dr. Parker."

It takes a full thirty seconds before I properly can process what my Tax Man has just said. I jump up in alarm from the sofa. "Just hold on a minute! What the hell is going on here?" I stick my thumb out at D.P. "Did he just say I was the intended target? That these guys who broke into my house wanted to...abduct me? For what damn reason?"

"I will explain everything in due time, Dr. Parker," the Black Knight says. "But first, I'm going to ask you to show us where you keep your collected baby teeth. I need to verify they haven't been stolen."

By this time, I'm shaking. I want to know why someone like me, someone with little to no magical skill, is being hunted by Chechen bad guys. What the hell did D.P. mean by injectables, and just how is the Tax Man even involved in any of this? I don't care whether either of them can read my thoughts right now. I damn well want answers of my own, but I'm guessing neither of them will be happy with what I'm about to show them. I know for a fact the bad guys did not find my overly large stash of baby teeth. My hiding place is remarkably clever, and they didn't come close to finding it.

I lead them upstairs to the loft, expecting to find it in the state of complete mess that the bad guys left it. I stop in total surprise at the doorway, finding that everything has been returned to its rightful spot and both smashed houses are whole again and standing where they belong. I didn't have the time or the heart to do this myself, so I am sure this was D.P.'s magical doing. I am unsure what to say, finding it difficult to say thank you, especially as everything was his fault to begin with. Thus, I say nothing and work to keep some kind of wholly inadequate mental shield in place.

If the Black Knight has anything to say about my dollhouses, he keeps it to himself. I stop in front of a very detailed wooden dollhouse deck with an unusual covered gazebo. While D.P. and the Sheriff watch, I pull out the stairs and lift the roof off the top of the gazebo, thus revealing several hidden compartments, each overflowing with baby teeth. I can almost guarantee what will happen next. I have triple the amount of baby teeth Cadets are supposed to keep at home; I've broken several rules by not returning often enough to *I Idir* to make my deposits, and I've been caught by none other than the Big Boss himself. My tooth fairy career currently is circling the drain.

D.P. runs a hand through his hair, and I see the look of exasperation on his face. The *Ridre Dubh* remains impassive and neutral. "Isn't this a rather large amount of teeth for a Cadet to keep at home, Dr. Parker?"

My face is hot and red. I stutter out an excuse. "Yes. It's definitely beyond the recommended amount, Sir…and I really meant to make my deposit in *I Idir* earlier…but… well…I got really sick, and then I fell way behind with my patients and…" I let the words trail off.

The Tax Man jumps to my defense. "That is true, Sir.

Dr. Parker was down for a week with the norovirus. Nasty bug, that one."

At first I am pleased that D.P. is sticking up for me, but then I'm annoyed. I don't need some big time, fancy-shmancy, Fae Lord making excuses for me. Especially not this one. "I take full responsibility for my actions, Sir. I understand that there will be consequences involved."

Expecting to be read the riot act, I brace myself for a lengthy lecture, but none comes. Instead, the Black Knight says, "Let's worry about those 'consequences' later, Dr. Parker. Who is your Cadet Squad Leader?"

Shit. The last person I want involved here is that asshole. "Erik Ashton, Sir."

For the third time, the Big Boss and D.P. exchange looks. Just what the hell is going on here? Pulling a plastic bag marked evidence from his pants pocket, the *Ridre Dubh* gathers up all the teeth and places them in the bag. I wonder what the teeth are evidence of and what this will mean for me. My stomach is now queasy, and I am more than a little afraid.

"Why don't we go back downstairs, Dr. Parker? We'll talk this all out, and I'll try to answer all of your questions. Then we can decide how best to proceed."

Proceed with what? Any way you look at this, I'm in deep doo-doo.

TOOTH 15

A SURPRISE PARTY FOR ROSIE

THE SHERIFF and D.P. head downstairs to the parlor. I stay behind because something curious in the loft has caught my eye. When the Tax Man repaired the damage to my dollhouses perpetrated by the intruders, he'd carefully returned everything to the same exact spot in which it originally had been. But I realize there's something new sitting on the dining room table inside my beach house. Something I hadn't put there. I bend over to get a closer look, and I see a tiny woven basket of pretty porcelain wild flowers, perfectly formed in shades of pink, yellow, and lavender, interspersed with shiny green leaves. It is an exquisite piece, and though I know it probably was magically created, I am tickled by how ideally it finishes that room. I pick it up and place it in the palm of my hand to examine it from all sides. That's when I see that there's a little card tucked in among the flowers. The writing is in scale and so small that I have to squint to read it. It says, 'To Rosie" and below my name is the letter D.

My face gets hot, which has nothing to do with the fact that bad guys just broke into my home or that I've inadvertently attracted the notice of the Black Knight Enforcer of *I Idir*. I received flowers from the Tax Man! Not the ordinary, run-of-the-mill, kind of flowers. Special flowers created specifically for me. If my feelings were in a jumble before, they now are playing an especially vigorous game of Twister in both my head and my stomach.

When I finally return to the parlor, I see that Sheriff Beckett and D.P. both are sitting on the couch, and I am left to take the armchair across from them. I try to catch the Tax Man's eye, but he looks away. Beckett leads the conversation. "As a Corps Cadet, I'm sure you understand the importance of the baby teeth you gather, Dr. Parker, and the service they provide to the people of *I Idir,* am I correct?"

I give a quick nod and then add, "Yes, Sir. I understand fully." I wish he would stop pointing out that I am a tooth fairy. It doesn't boost my self-confidence.

The Sheriff continues. "During your recently required professional development, I believe you were made aware that certain…foreign governments…are attempting to use DNA from mixed Fae teeth in an attempt to breach the divide between the Mundane World and the preternatural Otherworld, isn't that correct?" He waits for me to acknowledge that I am aware of this information.

"Yes. We were all told that, Sir. We were asked to be especially diligent regarding the security of our teeth and to be extra cautious to conceal our identities as tooth fairies." I want to profess that I am 100% on board with these mandates, but since these two gentlemen have just seen my overly large stash, any statements along these lines would no doubt sound lame.

D.P. jumps into the conversation. "Dr. Parker is at extra risk due to her professional life, Sir. She's an extremely popular pediatric dentist here in Salem."

This odd scenario is beginning to feel as if I'm starring in a *Law and Order* episode, with Beckett playing the bad cop and D.P. working the role of the good one. I wonder whether this would be a good time for me to ask for legal counsel, but realize, hell, I don't know any Fae lawyers. I'm not sure whether they even use attorneys in the Otherworld or whether the Black Knight automatically acts as judge, jury, and executioner. While I'm pondering this, the Sheriff stuns me with his next statement.

"Dr. Parker, we've received proof that someone in the Corps is 'outing' Cadets to unsavory parties willing to pay for this information. In light of what's happened here this evening, I'm concerned that your tooth fairy status may have been compromised. For your personal safety, and for the security of *I Idir,* I must recommend that you take up residence in the Otherworld for the time being. You will be perfectly safe there until we can get a better handle on this problem and apprehend those involved. It won't be a long-term situation. We've made a lot of progress in the matter within these past few weeks, but we don't yet have anyone in custody. You're a soft target here in Salem."

My mouth seems to have disengaged from my brain, because I am thinking of the words I want to say, but they are not physically coming out of my mouth like they should. *Is this freaking Sheriff guy out of his mind? Move to I Idir? I don't know a single person in I Idir! Those people there were my mom's relatives, and I can count on one hand the number of times I've met them. Where would I stay? How would I support myself? Plus, what would happen to my patients in the Mundane World? I don't have the type of job where I can just pick up and say "Adios, Amigos!" What the hell would I even say to Mel?* I don't know whether any of this is spilling out from my head like water in a colander or whether I still have any viable mental shield left in place, but I'm too upset to figure these things out.

It's a good guess they've both heard everything I was thinking. The Black Knight leans forward and does his best to look sympathetic. "I know this is a huge shock, Dr. Parker, as well as a big imposition for you. But I must be blunt here. The men who broke into your house today are not civilized people. They meant to abduct you. We're not sure for what purpose, but they are the type that routinely enjoy hurting people. I'm only looking out for your best interests."

The Tax Man has been quiet until now. He turns and speaks directly to the Sheriff. "Sir, if I may comment?"

"Of course. What are your thoughts, Declan?" the Black Knight asks. I resent that he's on a first name basis with my Tax Man, and I currently am not.

"I think we might be better served if Dr. Parker remains where she is," D.P. suggests. "If she goes underground, then the Chechens will know we're on to them. They thus could pull back, and we would lose our chance to catch the head of the snake. I propose that Dr. Parker remain here in Salem and continue her practice as if nothing has happened. I'll take on her security detail myself. If the Chechens make another attempt, I'll be here to apprehend them."

I can't believe what I'm hearing. The two of them are discussing my life as if I'm not even in the same room. This is the reason I've never had the slightest interest in Fae men, especially those with hoity-toity backgrounds like these two. Generally, I find them all to be like this: bossy, opinionated, and self-serving. My Mother warned me about Fae men. I'd always thought she over-exaggerated, but I now have first-hand knowledge that my mom was right as rain.

"Does your schedule allow for a one-on-one detail, Fitz?" the Sheriff asks. "I know you already have a pretty full plate."

"It will work out fine, Sir," D.P. answers. "I'm in the middle of straightening out Dr. Parker's major tax issues, so it will give me the opportunity to clear up that problem as well. She's one step away from the IRS intervening, and the last thing we need is Fed involvement of any kind."

"You make perfect sense, Fitz," the Sheriff says. "I agree. Yours is a much better plan of action."

Okay. Why in the hell did Lord Pompous the Tax Man feel the need to tell the Sheriff about my little tax problems? Now Beckett is sure to think me a total idiot if he hasn't already decided that Dr. Parker is a complete loser. I jump up from my seat. After all this back and forth between the two men, I am so angry that I lose my fear of standing up to the Black Knight. "Excuse me, gentlemen. But aren't you two forgetting to include my opinion in this little plan of yours? As far as I'm concerned, I don't need a full-time babysitter, and I have absolutely no desire to move to *I Idir*. Plus, I have no idea why you'd pick a damn tax accountant for my 'security' detail, Sheriff." I point a finger at D.P. "What's he gonna do? Stab them with a frickin' pencil? Throw his laptop at them?"

The corners of the Black Knight's mouth turn up in a definite smile. He looks at D.P., who all of a sudden becomes extraordinarily interested in a piece of lint on the arm of my sofa. The Tax Man doesn't look up when the Sheriff says, "No worries on that front, Dr. Parker. Declan Fitzpatrick is head of *I Idir* Intelligence here on the east coast. He's perfectly capable of keeping you safe and secure."

TOOTH 16

LIAR, LIAR... GUN FOR HIRE

I CAN ONLY IMAGINE what I look like, standing here with my mouth hanging open. I work like a maniac to keep my thoughts to myself. I don't want them to see how much this news hurts me. *You're a big dope, Rosie Parker! How in the names of all the goddesses could you possibly think that someone like him would be interested in someone like you? You're what they call a target. Nothing more. The Black Knight said so himself. A soft target. Soft in the head is more like it!* Busy as I am with this whole mental shield thing, I can't think of anything witty or clever to say, so I just mumble, "I wasn't aware that *I Idir* had an intelligence agency. It must be a new thing." *Duh! Nice going, Rose. Another dumb ass comment falls from your lips. If I Idir has spies in the Mundane World, they sure as hell wouldn't haven't gone around telling people about it. Especially tooth faries. So stupid!*

The Black Knight tries to look both sympathetic and

concerned. It seems fake, and I want to slap him silly; but frankly, he scares the shit out of me. I don't even look at the Tax Man. For all I care, he can go back to whatever spy hell he came from. "You are correct, Dr. Parker," Sheriff Beckett explains. "Organized intelligence of the Mundane World by the Otherworld is a relatively new necessity. With technology and science improving in the Mundane World at neck-breaking speed, we preternaturals need to be more proactive and diligent players in the espionage game if we want to keep *I Idir* safe from outside forces."

Bucking up some courage, I respond, "And if I don't want to participate in either of your 'plans,' Sheriff?"

He raises a dark eyebrow at me. "I'm afraid I'm going to have to insist, Dr. Parker. The security of *I Idir* and its citizens, both here and abroad, are my responsibility. I'm leaving the choice up to you as to whether you stay here in Salem with Mr. Fitzpatrick as your security detail or you move to *I Idir* until we've worked out why these tooth fairy abductions have been occurring and who is behind them. There really are no other alternatives."

Again with the damn tooth fairy reference. That man is not going to let me forget my place, is he? I absolutely do not want to move to *I Idir*. My place is here in Salem, so if that means I have to share my space with the Tax Man, so be it. I'm an adult. I can handle these things in an adult manner, especially now that I know the truth about him. "Then I suppose I'd rather stay here, Sheriff. There's no place for me in *I Idir*. I have responsibilities here in Salem, just as you say you have yours."

My answer sounds as flippant and sarcastic as it was

meant, but the Black Knight seemingly ignores the disrespect. He smiles congenially and thanks me for my service to *I Idir*. "By staying here in Salem and putting yourself at risk, you really are doing us a great favor, Dr. Parker," the Sheriff says. "If we can catch the men who broke into your house tonight, hopefully then we can follow the trail back to whomever is behind these atrocities. I commend your courage in helping us."

Blah, blah, blah. It's not like you left me a lot of choice, Black Knight. "Thank you, Sir. I'm glad we could reach an acceptable arrangement," I mutter.

D.P. walks the Sheriff out my front door as if he owns the place and follows him to his squad car. I pull back the curtains a bit and watch them through my front window. They stand and talk for a few moments and then move to the back of the Sheriff's squad car. Beckett opens the trunk and the Tax Man reaches in and pulls something out. It is past dusk, so I can barely make out what's going on in the dim light, but when D. P. holds it up and fiddles with it, the street light shines on the object in his hand. I can clearly see that it's a gun he's examining before sticking it in the waistband of his khakis.

Shit. If D.P. needs to carry a gun, then this is a lot more dangerous than I thought. I wonder if I've made a mistake by not just going to *I Idir*. Not only are bad guys trying to abduct me, I have to have the Tax Man under my feet indefinitely, reminding me of what a frickin' fool I've been. It occurs to me that I have only the one Queen-sized bed in my bedroom and one very narrow, lumpy, Murphy bed in the loft. I wonder where in the hell D.P. expects to sleep. *What the fuck's wrong with you Rosie? Don't you have a single brain cell left? He's not interested in anything going on in your bed, you idiot. You're just a soft target. He'll be damn comfortable anywhere away from you.*

There's no more time left for my brain to scold me. The Sheriff's car has pulled away, and Agent Fitzpatrick is walking back to my front door. There's only the smallest fraction of time to pull a composed face together before we're back to being alone in my house. I hop back into the armchair. The last thing I want is to be caught spying out the window, then I shake my head over my ridiculous choice of words.

At least the Tax Man has the courtesy to look a tad sheepish. He shuts and locks the door, which, by the way, magically is fixed, and takes a seat back on the sofa, working his hardest, I presume, to look contrite. "I suppose you have a lot of things to say to me, Dr. Parker," he states.

Actually, you condescending asshole, I want to take my fists and pummel you for making me believe there might be something between us. You hurt me, you bastard. I wonder if my mental shield thing isn't working so well, because the Tax Man goes a bit pale. Whatever. He can't begin to feel as rotten as I do. "As a matter of fact, I really have nothing at all to say to you, Mr. Fitzpatrick. Why bother talking when everything out of your mouth is a lie anyway?"

He leans forward and folds his hands. "That's very unfair, Ros...Dr. Parker. I haven't 'lied' to you at all."

He isn't really going to try to play a game of semantics with me, is he? "That's not how I see it, Mr. Fitzpatrick. You told me you were a tax accountant, one of the best in Salem. A frickin' enrolled agent. I expected someone who would help me with my IRS problems, not someone who was gonna screw me over." I regret my choice of words. Screw and D.P. should not be in the same thought together. It fucks with my head.

The man now has the balls to look offended, as if he is the wounded party here. His ears, which I now can see definitely are too pointy for my taste, are pink in color. He's either upset or he doesn't care for the use of the word screw in my diatribe either. It's obvious when he's agitated: he can't keep the brogue out of his voice. The Rs in his words are rolling like tumbleweeds. "I did not lie to you, Dr. Parker. I AM an excellent tax accountant and a highly sought-after enrolled agent. I've helped hundreds of people with problems like yours work something out with the IRS."

"Hmmm…you just conveniently left out the part about being a secret agent man for the Fae Otherworld, right? Forgot all about that side job, did we? Face it, Tax Man, you wormed your way into my house and my life just so you could spy on me." I spit the words out like venom while at the same time they're cutting an aching hole in my heart, but I can't seem to stop myself. "I bet you thought I might be that snitch who's been 'outing' other Cadets. You actually thought that I possibly could do something like that. But why the hell wouldn't you think that, Mr. High and Mighty, Lord *Nuada?* Everyone knows that according to the secrets of Otherworld hierarchy, tooth fairies are the lowest of the lows. We're capable of anything downright dastardly, aren't we, so why not cut the heart out of one of us? Who the hell cares about tooth fairies? You sure as hell don't."

TOOTH 17

A MOMENT... LOST

THE TAX MAN folds his arms across his chest and leans comfortably against the cushions of my sofa, making himself look far too much at home. I feel like I've completely lost control of this whole situation...of my home, my life, and especially my emotions. He begins with the pathetic, overused cliche, "I know this is upsetting, Dr. Parker, but..."

I don't let him finish. Instead, I make a noise demonstrating extreme frustration while grabbing a fringed throw pillow from my armchair and lobbing it at his head. "You don't know anything about me, you self-serving, lying bastard!" I have terrible aim. The pillow misses his head and hits the lamp on the side table next to him, knocking it to the floor and plunging the room into total darkness.

Before I can move to fix the damage, a hand is clamped over my mouth and nose, and someone roughly grabs me around my waist and pulls me against them. I panic and begin struggling, twisting and kicking to loosen myself and slapping at my assailant. The hand and arm holding me are like steel bands that I can't budge, and I begin to be dragged toward the front door. Cut off from normal breathing, I am slightly dizzy and disorientated. Then, a familiar voice whispers in my ear. "Do you see just how easy it would be, Dr. Parker?"

The hand and arm are removed, and I am free. The light in the dining room goes on by itself, casting an eerie glow over the darkened parlor. I am rocky on my feet, and the Tax Man puts his hands on my shoulders to keep me from falling. I push him away. "Get away from me. I don't want your hands on me."

He ignores me, picking me up under the knees and easily carrying me to the sofa as if I don't weigh close to two hundred pounds. "Take deep breaths," D.P. instructs, "in through the nose and out through the mouth." He models it, and I find myself following his actions without thinking about it. In the meantime, he rights the lamp and tightens the bulb, then takes a seat across from me. "I'm sorry I had to resort to such extreme measures, Dr. Parker, but you simply refuse to understand just how serious this situation has become."

"Your theatrics don't change anything." I spit the words out, breathing normally but now angry and embarrassed. "The fact is, Declan Fitzpatrick, you set me up to use me for your investigation. I freely invited you into my home and offered you my genuine hospitality, and you used it against me." If D.P. is as Fae-minded as I think he is, then this should cause him no little shame. The Fae take their protocols for proper behavior extremely seriously. One must never, under any circumstances, take advantage of a host's hospitality. To do so is considered a serious breach of one's character. The Tax Man's ears turn a light shade of pink, and I know my words have hit home.

"As I said, Dr. Parker, I am truly sorry that I felt I needed to frighten you to make you understand," the Tax Man explains. "And I never 'set you up' as you claim. It was a mere coincidence."

I don't wait for him to continue. "Liar. I call bullshit on that one! B-U-L-L-S-H-I-T! I might be just a lowly tooth fairy, but I am fully aware of the Tenets of Sacred Magic. Tenet #1 states that there is no such thing as coincidence. Everything that happens, happens for a reason and is part of the Sacred Plan of the Universe. You can't make me think for one minute, 'Lord *Nuada*,' that you believe in mere coincidences."

I figure I've got him on this one, but he calmly steeples his fingertips. "And now you understand exactly what I'm trying to tell you, Dr. Parker, though you keep rudely interrupting me. You are correct. I do not believe in coincidences. Not in the least. So when your office assistant contacted me about your tax issues just moments after I received a list containing the names of tooth fairies in the local area, with your name at the very top of that list, I saw it for what it truly was…a call to action from the Universe that I somehow was required to intercede. Thus began our interactions. And may I remind you that it was a damn good thing I was here this afternoon when those two men broke into your house." He pauses and looks away. "I shudder to think of what might have happened if I hadn't been here."

Everything he's just said makes perfect sense according to his belief system. I know this because it is the same belief system I hold dear. My parents let both my sister and I, when we came of age, decide for ourselves what spiritual path we wanted to take, as long as we chose something. Unlike my sister, Claire, I didn't find much of a connection to my father's Judeo-Christian philosophies, and Sunday services at his Episcopalian church left me too full of additional questions. I found the Fae Tenets of Sacred Magic more in line with my personal thinking. I spent nearly two years studying with a local Druid, and though my use of magic is pretty non-existent, I find its knowledge a practical life guide.

The sensibility of his explanation catches me off guard, and I can't think of a counter-argument. Instead, I hammer on about his manhandling of me. "Hmmm...I guess I believe you about this not being a purposeful plot, but frankly, I think you and the Black Knight are exaggerating my need for around the clock 'security.' For Pete's sake, was it really necessary to grab me the way you did?"

Obviously, I have pushed the right buttons. The Tax Man jumps from his chair and begins pacing, repeatedly running a hand through his ginger hair. "For the love of everything I hold dear, I cannot for the life of me make you understand just what kind of danger you actually are in, Rosie Lass." He's very agitated, so I don't think he even realizes he's just called me Rosie Lass. *Oh boy! There's just something about the way he says it...* He plops back down on the sofa next to me. "They're sending us parts, Lass! Literally parts…fingers, ears, eyeballs…of what we presume are the missing tooth fairies!" D.P. grabs my left hand and holds it up in front of my face. "Do you think I want to open one of those boxes and see these fingers inside? Do you, Rosie?"

One of us should probably pull their hand away, but neither of us does. Are we actually having a moment here? Reluctantly, I am the first to break contact. I sigh and say, "I guess I didn't think it was as serious as you both said."

I seem to have broken whatever spell of truce we were under. The Tax Man leaves the sofa and wanders over to the window, pulling the curtains away and looking out towards the front of the house. He speaks so low I can barely hear him, but it's loud enough to piss me off. "That's your problem, Dr. Parker. For a woman as intelligent as you are, you don't think things out clearly."

And there goes our moment. Lost because…well… when one is the high and mighty Lord *Nuada*, it's easy to sit in judgment of lowly tooth fairies. "You can stuff it, Fitzpatrick. You saved my life…big whoopee shit. I guess I should fall on my knees in front of you, shouldn't I?"

The Tax Man looks at me oddly but doesn't answer. I get up from the sofa. "I'm hungry. I'm going to the kitchen to make some dinner… if that's alright with Your Lordship?"

"I can take care of getting us something if you'd prefer?" he asks.

I tisk loudly and roll my eyes. "Sorry, but I have no intention of eating any of your magically produced Otherworld fare. The thought of it turns my stomach."

It's D.P.'s turn to tisk. "I was just going to order something from Grubhub, Dr. Parker. I don't waste my magical ability on nonsense."

"Of course you don't. So sorry you were forced to 'waste' it on me," I counter. "Never mind about the Grubhub. I'd rather do the cooking myself. It helps me blow off steam, and right now I'm about as steamed as one tooth fairy can get." I think of something and add, "You know I have Corps orders for tonight, right?"

Tax Man shakes his head no. "You're on leave until further notice, Cadet. Your squad leader has been notified. The Black Knight has seen to that."

Getting out of tooth retrieval duty is a bonus, but I don't let on how much that pleases me. "Once again, I'm not consulted about these decisions that affect me, am I?"

Now the Lord *Mac Nuada* looks down right pissed himself. "I don't presume the Black Knight needs to discuss his orders with a tooth fairy."

Ouch. That one hurt. I walk toward the kitchen. "Do I have your permission to go and make dinner, Oh Lordly One?"

"Do whatever you like, Dr. Parker," he sarcastically replies.

I think about what I have in the fridge. "Would you prefer chicken or fish for dinner?"

The Tax Man thinks for a moment. "I guess I'd prefer the fish."

I smile as I walk away and mutter under my breath, "Then chicken it is, your Lordship."

TOOTH 18

TRUCE

I WASN'T KIDDING when I said that cooking is a great way for me to let off steam. I find the repetitive motions of cutting, slicing, chopping, and grating soothing and somewhat meditative. Despite the fact I hadn't expected a dinner guest this evening, I'm confident I can pull together a damn tasty meal with whatever I have on hand. As someone who enjoys cooking, I routinely keep a good supply of basics in stock and can improvise when necessary. Plus, a small part of me still wants to impress the hell out of the Tax Man with my culinary talent. Don't ask me to explain this. I can't.

My dinner guest wanders into the kitchen, but when he sees me pounding away at the chicken with a meat tenderizer, perhaps with more vigor than the poor breasts deserve, he turns around and heads back to the parlor without a word. An hour later, I set the kitchen table for two. Truthfully, I had thought about setting D.P. up in the dining room and seating myself in the kitchen, but that seemed beyond childish. Plus, it's been such a long day that I just want to eat my meal in peace without more fuss.

"Dinner's ready," I call out. The Tax Man enters the kitchen and then stands awkwardly until I point out a particular chair at the table. "Why don't you sit there," I say. I set down a platter with chicken piccata and a bowl of warm pasta tossed with olive oil, fresh tomatoes, basil and a handful of aged parmesan. If D.P. is annoyed that I made chicken instead of fish, he's wise enough not to say anything. Instead, he looks at me with what clearly is a sense of wonder. "You made all of this in an hour?" he asks. "Without any magic? That's simply remarkable!"

I quickly turn away to take the garlic bread from the oven. It wouldn't do to have the Tax Man see me blush over his compliment. "It was nothing," I mumble.

"You really don't give yourself enough credit. You have a demanding job helping people, you can make exquisite tiny things with only your hands and creativity, and you're able to put together a gourmet meal in your kitchen in less than an hour. It's quite impressive…Rosie." He says my name with some hesitancy, as if testing how I will react to it. I have every reason to remain angry with Mr. D.P. Fitzpatrick, but I just don't have the energy to keep going toe to toe with this man. The time I spent alone in the kitchen has allowed me to cool my temper and think about things with more of an open mind. Plus, when he took my hand in the parlor, I got the distinct feeling that he was truly afraid of something terrible happening to me, and I haven't been able to shake the feeling of having his fingers wrapped around mine. I know. I'm a hopeless case. An embarrassment to every independent, self-reliant, professional woman.

I try my hardest to make it seem like I get compliments from hot men sitting at my kitchen table every day. "That's very nice of you to say…Declan." Then I hand him the basket of warm bread because I'm out of any further witty repartee. At least the ice between us has thawed a bit and thus we are able to eat in somewhat of a relaxed state. Eventually, I get enough courage to initiate a neutral conversation. "I'm guessing you're originally from Ireland?"

In his heaviest brogue he answers, "Now whatever gave you that idea, *mo chailin* (my girl)?"

We both laugh at that, and I ask, "What part of Ireland?"

"County Donegal. My mother's people are O'Donnells. We've been in that part of Ireland for several generations," he replies.

It's not shocking to learn the Tax Man is from that part of the country. There's a significant fairy mound in County Donegal, and there have been O'Donnells in both Irish history and mythology from its earliest recorded stories. Although his last name is Fitzpatrick, I'm already aware he is a descendant of House *Nuada*. The Tax Man has a helluva pedigree. "So what brings you to the US? Why did you leave Ireland?"

A look passes across his face. It's one I can't easily read, but if I had to guess, I'd say it was one of annoyance. I wonder for a second whether it's directed towards me for being too darn nosey. *Good going, Rosie, you dumb ass!*

Couldn't just talk about the weather...or baseball. Men like to talk about baseball. They don't like to be grilled.

D.P. clarifies his expression. "To be blunt, my parents were driving me crazy, both in Ireland and the Otherworld: sticking their noses into my personal life, questioning everything I did. I am my father's only son, and both he and my mother are obsessed with fussing over my single, childless state. I couldn't stand the constant 'suggestions' about how I should be living my life, so I figured it best to put 3000 miles, and another dimension, between us, though my father does 'pop in and out' regularly."

I can't help but think it odd that a guy his age has to take such extraordinary actions to escape his parents' chronic nagging; he has to be at least thirty years old. Obviously, I also forget to shield my thoughts because he adds, "Actually, I'm 35. And you have no idea how controlling and disagreeable my parents can be. My mother keeps a notebook in which she writes down the names and contact information about various 'perfect' women she thinks I should meet."

"Okay, you're right. That's pretty over-the-top meddling," I respond with a laugh. "My folks were the exact opposite."

"Were?" he asks.

I nod my head. "My mom's gone. Cancer got her five years ago. And my dad had a stroke shortly after she passed into her next life. He went into nursing care and then quietly slid into dementia. Most days he doesn't remember who I am."

Declan puts down his fork and lays a hand over mine. "I'm very sorry to hear that, Rosie. I do a lot of complaining about my family, but I can't imagine not having them. You must feel...lost sometimes?"

This is going to appear extremely crass, like I'm a terrible, heartless daughter, but all I can think of right now is that D.P.'s hand is over mine. Should I leave it, or pull it away? I don't want to decide wrongly again. I venture to leave it under his. "Thank you, but I find myself doing okay. I try to stay in touch with my sister and her family. She just had twin boys. She and her husband have their hands full."

The Tax Man pulls his hand away and picks up his fork. "Universe be praised! Twins? Your family must feel quite blessed to be graced as such!" He's smiling, but there's something strange about the way he says it, a bitter undertone to his statement.

If I didn't know that Declan was Fae...like really, really Otherworld Fae...I would think his exuberance over my sister's twins was a ridiculous attempt at making conversation. I'm pretty sure it's not. The Fae have an obsession with progeny and family lines. Twins are rare among the Fae and thus are considered to be an especially good omen for any House. Still, I'd rather have his hand on mine instead of his appreciation of my family's genetics. *You surely are a piece of work, Rosie Parker. It was just a friendly gesture. Did you think he was going to hop over the table and ravish you in your kitchen?*

Talking about my family ultimately will lead to a discussion about why I'm a tooth fairy instead of my older sister, and my tooth fairy designation is not something I want to talk about with Declan. Therefore, I quickly change the subject to accounting. It's a good choice. He waxes on about his foray into the business and how he ended up on the east coast of the United States. The Tax Man is careful not to bring up his other "profession." It is like we have both purposely set up the perimeters of our relationship, drawing boundaries around what we are willing to share and what is off limits. Finally, dinner is over and we've already worked our way through tea and dessert. I try to stifle a yawn; I'm not sure exactly what time it is, but I know it's late, and my butt has gotten numb from sitting so long on my hard wooden, kitchen chairs. Still, I am not inclined to be the first one to move, lest I break the carefully arranged truce the two of us have reached.

D.P. sees my yawn and pushes himself away from the table. "You look tired, Rosie. Don't let me keep you from your bed. Please allow me to clean this up for you. It's the least I can do after such a wonderful meal."

I try very hard not to focus on the word bed in case my shield isn't holding too well. That word rolling off my Tax Man's tongue sets off all kinds of nasty thoughts. *Oh Hell! Why did I just think about the word tongue? That's not helping me at all.* My leaking head and I need to escape the confines of the kitchen so I agree to his offer to take care of the dishes for me. I assume he'll do it magically, and I don't much care by this point in the night. I nod in agreement. "Thanks. That would be wonderful. I'll set up the Murphy bed in the loft for you, if that's okay?" *Shit. I hope my face isn't as red as it feels.*

"I don't want to put you to any trouble. I can just stretch out on the sofa downstairs if that's easier?" he offers.

"We both know that my 'sofa' is more like a loveseat, and you're…like…what…6'4?" He nods and I add, "You'd be crazy uncomfortable. The Murphy bed isn't very wide, but at least it's longer." I don't wait for an answer and hustle out of the kitchen and up to the loft across from my bedroom. There's only one bathroom up there, so I don't even want to think how that will work out. I thank the goddesses I took the time to change the Murphy bed's linens after Mel stayed the night a few months back. It's not in my nature to be so on top of things like that. I wonder whether the Universe has set this all up and then laugh at the absurdity of thinking that the grand Universe cares whether I have fresh linens for Declan Fitzpatrick.

As I finish plumping up the pillows, I catch the Tax Man in the doorway watching. Since he hadn't made a sound, his presence catches me off guard and I jump back a bit. He looks serious and says, "I apologize, Lass. I didn't mean to startle you. I know this has to be very difficult for you to deal with. Know this…I won't let anything bad happen to you. You have my solemn word on that."

And somehow, I know, deep in my soul, he means it.

TOOTH 19

TIT FOR TAT

As I BRUSH MY TEETH, I ponder the weird-ass situation in which I now find myself. D.P. and I already have said our goodnights. He passed through my bedroom, checking the window locks and warding the entire room with some kind of Fae magical security system before waltzing out with a passing "G'night, Lass" and instructions to lock the bedroom door before I went to sleep. *Too bad for you, Rosie. We know you'd prefer the warm-bodied, living, breathing kind of security system to be staying in that room with you all night, wouldn't you, Dr. Parker? You really are a big dreamer, aren't you? You'd think you would know better by now.* My Water Pik hums along as I inadvertently catch an interesting exhibition in the reflection of the bathroom mirror.

Lest you think me a Peeping Tina I will explain. The way the second floor of my house is configured, the bathroom mirror is angled in such a fashion that when both doors are open you can see into the loft in the bathroom mirror's reflection. The Tax Man left his door partially open, as I have done with the bathroom door since I'm only brushing my teeth. During the summer months, the second floor tends to get muggy and warm even with the AC running full blast. This is exactly the reason why I don't relish shutting and locking my bedroom door, but D.P. remains adamant that I do so. Now, while both doors remain open, I have a lovely view of my house guest performing multiple plank reps on my loft floor. *Hell, Rosie! When's the last time you had that carpet cleaned? Probably when you moved in. How embarrassing!*

D.P. is stripped down to his underwear, and I realize that my Tax Man is even more buff than his usual attire reveals. He does 3 reps of 10 in the regular fashion, and then he switches to doing them one handed. The bathroom suddenly feels 20 degrees warmer than it did five minutes ago. *What the hell is happening to you Rosie? You're a grown-ass woman, not some horny, teenage groupie.* I feel a tad guilty for watching, but I can't seem to take my eyes off the spectacle, especially since I've just noticed an amazing tattoo encircling his right bicep. I find it rather shocking, since Mr. Press-A-Crease-In-My-Khakis hasn't struck me as a person who would want to be ink adorned. Then I remember that Mel once had told me something about tattoos being a part of Fae magical culture. She, herself, has a small sigil tattooed on her right hip. Body art always has fascinated me, but since I'm not a fan of magic and the tattooing process itself makes me queasy, I've never considered getting one. *That's our Rosie girl. Always playing it safe and staying on the straight and narrow.*

I wish I could see D.P.'s tattoo up close. It looks, from

this perspective, to be a band of Celtic knotwork with some kind of figure in its center, facing outward. I consider asking him about it in the morning but then realize I would have to admit where and how I saw it. Can't do that. Maybe I will see it up close and in person someday. *Ever the optimist, aren't we Rosie?*

The Tax Man suddenly finishes his workout and jumps up from the floor. In a panic, I snap off the bathroom light and scuttle back to my bedroom, locking the door as I was told to do and trying to settle down for the night. However, sleep does not come easily. My mind is awhirl with bits and pieces from the entire day. When I finally do fall asleep, my brain remains awash with more than I can process...*I dream I'm in my office, working on a patient who is not a child. This is odd in itself, since I work strictly on pediatric patients. As I go to examine the inside of his mouth, he bites down, severing my finger and swallowing it. Then he grabs my entire hand and proceeds to chew each finger off, one after another. I call for the Tax Man to help but the door to my exam room is locked and all he can do is bang on it from the other side. A window pops open and into the room jumps another bad guy. He brought a saw with him and begins to cut my toes off right through my shoes. By now, I'm screaming bloody murder but no one comes to save me. The man in the chair grabs me by the shoulders, intending to bite the nose off my face. He calls my name over and over again... Rosie...Rosie...I do the best I can with my bloody, stumpy hand to fight him off, and I punch him right in the face as hard as I can. He immediately lets go and I hear him cuss in an angry brogue...* "Feckin' Hell! Stop, Rosie, it's me! Declan! Wake up! You're having a nightmare!"

My bedside lamp clicks on, and I bolt upright in my bed to see the Tax Man standing at the edge of it. I'm awake enough to see that he's holding his nose, which is bleeding profusely, and I realize that I have just punched him square in the face. "Oh my Universe! I'm so sorry! I must have been dreaming," I stammer. "I thought I was fighting off one of those bad guys from this afternoon. They were cutting off parts of me." I notice that the door is still shut, and the lock is still turned up. "Wait…the door was locked. How did you get in here?"

He wipes his bloody nose with the back of his hand, the one that is holding a gun. "A locked door will slow down a human intruder but doesn't pose a problem for me. That's why I had you lock it. It gives humans a barrier and me a few extra seconds."

It's at that moment I notice that my Tax Man is a boxer brief kind of guy. Boxer briefs that cling rather snuggly around his manly bits. It's not really my fault I'm staring. From where I'm sitting in bed, my eyes are in the most optimum position for viewing his…uhmmm… package, which, by the way is…uhmmm…quite impressive.

"I really am sorry, Declan. Do you want me to get you some ice for your nose?"

"No. It will be fine. I'm just glad it was a false alarm. Your screaming made me jump out of my skin." He makes a high-pitched, screeching noise in a rather silly attempt at mocking my distress.

His doing that not only embarrasses me but also puts me on the defensive. "Well, it's your fault, you know. You kept filling my head with stories about fairy parts being mailed out in boxes. It's no wonder I'm having nightmares."

He laughs off my petulance. "You're probably right, Rosie. I was a bit graphic in my attempt to have you take me seriously."

I wasn't expecting an apology so quickly. I am lost for words. I think about his tattoo, and say, "That's really a beautiful ink job on your arm. Did you have it done in *I Idir?*"

He laughs slyly. "I'm surprised you even noticed my arm, Dr. Parker. Your attention seems directed…lower."

My face goes red and hot. "Well…it's hard to…" He laughs again and I quickly realize my poor choice of words. "I mean…it's 'difficult'…to miss it. It's practically in my…face." At this point, I'm totally discombobulated and completely mortified that all my words are sounding… dirty. I'm having a flashback moment to our very first meeting in my office.

The Tax Man smiles. "No worries, Rosie. I'm enjoying my eyeful as well, so I suppose fair is fair."

I look down and notice that all of my tossing and turning has caused every button on my pajama top to come undone and no doubt D.P. has been enjoying a top-notch view of the sisters in all their glory. I hurry to button up. "It's really ungentlemanly to look, you know!"

This just makes him laugh harder. "I guess we'll have to call it 'tit for tat,' Lass." He turns arounds to leave. "I hope the rest of your dreams are pleasant, Rosie. I know mine will be." Then, he just disappears, gone in the blink of an eye.

I turn off my light and lay in the dark. I hear the Tax

Man laughing to himself for several minutes before I hear footsteps in the hall and then the shower running in the bathroom next door. The water runs for a long, long time, and because I know I don't have an outrageously large hot water tank, I'm pretty sure he's running the water cold.

TOOTH 20

HARD CAUCUS

I USUALLY RESERVE my Sundays for doing errands. It's my go-to day for grocery shopping, attending the farmer's market, and, of course, taking a happy gander through the local hobby store. I have no idea whether I'll get to do any of these on this particular Sunday, as I have the distinct feeling I've been put under some type of house arrest. I don't hear any sounds from the loft, so I assume my house guest is still asleep. I am relieved. I'm not quite ready to face him after last night's debacle. This is why I groan inwardly when I reach the first floor and see D.P. camped out at my dining room table.

The Tax Man already is showered and dressed. *Too bad for you, Rosie...a missed opportunity for another free show!* There are a variety of East Coast maps laid out in front of him, with multiple red dots pinpointed in various locations all over them. He also has two different laptops open beside him, one to his right and one to his left. He notices my presence and looks up, holding a mug in his hand. "Good morning, Rosie. I hope you don't mind. I took the liberty of making coffee and picking us up some breakfast. Nothing as glamorous or delicious as I know you'd whip up, but I thought you might like to take it easy this morning."

I mumble a word of thanks, and D.P. turns his attention back to his work. I'm a tad disappointed that he doesn't mention anything, not a single word, about last night, even jokingly. Though pleasant, he seems coolly all business this morning, and I'm confused regarding how I feel about this, or even what I had expected. On my kitchen table I find a shopping bag from Caramel French Patisserie, the best bakery in Salem, which generally has lines going down the block on Sunday mornings. Inside the bag are apricot filled croissants and several kinds of delicate pastel macarons, both of which are my absolute favorites. How the Tax Man knew this leaves me stumped; with everything going on, I am quite sure pastries never crossed my mind, so it wasn't like this information accidentally leaked out of my head.

I select a croissant and pour myself a cup of coffee before returning to the dining room to take a seat around the table. I wonder whether the red dots on the maps represent missing tooth fairies or perhaps where boxes with various severed fairy parts were sent, but I don't ask. I don't really want to think about how close I came to being a tooth fairy special delivery. The silence between us feels like a weird vacuum, similar to how it feels when you try to squeeze all of the air out of a Ziploc baggie but the last bit remains no matter how hard you try to remove it. This situation is utterly ridiculous, because nothing unseemly happened last night. It was all just a silly mistake...me and my over-zealous imagination and the Tax Man just doing his job.

I try to be funny. "Hello? Earth to the Otherworld, come in Declan. Can you hear me?" He doesn't even look up, so I try discreetly clearing my throat. He finally notices and says, "Oh, I'm sorry, Rosie. I wasn't paying attention to you." *Ouch, Tax Man. Just what a girl wants to hear.* He glues his eyes back to the computer screens but adds, "I know there's a pattern to these events, but I just can't seem to recognize what it is."

It's obviously him just talking out loud, so I don't respond. I can't let myself forget that D.P. is here to do a job and not to romance some random tooth fairy. My coffee needs a refill and, ever the polite hostess, I grab Declan's as well. "Do you want another cup?" I ask.

The Tax Man nods his head in the affirmative, but before I can run off to the kitchen, he looks up at me and asks, "I have a big favor to ask, Rosie, and I hate doing it, but I don't see any safe way around it."

Well, this is a positive turn of events. I like the idea of being able to do a favor for D.P., but the safe part of the equation worries me a bit. *Who are you kidding, Roslinda Parker? It's an absolute fact that if the Tax Man wanted to tie a rope around your waist and dangle you from a second-floor window as Chechen fairy bait, you'd happily agree. Damn, girl! One semi half peek at his private parts and you've just about lost all control of your common sense and intelligence.* "Uhmm...sure. What is it you need from me?"

"I need to meet with some colleagues regarding this

ongoing investigation. Normally, I'd meet with them at my office or home, but I don't think the targets have me on their radar yet and I'd hate to clue them in on my involvement or lead them to my residence. I was hoping you might allow us to gather here?"

"I suppose that would be okay. Are your colleagues also Fae?" I ask.

"They are. Of course we'd follow all necessary and directed protocols regarding entry and behavior," D.P. promises.

"That's fine," I answer. *And there you go, you horny dimwit! Volunteering to host a frickin' fairy ring in your home. Throwing everything your mother ever warned you against when dealing with the Fae right out the window just so you can let your girlie hormones run away with you.* "Will your colleagues require anything special? A casting circle… magic instrumentals…refreshments, maybe?" *Or even perhaps for Dr. Parker to lie down and be your doormat?*

Declan laughs, which makes the corners of his eyes crinkle up. *How did you ever not recognize him as Fae, Rosie?* "None of that will be necessary, Lass," Declan says. "We don't use any of that stuff with our magic. Plus, we're just getting together to talk and bounce around some ideas. No hocus-pocus, I promise. They won't be here long, and I certainly don't want to cause you any additional inconvenience."

"No. It's all good," I blabber.

"Thank you, Rosie. I really do appreciate your cooperation. I'm just so very sorry this all had to happen to such a nice person as yourself."

I smile. How should a person in my situation respond

to a comment like that? *Oh goody! You're a nice person, Rosalinda...# 1 sucker.*

Maybe my face betrays me because Declan asks, "Is there someplace you absolutely need to be today? I'd prefer that we stay here, but perhaps we could work something out," he offers.

"Well, Sunday is my usual day to go to the Salem Farmers Market in Derby Square," I offer.

D.P. shakes his head left to right. "That's too much of an open space...too many people. I can't secure your safety there."

"Then maybe Hobby World in the mall?" I suggest.

Again he answers in the negative. "No malls. Same reasons."

Frankly, I'm tired of being Little Miss Agreeable. "Then, I absolutely must insist I be allowed to go to the grocery store. Sundays are my day for grocery shopping, and I don't want any of your magically produced shit." *Okay. Maybe shit was a bit too harsh, Rosie. I'm sure these Fae types are quite proud of their magical abilities.*

He frowns, but I'm not sure whether it's because I've insisted on going out or because I've hurt his feelings with my comment about his magic being shit. "Which grocery store are we talking about?" he asks.

"Steve's Quality Market," I reply.

"The little Italian place on Margin Street?"

"That's the one. I think I can get everything I need for the week there," I suggest.

The Tax Man thinks about it for a moment and says, "I suppose that would be okay. Plan on us going right after my meeting, then." He quickly adds, "Of course, only if that time works for you as well, Rosie?"

I try to ignore the rigid politeness in his tone. *What the hell, Tax Man? Last night you danced around in your boxer briefs, wagging your package in front of my face and partaking in a free topless show. Now, this morning, you've gone all Miss Manners on me? You're a teasing jerk, Declan Fitzpatrick.* Despite my annoyance, I am more than a little curious to see the types of colleagues with whom the Tax Man works. And even though they're all Fae, and some may be freakishly ugly to boot, I plan to flirt outrageously with every single male in attendance. *So there! You can kiss my ass, Mr. Tax Man!*

TOOTH 21

FAE BRAIDS

THE TAX MAN totally is engrossed in his maps and data, and I feel like a dummy sitting at my dining room table in silence, waiting for the prospect of obtaining even a measly nugget of interaction. Thus, I get up from my chair, leave the table, deposit my coffee cup and plate in the kitchen, and head back upstairs to the loft. I initially planned to busy myself working on the plank-flooring of my newest dollhouse until D.P.'s colleagues arrive, but when I accidentally catch my reflection in the bathroom mirror, I change my mind.

Most days, I wear my long hair up in a messy bun thingy on the top of my head, or I pull it into a tight pony-tail in the back. These are the simplest ways to keep my unmanageable tresses off the faces of my patients when I'm bent over their mouths. But today, I decide that in honor of the Tax Man's meeting I will braid it Celtic style. In the Fae Otherworld, hair grows at double the speed it does in the Mundane World. Both men and women routinely braid their hair, lest loose strands fall into the wrong magical hands. Of course, in this day and age, there are laws in *I Idir* against practicing hair magic, strictly enforced, I'm sure, by the Black Knight himself. But old habits and traditions die hard, so braided hair is still the norm.

It's only because of Mel that I even know how to do this. For a period of time, my BFF was gung-ho over Fae culture and even thought seriously about moving permanently to the Otherworld. Thankfully, she retained her senses and decided that the grass still is greener on the Mundane side of the lawn, but not before signing up for a barrage of Otherworld instruction. The hair braiding class was just one of the many she took, but thankfully it was the only one she successfully convinced me to take with her. It's simply easier to practice braiding someone else's hair before attempting to braid your own, so the fact that we were paired up made the class an enjoyable success for both of us.

Deciding on a semi-elaborate style that I have the most confidence with, I plait two long half braids on either side of my head, leaving about half of the hair loose at the ends of each braid. Then I take the two ends and work them together into a Celtic knot at the back of my head. Getting the knot part done correctly without seeing what my hands are doing is difficult, so by the time I finish, I am sweating from my effort. But I am more than satisfied with the end results, so the effort was worth it. I use my phone to get a good look at the knot's reflection in the mirror and smile. It's damn near perfect. I consider taking a selfie and sending it to Mel but realize I'd have to explain why I've made the effort to tie a fancy Celtic braid in my hair on an ordinary Sunday morning. Instead, I just snap a photo for myself to memorialize this day.

My timing is nearly as impeccable as my handiwork. I barely snap the photo before I hear the Tax Man's voice from the bottom of the stairs. "Rosie, did you go upstairs? I need you to come down and allow my colleagues entry to your house."

Well, look at that. You finally realized I'm not sitting there, huh, Tax Man? But you've only noticed because you have a need for me. "I'm in the middle of a project, Declan. I'll be down in a few minutes." Then, I stand there and silently count to one hundred. I imagine the Tax Man standing at the foot of the stairs tapping his foot impatiently while his friends wait on the porch, and I smile. Sometimes, I can be a real bitch.

When I finally do come down the stairs, I can see a look of annoyance plainly on D.P.'s face, but when he sees me his eyes go wide, and I would swear that his skin color turns a shade paler. For someone who supposedly is a Fae super spy, he sure doesn't have much of a poker face. He opens his mouth as though to speak but immediately clamps it shut. Instead, he walks silently to the front door. I know what's expected. The Fae cannot enter a home in the Mundane World unless they are invited to do so. What constitutes an actual invitation is open to debate, but essentially the owner of the home must give permission for guests to enter. Once that is accepted, rules of hospitality for both sides are expected to be followed.

I open my door to find a group of men standing on the

stoop. If one were to see them individually on the street, one probably would take it for granted that each of them was an ordinary person amidst a swollen mass of humanity. Well, maybe all except one. Towards the back of the crowd is a young man who prominently stands out. The term Dark Fae springs to mind, but I immediately wipe it away because it's considered a racial slur in the Otherworld. His hair is jet black and wavy, and his eyes are a startling shade of blue-gray, enhanced by the snug fitting t-shirt he's wearing in the exact same shade. His face is perfectly symmetrical as though it was chiseled from some type of marble, and if I ever were to meet the devil that I was endlessly admonished against in my daddy's church, this is what I imagine he'd look like. I must be staring a bit too long, because next to me D.P. impatiently whispers my name and awakens me from my reveries.

I snap out of my mini-trance with a pleasant smile. "Do come in, Gentlemen. Welcome to my home." I have just given entry to a myriad of only the Universe knows what types of Fae characters. I assume that because the Tax Man is standing next to me I am perfectly safe, but if the stink eye he's giving me is any indication, he's none too happy with me right now.

Proper etiquette requires introductions, and D.P. does the honors. "Dr. Parker, I'd like you to meet my colleagues." *Uh oh...I've been relegated to Dr. Parker once again.* He points to a very short man with a full ginger beard and bald head and introduces him as Mac O'Kelly.

D.P. moves closer to me so that our hip bones are touching. I start to put my hand out, but I feel Declan stiffen and remember the Fae do not shake hands lest there be an unwitting transfer of magical energy. I think back to the first time I met the Tax Man in my office. He'd refused my offer of a handshake. Now it makes sense. I drop my arm and give a nod of my head in greeting "Welcome to my home, Mr. O'Kelly." The man scowls at me, and I suddenly realize he's a leprechaun. Despite the silly commercialization of them in the Mundane World, leprechauns are notoriously grumpy, anti-social, and alarmingly quick to anger.

Declan continues around the group in the same manner, introducing me to Sean Callighan, Dennis Flaherty, and Connor Dell, all of whom are various types of *Sidhe*. Finally, he reaches the dark-haired man, who's been winking and smiling at me since his arrival. "And this, Dr. Parker, is Duncan Fitzpatrick." D.P. must register the surprise on my face, because he adds, "Duncan is my second cousin."

Family or not, there appears to be no love lost between the two of them. Even with only our hip bones touching, I perceive an overwhelming sense of dislike towards Duncan radiating from the Tax Man. The man in question doesn't seem to care a whit regarding his cousin's chilly reception of him. He steps forward, takes my hand in his, and brings it to his lips. "It is a pleasure to meet you, Dr. Parker. I had no idea this day would hold so much promise." A tingling sensation runs from the touch of his lips, down my arm and proceeds...lower. I now understand that D.P.'s cousin is a *Gancanagh*, a *Sidhe* incubus. I quickly pull my hand away, and I swear, I literally can hear the Tax Man growl under his breath.

As quickly as Declan's anger flares, it disappears, and

he directs the men to my dining room where they take seats around the table. The Tax Man sits at its head. One doesn't need a Fae book of Who's Who to understand the hierarchy in this group. All of the men, the bold Duncan included, obviously defer to my Tax Man. He is without doubt their superior...the Big Cheese...the Head Honcho...the Boss Man. This is evident from D.P.'s body language, the tone of his voice, and the stern expression I experienced first-hand when we originally met that day in my office. I start to sit, and everyone goes silent and subtly look away.

D.P. smiles blandly at me. "I know this is all a huge imposition, Dr. Parker, and I surely hate to ask, but I'm afraid we could all do with a nice, cold drink. Perhaps we could bother you to fetch some ice water for the group?"

It's my turn to be annoyed. I want to tell the Tax Man to go fetch the damn water himself. I am surely not his maid. But the few brain cells I have left after Duncan's unwanted advances warn me against doing this. To say such a thing would embarrass him greatly in front of his team. And as pissed off as I currently am towards him for treating me this way in my own house, I also understand that acting out my feelings now would be to cross a line between us I couldn't later fix; I am not ready to burn all my bridges with the Tax Man. Therefore, I give the group the sweetest, most feminine smile I can muster. I even consider dropping a curtsy but figure that might be overkill. Instead, I bob my head towards the Tax Man and say with just the slightest hint of sarcasm, "Of course, Lord *Mac Nuada.* Whatever you say; it would be my pleasure."

TOOTH 22

BE CAREFUL WHERE YOU PUT YOUR EARS

WHEN I GET to the kitchen, I try not to slam the cabinet doors as I take out water glasses for everyone in the group and a tall pitcher to fill with water. The whole situation makes me begin to seriously question whether something isn't wrong with my mental health status. For as far back as I can remember, I have been fiercely independent. Even as a kid, I fought against the boundaries my parents set regarding my expected behavior. The fact that I was their only child to inherit a Fae gene pool made it harder for me. There were rules for me that didn't apply to my sister. Rules about using magic, rules about traveling to *I Idir*, even rules prohibiting me from becoming too chummy with my fully human friends. I rebelled by spending more and more time by myself, relying on personal goals and hobbies to fill the voids I felt in my life. To date, Mel is the only person I ever try to adapt for... until the Tax Man.

It's not like I haven't had romantic relationships. I am

by no means a neurotic, insecure virgin, and I've had more than my fair share of break-ups and heart aches. Up until now, I've always held to the philosophy: "Here I am...Rosalinda Parker...Like me for who I am or hit the road." And when people haven't played according to my rules, I haven't lost any sleep over their exits. So why is everything different for me regarding D.P. Fitzpatrick?

I understand he's crazy hot; no doubt about that. He's also super smart, successful, and rather funny, even if it's in a droll sort of way. On the other hand, he belongs to an entirely different spectrum of the Universe than me. We have nothing in common, and, frankly, if it weren't for the tooth fairy conspiracy that's going on right now, I'm pretty sure I never would have found myself on his radar. Guys like Declan Fitzpatrick, Lord *Mac Nuada*, do not chase after tooth fairies.

This little pity party I'm throwing in the kitchen has left me feeling rather sorry for myself. Thus, I've decided to drop the tray of ice water and glasses off in the dining room and hide out upstairs in the loft, burying myself in an all-day dollhouse project. To hell with the groceries. I really don't care what we eat. That's my plan, anyway, until I find I've become trapped in the kitchen. I head toward the dining room and run straight into a solid wall of...nothing. I set the tray down on the kitchen table and use both hands to push on the invisible barrier, but it doesn't budge. I head toward the back door that leads from my kitchen to the backyard and learn I am stopped there as well. In total frustration, I take one of the glasses and throw it at the barrier. It bounces off the barrier and onto the floor, shattering into a million tiny shards. I hear the muffled voices stop for a moment at the sound of breaking glass, then quietly resume.

I can't decide whether to throw a screaming tantrum or to cry. I do neither. I sit at the table and work my way through the entire selection of macarons. While I munch, I hear D.P.'s voice in my head. It is the third time the Tax Man has communicated with me in this manner since I've met him and it still feels strange to me. My mom infrequently used her Fae telepathy with me, mostly to scold, and when we were younger Mel and I would sometimes speak like this while we sat in our high school classes. It was our version of note-passing. But it's been a long time since anyone regularly has used this form of communication with me, so the sensation of it makes me jump.

"I'm sorry to keep you in the kitchen, Lass. I have no choice. It's better if you remain unaware of everything that's going on with this mission. It's standard protocol. Please don't be angry with me."

I don't like his talking to me in my head this way. It's far too…intimate. We're not friends. We're not…anything. *"Whatever, Declan. Please get out of my head. I didn't invite you in and I don't want you here."* Then, I use every bit of what meager concentration I can muster to pull up the tightest shield I can manage. Now I really want to cry.

Finally, I hear the drag of several chairs on the hardwood dining room floor, so I assume the meeting is over and D.P.'s colleagues are ready to leave. Apparently, I'm not required to grant them exit. I hear the front door open and close and then silence. When I check, I find the barrier gone and I'm free to leave the kitchen. I intend to head straight to the loft without a word and lock myself in there for the rest of the day. After leaving my kitchen prison I realize no one is left in the dining room, but I hear voices on the front porch. I know I probably should ignore them and just go about my business upstairs, but the allure of listening to something I'm not supposed to hear is too great, as if by doing so I am thwarting the Tax Man's secret plans. I creep closer to the front window and peek out. I can't see who's out there because they are standing too far to the left of the windows, but I can hear them perfectly. I recognize the voices as Declan's and his cousin Duncan's.

"You sure are one lucky bastard, Fitz," Duncan says with a sly laugh in his voice. "You draw a cushy security job like this one with a ripe little dolly just begging for it. I know tooth fairies aren't your standard fare, cuz, but I hope to Hades you're tapping some of that. If you're not interested, I might take a shot. Just the thought of burying my face in those luscious ti…"

I feel hot and queasy and start to turn away, but then I hear the jarring sound of flesh hitting flesh and a painful whoosh of breath coming from a pair of lungs. The Dark Fae cousin barely can get his next words out. "What the Feck, Fitz! There's no need for that! I didn't mean anything by it…"

I hear D.P spit out an onslaught of words. They obviously are angry, containing a boatload of obscenities, but he's speaking in Gaelic, so even if I could understand a few random words, he's talking so fast and with such a heavy brogue, I can't make out any of what he's saying. His cousin only answers, "Yes, Sir," and "No, Sir," and eventually I hear footsteps going down the wooden steps and some coming back towards the front door. I scuttle across the room and plop myself down in the armchair so I'm not caught eavesdropping just before the Tax Man comes back inside, looking angrier than I've ever seen him.

He notices I'm sitting there, and for a second he looks horrified. I feel hot and am sure my skin is flushed. My poker face must be as bad as the Tax Man's. There's no doubt he realizes I heard the entire conversation between Duncan and himself. I expect him to apologize or to make lame excuses for his rude cousin. He doesn't do either. Instead, he says, "I bet you are entirely sick of being stuck inside this house on such a glorious day, Rosie. Grab what you need and let's tackle those groceries."

TOOTH 23

THE SHOPPERS' RHUMBA

Thus far my normally enjoyable Sunday morning has been a complete disaster, and I want to tell the Tax Man to forget the grocery shopping idea. However, the prospect of spending the rest of the day inside with Mr. Pissy Pete doesn't strike me as a favorable alternative. Plus, I really do need groceries. Trying to shop for them during the week never works out well for me. I like to have everything I need on hand when I get home from work so I can start cooking dinner immediately. I grab my purse from the entryway table and head for the door. "I'm ready," I blandly reply. "Let's get this damn well over with."

D.P. stands directly behind me while I lock the door. Then he makes a strange wave movement with his hands which I assume produces some hinky-dink, magical security system. "I want you to know I'm only allowing this excursion because you insisted you need these things," he lectures, "and I don't want you to be inconvenienced any more than you already have been. I'm a tad concerned about the security risks we're taking in doing this. I expect you to follow all of my instructions and to stick to my side like glue. I must be able to move the both of us quickly should the need arise." With that the Tax Man takes my hand and leads me down the steps. This creates a tiny brush of energy…his big-time magic aura brushing up against my much softer one. It tickles my palm.

Someone with any amount of brains might be hyper alert to the possibility that the Chechen bad guys are watching us leave the house, but all I can think of is that the Tax Man and I are holding hands. Like a couple. On a date. To the grocery store. To buy our groceries for the week. *You've really gone around the bend, Rosie, girl! Why don't you just hang a sign around your neck that reads, Take Me.*

"We'll take my car," he says as he leads me half of the way down my block to a black Mercedes EQS parked at the curb. I try not to gape. Of course the Tax Man would drive such a car. One that costs over a hundred grand. Shit. He unlocks the passenger door and holds it open for me. After I get in, he quickly slips into the driver's seat, enters the address for Steve's Quality Market into the GPS, and pulls away from the curb.

We drive in silence, and I am grateful for it. I don't want to discuss what I heard…what he knows I heard. It's ever so much nicer in my fantasy world. The one where Declan and I are on a Sunday outing and not a covert mission to buy bananas and orange juice. Jazz music pours from the car's speakers, and I notice the Tax Man's long fingers tapping out the music's rhythm on the steering wheel. A musician, perhaps? I realize I know literally nothing about this man other than the most basic facts. He's male, Fae, 35 years old, and a tax accountant. Oh…and he's an Otherworld spy and an Otherworld celebrity. Let's not forget those key pieces of the Declan puzzle. Still, I don't want to think about any of that. Instead, I just want to listen to the music and catch sly side glances of his beautiful face out of the corner of my eye as he drives: the dark Ray Bans, the way the sun comes through the windshield and catches the reddish gold of his hair, the brush of razor burn on the back of his neck. *Razor burn? Goddesses help you, Rosie! You've completely lost it!*

We arrive at the market in a matter of minutes. D.P. parks the car and jumps out to open the door for me on the other side. I'm not sure whether this is normal for him when he has a female passenger, or whether it is just part of the security protocol. Either way, I kinda like it. He takes my hand again, and we stroll towards the grocery store's main entrance. I shop here pretty often. Steve, the owner, carries a great variety of ethnic ingredients, especially those needed for Italian cooking. His produce is the freshest in the area, and he has an excellent butcher. Plus, the staff always makes everyone feel welcome. As if to prove my theory correct, Stella, the cashier, greets us warmly as we enter the establishment. Stella is nearly 70 and a hoot. Her age doesn't hold her down. Today she's dressed in a fabulous cheetah print shift under her market apron, and her finger and toenails are painted blood red.

"Hey there, Dr. Rosie! Brought a friend today, I see."

The cashier winks at me and then turns to the Tax Man. "Hello to you, Dr. Rosie's good-lookin' friend. Welcome to Steve's Quality Market. Let me know if I can 'personally'…help you find…anything." She wags her eyebrows up and down, gives him a salacious grin, and then blows him a kiss. I watch D.P.'s face turn pink behind his sunglasses, and Stella laughs. "Steve got those Littleneck clams you wanted, Dr. Rosie." she adds. "Freddie has them behind the counter."

"Thanks, Stella. I'll be sure to ask for them." Declan continues to hold my hand, maybe even a little tighter, which probably will make the actual shopping part difficult. I raise up our clasped hands. "I don't think I can shop properly this way. It's kind of awkward."

The Tax Man frowns. "I was dead serious when I said 'stick like glue,' Rosie." He lets my hand loose and moves his to the small of my back, right above my ass. "Better?" he asks, maybe a touch too innocently.

I think my temperature rises about ten degrees, but I just smile pleasantly. "That'll work," I say. We maneuver our way through the produce department. Declan watches me tap a few melons, squeeze some lemons, and smell the cilantro. He wasn't kidding about the glue part. He is so close that I back into him several times, ass to groin. I swear to myself that it's not on purpose. *Sure, girlfriend…you keep telling yourself that!* Feeling emboldened, I select a particularly large zucchini and hold it up, batting my eyelashes as I ask, "I do enjoy a good squash; Declan, how 'bout you?"

He's still wearing his damn sunglasses, so I can't see his eyes, but I do hear him chuckle. Under his breath. He grabs a couple of cantaloupes and he holds them at chest level and with a perfectly straight face says to me, "I'm more of a cantaloupe sort of guy, Dr. Rosie."

Sure. It's totally juvenile. I get that. But after the morning we both just had, we're entitled to a little silly fun. From the produce section we head into the canned goods aisle. I immediately see something I want on the bottom shelf and quickly bend down to grab some large cans of San Marco whole tomatoes. Because of the way I've moved, the Tax Man's hand slips from the small of my back to the right cheek of my ass. I freeze, and I hear D.P. say, "Oops," but he doesn't remove his hand. He's definitely upping the game. I linger down by the bottom shelf, bent in half, searching for just the right can, until the blood rushes to my head and I'm forced to stand upright. Pushing the cart a few feet at a time, we continue to dance this dirty little rhumba as we traverse the entire store, backing into each other mixed with a generous amount of hand slipping. If anyone is watching, they've probably pegged us as a horny couple in the midst of kinky-ass-grocery-store-foreplay. They'd be more than partially right.

Finally, we make our way to the meat counter, and I am pleased to see that our game has caused the Tax Man to look as flushed as I feel. It's obvious he definitely is working hard to avoid providing me with a full-frontal view of himself. I step up to the counter more quickly than D.P. anticipates, and he literally has to slide on his feet to remain behind me. When he makes contact, I'm pretty sure there's more of him than there was a few minutes ago.

Steve's top-notch butcher/fishmonger is Freddy Carlisi. If anyone were to look for a stereotypical manifestation of a movie style Goombah, it would be Freddy. He checks all the right boxes: slick-backed hair, heavy gold chains, and diamond pinky ring. Despite the off-putting personae, Freddy is a great cook, an authority on Italian food and wines, and the best damn meat and fish guy in Salem. It's no secret that most of Steve's clientele shop at the store because of Freddy. I'm one of them. He sees me and comes directly over. "Dr. Rosie. It's so good to see you. You look especially fetching today, 'mi bello amor.' The new hairstyle suits you." Freddy notices Declan and adds, "I see you brought a young man with you today, bello? Friend of yours?"

"Yes. This is my friend, Declan Fitzpatrick, Freddy. He's helping me shop today," I explain.

Freddy gives Declan the once over. "You ain't one of those East Boston Fitzpatricks, are ya?" he asks.

In his heaviest brogue, Declan answers, "I'm 'fraid not, Mr. Freddy. Not from aroun' here."

I have no idea why Declan is over doing the brogue thing or why he's lying about not being from Salem. It causes the butcher to eye him suspiciously. "How do you come to know our Rosie then?" he questions.

I jump in before D.P. makes things any weirder. "Declan is my tax accountant, Freddy. He's helping me with some problems I'm having with the IRS. We've ended up...becoming friends because of it." *Sure, Rosie. The two of you are just friends. That's why the two of you have to play games to touch each other. Like you're both still in Middle School.*

My mention of the IRS causes Freddy to make an obscene gesture. "Those bastards. Always got their hands in our damn pockets. You any good at your job, Fitzie?" he asks D.P.

"I've been told I'm vera good," Declan answers. Then he drops a hand on my hip in what's obviously a very possessive manner.

Freddy grunts. "I know certain gentlemen who might be needin' a good tax guy. I'll keep you in mind, Fitzie."

At this point, I just want to get the hell out of this grocery store so I can get some fresh air. With the Tax Man's hand on my hip and his obvious 'presence' in back of me, I can feel sweat starting to run down my chest and into my bra. I quickly change the subject. "Stella said you have some Littlenecks for me, Freddy? I'm also gonna need two pounds of flank steak, tenderized of course, two rib eyes, heavy on the marbling, and two veal chops, the best you got."

Freddy laughs and says, "Marone, Fitzie! You must be somebody pretty special if our Rosie is making you her linguini with white clam sauce and Veal Chops Lombatina in the same week! Our 'belle a mia' really knows how to cook for a man. You better be treating our girl right, Tax Man, or you'll be answering to Freddy Carlisi." The butcher then looks at me and adds, "If things don't work out with this Mick, Dr. Rosie, I want you to remember that my oldest boy, Jimmy, is gettin' out of Essex County Corrections early for good behavior. He's gonna work the meat business with me. Be a good catch for a girl that can cook like you."

Before I can respond politely, Declan jumps in. "No

worries on that front, Mr. Carlisi. Nobody knows what a treasure Rosie is better than I." And then the Tax Man adds, in perfect Italian, *"Credo che questa donna mi abbia rubato il cuore."*

Freddy laughs and gives D.P. the thumbs up sign before heading off to work on my order. It's too bad I don't speak Italian any better than I speak Gaelic. Whatever the Tax Man said, it sounded lovely. I sigh loudly, but Declan looks away without translating a single word of it.

TOOTH 24

A QUESTION OF TRUST

THE RIDE back to my house is a tad awkward. I suppose it was inevitable given that we'd been playing grab-ass for the last hour and now realize how ridiculous we'd been behaving. Even Stella the cashier sensed something going on between us. As she hands me my receipt, she wishes me "a very pleasant afternoon," stressing the word pleasant and giving the Tax Man an obscene wink.

In all truth, I expect D.P. to say something about our little game in the grocery store, even if it's jokingly. But he remains mum except to ask me whether I have ever met Freddy's son, the infamous Jimmy Carlisi, in person. It seems a rather strange question to ask. "Nope. Never met the guy; though Stella thinks he's 'a total fox,' whatever that means. She likes to use old time phrases like that that no one knows the meanings of anymore. Why do you ask?"

"The meat man seemed very intent on brokering a match between you and his son. I am just curious to know whether there's any interest on your end?"

For a brief second, I think maybe the Tax Man is messing with me, but with his Ray Bans firmly in place it is impossible to see whether his Irish eyes are smiling. He remains silent, scratching his right bicep through his shirt as if he's suddenly developed some kind of rash, and waits for me to answer. "That's an odd thing to ask, Declan, given our activities for the past forty-five minutes."

His neck turns pink, and he shrugs. "I'm just asking a simple question, Rosie. You don't have to get all huffy about it. If you don't want to answer, then just say so."

All thoughts of any type of sexy romance disappear like smoke in a windstorm. *Of course they do, Rosie. Seriously, did you really expect a happily ever after? Did you really expect him to carry you off to the bedroom? No such thing is gonna happen, dummy! Those romance stories aren't real, silly girl!* It's become very evident to me during the past week and a half that if there is a perfectly wrong thing to say, Declan Fitzpatrick will say it. There's an ache in my throat as I say, "My relationships aren't any of your business, Mr. Fitzpatrick. Once this little security issue is taken care of, I expect you'll go your way and I'll go mine. You needn't worry about me after you're gone. Besides, I'm perfectly capable of making my own life decisions, and I don't need anyone 'brokering' me away like I'm a side of beef."

The Tax Man doesn't reply. We pull up to the curb by my house, and I feel as though the events of the past hour were a figment of my imagination. When D.P. opens my car door, I grab my bags from the back seat and head directly for my house, forcing him practically to run after me to catch up. My hands are full, and I make no attempt to take his. As I try to unlock the door, I am stopped once again by one of those frickin' invisible barrier things and must wait for D.P. do undo whatever magic he did when we left.

I ignore him entirely as I put away my groceries. Neither of us says a word as I try to figure out why the hell we are fighting. I don't give a rat's ass about Jimmy Carlisi, a guy whom I've never met in my life, and I can't understand why the Tax Man would think I need the neighborhood butcher to help me find a mate. In my mind, this is very insulting. Does he think I'm going to wither away and die when he leaves? When I finish unpacking and turn around, he is gone from the kitchen.

I quickly decide to bury myself in the loft for the rest of the day, out of sight, out of mind, but before I can sneak up there D.P. reappears and blocks me from exiting the kitchen. "Move," I say, "or I'm gonna sock you somewhere you're not gonna like. I'm damned tired of being held prisoner in my own home."

The Tax Man looks genuinely contrite but covers his groin with his hands. "Then, please, let me take you somewhere special for the afternoon."

I'm not in the mood for any more game playing. The last one badly hurt my feelings. "Not a chance," I reply. "Aren't you supposed to be working on my taxes? That's what I'm paying you to do, right? So why not go busy yourself with that, or with your super-secret spy business, or whatever it is you Fae types like to do and just leave me the hell alone. This nonsense will all be over soon, and then we can go back to pretending we don't know each other."

Again D.P. furiously begins to scratch at his right upper arm and then braces himself more firmly in the doorway. "I am very sorry, Rosie, if you felt my question about the Italian man was...inappropriate. In Fae culture, families and parents often are involved in making matches for their offspring. It's just that...with your hair like that, looking so Fae yourself, it made me forget you live entirely in the Mundane World where things are... different. I truly did not mean to insult you in any way. Let me make it up to you by taking you somewhere special for the afternoon."

Sensible, logical me knows I absolutely should say no. There's no way this will end pretty, and the more I let the Tax Man lead me on, the more painful it will be when he gives me the ole' *let's just be friends, Rosie,* brush off. Still, even if he's laying it on thick with the whole Fae hair thing, I realize he's not entirely wrong. I'm not completely ignorant of Fae tradition. I know enough to understand he's correct about family matchmaking. It's still done regularly in the Fae Otherworld, especially among older families like his. So maybe his question wasn't any more insulting than when a possible love interest asks whether a person they're interested in is seeing anyone special. But who the hell knows? To me, D.P. Fitzpatrick is a total enigma.

The Tax Man must sense my hesitancy. He takes my hands in his and says, "Come with me, Rosie, Lass. I promise it will be more fun than staying locked up in this house."

"Just where do you plan to take me, Declan?" I ask.

Smiling, he tugs me into the center of the kitchen. "It's a surprise! Do you trust me, Rosie Parker?"

Now, that's a loaded question, isn't it?

TOOTH 25

TAKING THE BAIT

THE TAX MAN looks at me with those killer green eyes of his. He's still holding my hand, waiting for an answer. I am in a losing position. *Who are you kidding, Rosie? You know damn well that if he asked you to walk across the backs of crocodiles you'd say yes.* I try to speak the words without stuttering. "Sure, Declan. I trust you." *I certainly hope you've got your affairs in order, dumb shit. You just gave this guy the green light to do whatever he wants with you. What if he decides he wants to go skydiving...or bungee jumping or something crazy-ass like that? Bye, Bye Dr. Parker!*

D.P. gives me the biggest grin. "You won't be sorry, Rosie. I promise! Now, just stand right there." He grabs a piece of chalk from a small board hanging on the south wall of my kitchen, steps in front of me, and draws a circle around the two of us. Now I'm really nervous. It looks very much like he's making some kind of casting circle, and it's obvious he's planning to use some heavy-duty magic. Before I can change my mind, Declan takes both of my hands in his and says, "Close your eyes and hold tight, Rosie. Don't open them until I tell you." He moves in closer, and I can feel his breath on my hair. "No fair peeking, Lass," he commands. I hear a whooshing sound, and my ears pop, but I keep my eyes closed. This is a good thing because I feel slightly dizzy and my mouth has gone dry, sure signs that I have passed into the Fae Otherworld. "You can open your eyes now, Rosie," the Tax Man says.

I open them and wobble a bit, my balance slightly off. This is normal for me when crossing into the Otherworld. Declan notices and props me up until I can shake off the vertigo. "Thanks. I'm better now," I say. "I always feel a little wonky when I cross over."

He nods and says, "You're at a much higher altitude than I'm sure you're used to when you normally visit *I Idir*. That probably doesn't help with your dizziness."

I finally feel well enough to take in my surroundings. We are obviously on top of a mountain. Below me, I see miles and miles of green valleys, winding roads, and the shimmer of lakes and rivers. The view is unlike any I have ever seen in any previous trips to *I Idir*. My visits all have been limited to the city center with its bustling markets and wooden buildings teeming with every type of Fae one can imagine. Despite being a tooth fairy, I've always felt out of place in *I Idir*. Being here is like going to the most authentic Renaissance Faire ever, with the addition of magic occurring in every corner. I've always felt strange whenever I've gone, as if I've just walked into some kind of Brothers Grimm fairytale that I couldn't quite remember.

But this place D.P. has brought me to is different. It's vast and beautiful and reminds me of the Smoky Mountains of Tennessee, only ten times more awe inspiring. "Where are we, Declan?" I ask. "I know for a fact I've never been here before. It's incredibly beautiful."

"This is the top of *Tir na Fathach,*" he explains. "It's the final resting place of *Ysbaddaden.* This range of mountains sits between *I Idir* and *Avalon*...sort of the unofficial boundary between both countries. My family has been its caretakers for nearly a thousand years."

Our being here is a powerful reminder that my Tax Man is *Tuatha de Danann*, one of the oldest and most powerful magical families in the Otherworld. I consider how reckless I've been, actually threatening to sock him in the balls earlier today. Shit. Still, he doesn't seem to mind my "relaxed" Fae protocol regarding his family status. In fact, he looks happier than I've ever seen him. "Wait," he says, "you haven't even seen the best part of the surprise yet, Rosie." He drags me by the hand into a wooded glade a few feet from the mountain's edge. Within, the trees form a leafy canopy overhead, with just the tiniest rays of sunlight breaking through. There is a rocky overhang with a small waterfall dropping into a narrow stream that winds its way through the woods. I see flashes of silver and red fish in the water, and from the trees' branches I hear the songs of several kinds of birds.

"Do you like it?" he asks, suddenly sounding shy.

"Oh Declan...it's amazing! Thank you for bringing me here."

The Tax Man looks pleased. "Tis my most favorite spot in either world, Lass. I had hoped you would like it." A woven hamper suddenly appears at our feet. "I thought we could have lunch here, if you'd like? It won't be anything as grand as you might create in your kitchen, but it certainly will do for an afternoon meal. All that shopping has given me quite an appetite."

D.P. removes a large cloth from the hamper and spreads it next to the stream. We sit on opposite sides, and he unpacks the rest of the items from inside. There are a few chunks of cheese, some peaches and grapes, a loaf of some type of multigrain bread, bags of almonds and pistachios, and two earthenware jugs, which he promptly plops into the stream, explaining that they need to chill for a bit.

While we eat, Declan points out a few of the birds we can see and matches them with their Mundane World counterparts, explaining how the two worlds share much of the same physical make-up yet differ in a hundred subtle ways. It's easy to see that he's much more comfortable and content in the Otherworld. This realization cuts me deep. It's clear that on the opposite side of the spectrum, I consider the Mundane World to be my true home, and it's unlikely at this point in our lives either of us will change our preferences. It's a pipe dream to think we possibly could forge any type of long-term relationship with such monumental differences between us. I shove these unpleasant thoughts from my mind, lest they leak out and ruin the joy of the moment. Again, I notice him scratching at his right arm, and the physician in me feels compelled to ask: "Is something wrong with your arm? A rash or perhaps an allergy of some sort?"

He pulls up his shirt sleeve and looks at it himself. "I don't see anything out of the ordinary," he says, but I notice a look of concern pass over his face. It happens to be the arm with the gorgeous tattoo I noticed the night before. The one he hasn't explained yet.

I again try to get some information out of him, this time in a more relaxed setting. "Your ink is beautiful, Declan. It's very elaborate and unusual. Did you have it done in Ireland or here in the Otherworld?" He looks away before answering, which I find to be slightly curious.

"It was done here in the Otherworld, at my ancestral home in *I Idir*, which actually is not very far from where we are sitting. It's a family tradition," he explains. "Every male in my line has this same design applied by a mage artist when they turn fourteen. The same family of mages has been doing the inking for House *Nuada* for a thousand years."

I can't imagine having a family history like that. I never knew my mother's parents, and my fraternal grandparents were gone by the time I was six. "It must have taken a long time to finish," I comment. "I love the idea of body art, but I'm afraid I'm too much of a chicken actually to get any. Did yours hurt?"

He looks away again, and now I definitely feel he's leaving out a big part of the story, but I'd rather not have Pissy Pete Declan return, so I decide not to push the conversation further. His answer is quick and to the point. "It hurt a bit, but I got over it." Then, he stands abruptly, and I worry I've already gone and screwed up the moment. I'm wrong. The Tax Man has more surprises in store. "And now...for the very best part of our day," he proclaims. A fishing pole complete with reel appears in his hand out of the blue. "Have you ever fished for *Iasc Dearg*, Rosie? It's great fun! They do like to put up a fight."

I recognize the word *dearg* as meaning red in Gaelic, so I assume he's referring to the fish I saw in the stream. I've never been what you might call an outdoorsy kind of girl, and I usually prefer my fish dead: cleaned, boned, and waiting in Freddy's case for me to select as dinner. But I don't want the Tax Man to think I'm a bourgeois, stuck-up, city girl, so I work at appearing excited at the prospect of waiting around for a dumb ass fish to take my bait. *Wow...a situation you can relate to, huh, Rosie? Sitting around waiting for the Big Kahuna to take your bait.* "To be honest, Declan, I can't say I've ever tried fishing at all. My dad wasn't much into the outdoors, so we didn't spend a lot of time doing things like that."

"Ah, Lass, you've been missing out! Let me teach you today?"

For Pete's sake! How could I ever resist that damn boyish grin. "Well, how 'bout I just watch you for a while, and then maybe I'll give it a try, okay?"

"I'm holding you to that, Rosie!" With that, he turned toward the stream, fiddled a bit with a lever on the reel, and whipped the line directly into the stream's center. And then we waited. And waited. In my opinion, fishing seems like a rather boring hobby, with a lot of time spent waiting on the fish. Still, I had a great view of the Tax Man's ass and his shoulder span from where I was sitting, the setting was amazingly beautiful, and I had D.P. all to myself. Well, I was sharing him with the fish, but that was competition I felt I could handle.

Suddenly, he shouted and reeled the line out of the stream. Hanging onto the end of the line was a red and silver fish, jumping and twitching, which he insisted on showing me close up. The fish looked up at me with wide panicked eyes, and I literally could sense its terror. "It's a lovely fish, Declan. But maybe you should put it back in the water now. It looks like it's terrified."

He smiled. "Aye, it is merely a game between the fish and me. I always release them, Lass. *Iasc Dearg* are in the Universe for sport alone. They are not very tasty." The Tax Man removed the fish from the hook, then strangely he kissed it and threw it back in the water. *"Tapadh leibh airson an dùbhlain beagan air adhart* (Thanks for the challenges ahead)."

The scene made me feel all squishy inside, though I will admit to being jealous of the kiss the fish received before I did. From what I could decipher in his words, Declan had thanked the fish for their game before returning it to the water. This was a side of him I hadn't seen before, and it added to the mystique surrounding my Tax Man. After he assured himself the fish was okay and safely swimming away, he turned his attention to me. "Now it's your chance to play, Rosie," he said, as he rubbed at the same arm again.

"I'm not sure I can get the line out into the water like you did. Maybe you should do it a few more times so I can learn your wrist movements?" I suggest.

D.P. laughs and extends a hand to help pull me from

the ground. "You'll do just fine. I'll be right there helping you."

The idea of the Tax Man helping me quickly gets my ass off the blanket. He sets up the bait and pole for me and then puts it in my hand. "I don't know how to do that 'whippy' thing you did to get the line into the middle of the stream," I protest.

"Patience, Lass, " he says, "fishing is all about waiting for the right moment." Then he steps directly behind me, and I can feel him pressed against my backside. He puts his arms and hands over mine. "Just follow my movement," he suggests. He pulls my arms along with his and snaps the line out into the water. "Now, we wait for the fish to take interest," he says, but he doesn't remove himself from behind me. For all intents and purposes, I am in the Tax Man's arms, and it feels damn nice. I hope every frickin' fish in this stream avoids my bait like it's poison, and if I had the magical ability to do so, I'd put the biggest whammy on that hook so not a single fish would come near it. Unfortunately, my luck holds true and soon we both feel a pull on the line. "Easy, Lass. Don't spook him," Declan instructs.

Out of the blue, the reel begins to spin in my hand as the fish races away from us, heading downstream with the hook still in its mouth. "Hold on tight, Rosie. Mr. Fish wants to play hard." My mind goes in an opposite direction and the words coming from the Tax Man's mouth have nothing to do with fish and everything to do with more intimate types of pastimes, which is why I'm not prepared for what happens next. The line breaks with a snapping sound, and the force we were using to hold onto the pole works against us, pushing us both backwards until the Tax Man falls and I tumble on top of him.

We lay there laughing hysterically for a moment, not moving at all, until I worry that I am probably too heavy to be laying on top of him and discreetly roll to the side. D.P. looks at me intently and moves a stray hair that has come loose from my braid, tucking it behind my ear. I hold my breath, wondering if this is the right moment for the fish finally to take the bait.

TOOTH 26

SUNDAY FUNDAY

BEFORE I even can attempt to formulate another witty fishing metaphor, a wave of nausea passes through me, and the world seems to be spinning while I remain unmoving. I have a feeling I might be sick so I bolt upright to a sitting position.

I must look unwell, because the Tax Man also sits up and takes my hand in his. "Are you alright, Lass?" You suddenly are very pale."

"I...I seem not to be feeling good all of a sudden, Declan. Maybe I ate or drank something that didn't agree with me?"

He shakes his head. "No, I don't believe our food is the cause. Does your chest feel tight? As if you can't get a full, deep breath?"

This is not how I imagined it would go the second time the Tax Man drew his attention towards my chest. But he's not wrong; I do feel as though my breathing is much shallower than it was just a few minutes before, and I don't think it has anything to do with the excitement of lying next to D.P. "Yes…you're right. I feel as if I can't take a deep breath."

"Altitude sickness," he says. "*Cac*! We are at an elevation of 2,600 meters. I should have realized this might be too high for you, especially since we're in the Otherworld and you've been here a few hours. Wrestling with the fish must have been more than you physically could manage at this height." D.P. stands up, and I try to do the same before dizziness stops me. "No, Lass. You sit here. I'm going to take you home now."

He uses the heel of his boot to once again make an energy circle, careful to stay within its boundaries. Then he sits down and pulls me into his lap, wrapping his arms around my waist. "Put your arms around my neck and hold tight," he says. "We'll be back to your house in just a few seconds."

This would be a very sexy moment if I didn't feel so wretched and if the Tax Man didn't look so panicked. I put my arms around D.P.'s neck and bury my head against his chest. I would like to take credit for the idea of adding the chest part to the moment, but the truth is, I feel very strange, as if my head is too heavy to keep from wobbling, and before I can figure out why, the world goes dark.

* * *

I wake up in my own bed with a damp cloth on my forehead and the Tax Man sitting in a chair pulled next to me. I have no idea how long I've been out of it or what time of day it is. I remember that there is a difference in time between the Otherworld and the Mundane, but I can't remember which is ahead and which is behind. Outside my bedroom windows, the sky is a dark, inky blue, so I am guessing that it must be around 9:00 PM.

"Welcome back, Lass. How are you feeling?" D.P. leans over and takes my hand.

"Better, I think. My stomach is not nearly as queasy, and I don't seem to be dizzy or breathing strangely. How long have I been out?"

"About three hours," Declan says as he rakes his fingernails over the shirt sleeve covering his right arm. "I considered taking you to the hospital, but I'm familiar with Otherworld altitude sickness, and I knew you'd likely feel better once you were home and rested a bit. Besides, I wasn't sure how I would ever explain to the ER doctor how you came to be at such a high altitude here in Salem. It would have been a tad awkward. I'm so sorry I dragged you there. I should have realized it might not have been safe for you."

"Oh, please…don't be sorry! It's an amazing place and I'm thrilled you shared it with me. I had a wonderful afternoon. Maybe we could go back someday…" My words trail off. *Oh for Pete's sake, Rosie. Don't carry on like you're begging. You sound so desperate. You had your chance. It's over.* I change the subject before D.P. can answer. "What time is it, anyway?"

"A little before nine," he says. "Are you hungry? Thirsty? Can I get you anything?"

As much as I want to spend time with the Tax Man, his hovering makes me nervous. I need to get up and make my way to the bathroom to pee, and I'd rather not have to explain this to him. "No. I'm good. Look, Declan, I'm feeling a lot better now, so if there's something you have to do...you know...with my taxes...or maybe with your spy stuff...you just go ahead and do it. I'll be fine here. I'll watch television or something." I start to sit up and swing my legs over the side of the bed, but I sway and need to grab the headboard to keep myself upright.

"Whoa! Not a hundred percent yet, I see. Why are you trying to get up?" he asks.

I really have to go, so I have no choice but to be honest. "I sort of need to use the bathroom."

"I understand." Declan puts his arms out and the right sleeve of his shirt rides up, revealing part of his tattoo. It might be my woozy head, but the damn thing seems to be darker in color than I remember it being. He sees me staring and pulls his sleeve down to cover it. Something about that ink job bothers him. No doubt. "Grab my arms, and I'll help you to the bathroom," he instructs.

We inch our way across the bedroom to the bathroom next door. I sure as hell hope he doesn't think he's staying in here with me. My thoughts must be leaking from my head, because he smiles and says, "I'll be right outside the door if you need me. Use the sink to hang on to." He leaves and closes the door behind him.

All I can think of is that this hottie of a man is outside my door listening to me pee. It's got to be one of the most unsexy, unromantic situations I can think of, but then I remember he heard me puking a week ago and thinks that now we've run the entire gamut of how to make Rosie Parker look like a total dope. I can't wait to pee any longer, so I turn on the water in the sink full blast, hoping it masks the sound.

If The Tax Man realized why the water in the sink ran for such a long time, he doesn't comment on it, and I am grateful. He helps me back to my bedroom and into bed and hands me a banana and a glass of orange juice, both of which he orders me to finish before I fall asleep again. Then he plops down into the chair next to my bed and turns on the TV. We agree on old reruns of CSI: Las Vegas, which I usually find pretty intriguing, but tonight I have trouble staying awake. At some point, I must doze off, but the sound of the television clicking off awakens me.

"Jeez, I'm sorry to fall asleep on you again," I apologize. "Just can't seem to keep my eyes open."

"No worries, Rosie. It's to be expected. I'm sure you'll be fine by morning. I'm going to stay right here tonight in case you need to get up again. The last thing we need is for you to trip or fall in the dark if you're still dizzy," the Tax Man says.

I look at him stretched out in the chair. His legs are hanging over the arm, and only half his butt fits on the seat. It looks to be ridiculously uncomfortable. Before I change my mind, I push out the offer: "You'll never be able to get any sleep in that chair. Why don't you just lay on the other side of my bed? It's fine," I say, then quickly add, "I promise not to infringe on your virtue."

D.P. puts his head back and laughs, and when he answers his heavy brogue is back. "Only a fool would turn down such an enticing offer, Rosie, and I suppose it's penance for my dumb judgement making me play the fool. I don't think sharin' your bed tonight is a good idea for either of us, but that doesn't mean I won't expect a rain check, Lass." The Tax Man leans over and presses a kiss to my forehead. "Pleasant dreams, Rosalinda," he says, then clicks off the light.

TOOTH 27

MANIC MONDAY

FOR MOST PEOPLE, myself included, Mondays are not good. As days of the week go, it has a well-deserved infamous reputation for being the most troublesome day of the week. I don't expect this particular Monday to be an exception. Needleless to say, I did not sleep well. There were a lot of factors involved. For one, I'd been napping on and off all evening, and I wasn't particularly sleepy anymore. Secondly, there was that little faux pas of my invitation to D.P. to share my bed, his polite refusal followed by his request for a raincheck, and that ridiculous brotherly peck on my forehead that in no way counts as a first kiss. Lastly, it was extremely hard for me to sleep while a man I'm wildly attracted to was sleeping on his back in a chair inches away from me, snoring so loudly he could put wood chippers to shame.

On top of all that, my bedroom is overcast and gray, and I can hear rain drops beating against the windows with the power of coastal force winds. The sound makes me edgy and tense. Or, is it possible that the idea of rain leads me back to that stupid word raincheck? Which, by the way, was an ambiguous response to an innocent offer. I simply thought D.P. would be more comfortable on my bed than scrunched up in that little chair. It certainly was not an offer of intended sexual favors. *Sure, Rosie. You go ahead and keep telling yourself that. No one believes it; not even you.*

The man in question is nowhere to be seen. He was, however, correct when he told me I would feel much better today than when we first returned from *I Idir*. I no longer feel any sense of dizziness, and my breathing is perfectly normal. Since he's not in the loft or the bathroom, I assume he's already showered and dressed and somewhere downstairs. I am relieved to be able to get ready in total privacy. I have a bad habit of singing along with the Alexa in my bathroom while I shower, and I don't feel ready to share this fun little fact about me with D.P. Today, I ask Alexa to play the best of Streisand and belt out "Don't Rain On My Parade" at the top of my lungs while I soap up. Thirty minutes later, I'm dressed and polished and ready to start this monumentally miserable Monday.

I find my house guest standing in the kitchen with a cup of coffee in his hand and a copy of the *Salem News* spread out on my island. For a second, I stop dead in my tracks. The Declan from yesterday is gone, and D.P. Fitzpatrick, E.A., is standing in his place, complete with three-piece suit, monogrammed cufflinks, and polished oxfords. He's wearing the tortoise framed glasses I remember from our first meeting that I don't recall ever seeing him don once this past weekend. Either he also wears contacts, or the glasses are just for show. The whole spy side of him is obvious now, and I don't know how I feel about it. Still, there's no doubt the man fills out a suit rather nicely.

He looks up from the newspaper with a smirk. "Good morning, Barbara. Care for a cup of coffee, or can I talk you into an encore?"

I'm caught off guard for a second and then realize he must have heard me in the shower. "Coffee would be lovely. Where did you get that suit, Magic Mike? I don't recall you crashing my pad with any luggage."

He looks at me as if I'm an idiot. "Ah, ye of little faith. From my closet, of course. By the way, who is Magic Mike?"

It really sucks when you're trying to toss out a zinger and the recipient doesn't even get the implication. "He's a character from a movie," I explain. "You know...*Magic Mike*? Don't tell me you never saw it? It's a cult classic."

D.P. shakes his head, looking completely innocent. "Nope. Never saw it. What's it about?"

I fall for his feigned innocence. "It's about...well... these guys who work as male strippers."

"Oh, I see. So can I assume by your reference to that movie you'd like me to strip off my clothes?" the Tax Man not-so-innocently asks.

Suddenly I'm at a loss for words. D.P. unclips his cuff-links and tosses them on the counter, then begins to unwork the knot in his tie. I feel like I'm going to combust into flames right there in my frickin' kitchen. Then, I remember last night's little game. I refuse to be on the receiving end of another big tease. Besides, it's late and I have a full schedule of patients this morning. It's my turn to douse the flames.

"As lovely as that sounds, Declan, if you're going to take your clothes off for me, I'd rather have the time to… fully enjoy it. Unfortunately, I have a molar extraction at 9:00 AM, so we really need to get going; otherwise I'm going to be late."

He smiles as he readjusts his tie, and then he returns the cufflinks back to his shirt. "As you wish, Lass."

I dump the rest of the coffee down the drain and turn the pot off before heading out the front door. The Tax Man does the same motion thingy in front of my door, then takes my hand as we head to his car under the shelter of one umbrella. As he opens the passenger door for me, I turn to him and say, "Oh…and by the way, Mr. Fitzpatrick, I'm gonna need a raincheck on that whole stripping thing."

"Of course, Dr. Parker," the Tax Man replies. "A raincheck, indeed." And then we laugh all the way to the office.

TOOTH 28

DID I MENTION IT WAS MONDAY?

WE'D ORIGINALLY PLANNED to stagger our arrival at my office. The Black Knight had been adamant that we keep the whole tooth fairy conspiracy under wraps, and I thought it might be more than a little difficult to explain how the Tax Man and I just so happened to have walked in the door at the same exact moment. The women in my office definitely would notice something like that. On their best days they're a group of busy-bodies, but anything out of the ordinary that might perk up a dismal Monday morning would be fair game for a heavy dose of office gossip.

As things went, the normally nightmarish Monday Salem rush hour traffic was made worse by this morning's terrible weather, and it was quite late when we finally arrived at Witch City Mall. Add to that a ten minute discussion the two of us have regarding his concerns about me walking alone across the courtyard to the front entrance. Altogether, this leaves me barely enough time to rush in, grab my coffee, and still make my 9:00 AM appointment on schedule.

That's not to say that everyone didn't gape at us as we walked in. Not only does the Tax Man look like the latest cover of GQ, he also holds open the door for me with a slight tilt of his head and greets the staff with just enough of Ireland in his voice to make them all blush into their coffee mugs. I could tell Mel is bursting at the seams with questions, but with patients already in Exam Rooms 1 and 2, plus a handful in the waiting room, I have no time to give her explanations.

I instruct Mel to set Mr. Fitzpatrick up with any spare space she can find in my office, with the excuse that I would be able to pop in whenever possible to help him locate whatever paperwork he might need and to answer any questions he might have. In truth, everything he needs for his tax work can be found online in our book-keeping program. His being in my office mostly gives me the opportunity to stop by privately in between patients so that my hungry eyes and naughty thoughts can drift to the cufflinks he'd earlier taken off and tossed on my kitchen island. Unbeknownst to me, D.P. ordered brunch for the entire staff delivered from The Village Tavern, keeping them glued to the staff room when they aren't busy with patients and thus keeping us off their radar. Unfortunately, this doesn't stop Mel from pulling me into the utility closet the first opportunity she has.

Shutting the door, my PA shoots a barrage of ques-tions at me. "What's going on, Rosie? With you and the tax accountant? Did you ride in together? Why haven't I heard from you all weekend? How did you convince him to come back here? I can tell something is going on between you two. Spill it, girlfriend!"

The only thing I can do is to tell her the truth, or at least part of it. "It's a very long, very complicated story. One I can't tell you. You'll just have to trust me on this."

The look she gives me demonstrates that she's clearly unhappy with my answer. "Rosalinda Parker, we've been best friends since we were eight years old! How can you keep things from me?"

I have no choice but to play my trump card. "Mel, you know I would tell you if I could, but I've been ordered by the Black Knight of *I Idir* himself to keep silent on the matter. You'll just have to believe me on this."

At the mention of the Black Knight, her mouth makes the letter O, and she hugs me. "Oh, Rosie, I'm so worried now! The Black Knight? Oh hell, Rosie!"

Like I've mentioned before, the *Ridre Dubh* of *I Idir* has the reputation for a strict no-nonsense attitude regarding anything to do with Otherworld security. Now that I've met him in person, I realize he's not nearly as scary as the stories told about him, but then again, I've been pretty compliant regarding his orders. I venture to say he'd be different if I were not. Mel hugs me and says, "Promise me you'll be okay, Rosie? If the Black Knight is involved, it must be pretty serious."

I figure I better mention the Tax Man somewhere in this conversation. "Thanks, Mel. I'm hoping this all will be over soon. In the meantime, I'm trying to take care of that IRS problem as quickly as I can. By the way, did you realize that Mr. Fitzpatrick was Fae when you sought him out?"

She snorts, and I can tell she thinks this is a dumb question. "Of course! It's the main reason I called him before anyone else. I was worried about the tooth fairy thing becoming an issue, so I went with someone I knew would understand fully. Don't tell me you didn't recognize he was Fae, Rosie Posie?"

I blush on cue. "Not at first. It was a bit of a shock, but we've put the coffee incident behind us and seem to be getting along okay." *Yeah...that's about all you're getting, Rosie. Lots of teasing and grabby-ass.* I carefully don't answer her question about whether we drove in together. She'd be like a dog with a bone if she knew we'd been living under the same roof all weekend. "Look, Mel, I have to get back to work, but as soon as I can, I'll explain everything, okay?"

She hugs me again. "You know you mean the world to me, Rosie. I just want you to be safe and happy. And I know you don't care much for Fae men, but this tax guy is a real hottie! I hope you're at least enjoying the view."

View? It's been more like views, plural. Poor Mel. She doesn't know the half of it.

TOOTH 29

A TOAST TO MONDAY MARGARITAS AND
MAGICAL MOMENTS

IT's a difficult afternoon for more than a few reasons. The WiFi keeps dropping in and out, playing havoc with our records system, while the lights constantly are flickering, going off and then back on multiple times. Both issues are due, no doubt, to the summer storm raging outside. Plus, a handful of patients are late for their post-lunch appointments, throwing the entire afternoon schedule off, and there appears to be a strange man sitting on a mall bench directly across from my office entrance that the Tax Man definitely does not like the looks of. A call to the Sheriff's office results in the man being told to move along, causing D.P. the Spy to be frustrated and cranky that he wasn't able to tail him, obligated to stay glued to my side as he was.

As a result, he decides it would be great fun to tease me all afternoon, finding a multitude of ways to make physical contact every chance he can. He brushes up against me as he shuffles around the tight space of my office searching for files, reaching for things that require his arm to make direct contact with my boobs, and boldly pressing his thigh up against mine when we sit down to eat lunch. Somehow, his tie winds up in an exam room storage cabinet where I need to go for gauze, and his cuff links find their way into the pocket of my lab coat on three different occasions.

Apparently, my Tax Man loves to play games. This should have been obvious to me during our picnic the previous day when he referred to our activities as playing a game with the fish. I also got the distinct impression that he does not like to lose. That's okay. Neither do I. By the end of the day, I finally decide that it is high time to hook my damn fish or leave the pond for good, and if a little tequila was needed to grease the pole, then I wasn't above using it.

Thankfully, Mel had a Monday night date, so she leaves the office the moment the clock strikes five and doesn't hang around to notice whether Declan and I leave together. The rest of the staff never lingers at the end of a work day, so by 5:10 D.P. and I are the only ones left in the office. He'd been informed an hour earlier that Duncan Fitzpatrick had apprehended the man on the mall bench and that the guy was now safely in the Black Knight's custody. This didn't mean I was in the free and clear, but it was solid progress, and this knowledge seemed to put my Spy Guy a bit more at ease.

We barely leave the mall parking lot when I bring up the subject of dinner. "I know it's only Monday, Declan, but I'm kinda in the mood for 'Taco Tuesday.' After the day it's been, I could really use a giant-sized margarita. How 'bout you?"

It was too dark for his usual Ray Bans, so I am able to get a better look at his eyes. I'm pretty sure I see an eyebrow arch at the mention of alcohol being involved, though he answers positively. "I'm sure whatever you serve, Rosie, it will be the best I've ever had. As to the margaritas…I must admit that I've never had one. But if you would enjoy it, then I'm…game."

This is a boon I hadn't expected. "Truly, Declan?" I question. "You've never, ever had a margarita? Unbelievable! I suppose that makes you a 'margarita virgin,' doesn't it?"

He chuckles but doesn't seem the least embarrassed by his lack of "fiesta experience." "I am not much of a drinker, Lass," the Tax Man confesses. "Some ale or wine with a meal or an occasional nip of Irish whiskey is what I'm usually about." He takes his eyes off the road for a second and stares straight at me. "But if this is to be my first experience with tequila, Rosie, I'll be glad to be sharing the moment with you."

I suddenly feel way too warm, and I'm pretty sure that the fog on the windshield has nothing to do with the AC in the car or the humidity on the outside of it. Neither of us has much to say after that last statement, and I'm glad when D.P. puts on the radio to break the weird, awkward silence in the car. When we finally pull up to my house, no one is happier to be home than me, and the Spy Guy doesn't even bother to hide his car down the block.

I head upstairs to change clothes, and when I come

back down, D.P. also is out of his work attire. Yet again, I am shocked at his appearance. This is an entirely different Declan than I have seen in the past two weeks. He is now wearing a pair of very faded jeans and a white T-shirt, barefoot, and, as I live and breathe, looking years younger than he did ten minutes ago. I'm starting to wonder which of the men I've met over the past week is the real D.P. Fitzpatrick.

Heading to the kitchen, I pull out everything I need for the margaritas and mix up a pitcher so it can chill before we are ready to eat. The Tax Man watches me but is unusually quiet and subconsciously scratches his arm again. I'm a mite concerned that whatever is causing that itching might be contagious, but I figure I will cross that bridge when we get to it. I pull the flank steak I bought yesterday out of the fridge, squeeze the juice of a lime over it, then add some fresh garlic, salt, and pepper. My plan is to grill the meat outdoors, but the rain is still coming down in a steady stream, so I ask D.P. if he's willing to hold an umbrella over me while I cook.

This gives us something to do and helps keep the elephant in the room busy enough so we don't have to talk about it. If the Tax Man suspects I'm out to seduce him, he feigns ignorance. Instead, he chit-chats about his experience with Mexican food while rain rolls off the end of the umbrella and soaks the back and the sleeves of his t-shirt. The wet sleeve makes his tattoo easily visible through the cloth, and I am nearly certain the damn thing is darker than it was when I originally caught a look at it.

When the steak is finished cooking, we head back inside. I set up everything for the tacos and pour each of us a very large margarita in salt rimmed glasses. Declan pulls off his wet t-shirt but makes no attempt to don a fresh one, and my heart just about leaps out of my chest as he wanders around my kitchen wearing only faded jeans. One would have to be a complete moron to think he hasn't joined the game. It's also obvious he's not willing to play fair either. I lift my glass in salute. "Here's to a memorable Monday," I toast. The Tax Man raises his glass as well, "And to sharing more of them with you, Lass."

I hide my blush behind the large glass while I watch Declan taste his supposed "first ever margarita." He smacks his lips. "Not bad. Very tart and refreshing," he says. "I think I could like these."

"I guess this means I've popped your 'margarita cherry,' huh, Tax Man?" Even I'm a little shocked at my boldness, but I figure if he's going to dance around me shirtless, I need to "up my own game."

He laughs at my statement, then puts his glass down on the island and takes mine out of my hand as well. He moves in closer, putting one hand on the wall and backing me up into it. The brogue is out in full force. "For someone with the face of an angel, ya surely talk like a troll warrior, Lass. Still, I can't ever remember kissing an angel, and I'd like vera much to do so now." My heart is pounding, but before I say a word, Declan, being Declan, adds, "Unless, of course, you'd be savin' all your kisses for the butcher's son, Rosie?"

Instead of dousing the flames, his comment about Jimmy Carlisi fans them. "I don't know, Tax Man…there's something to be said for a lifetime of free beef. Got anything that can beat that?"

"Hmmm…you tell me, Lass." Then, he leans in and kisses me, a kiss with nothing brotherly about it. I've never kissed a Fae man before, and I'm not sure whether his magical DNA has anything to do with it or whether the Tax Man is just that damn good of a kisser. He pulls away and asks, "What do you think? Better than free beef, Rosie?"

It's a good thing the wall is at my back, because I'm sure my knees are wobbly. However, one kiss definitely is not enough. "You know, Tax Man, I'm not quite sure yet. You seem to be a head taller than me, and I have to sort of strain my neck reaching up to kiss you. It's kinda hard to tell from that angle. It's a big decision…you or a lifetime of free beef. I want to be sure, you know?"

In a flash, I'm no longer against the wall. Now I'm sitting on the edge of my island, the Tax Man is between my knees and he and I are face to face. If kiss number one was wonderful, kiss number two is astonishing. We play this game for what seems like a very long time: testing out kissing on the living room sofa, the dining room table, the stairs up to the second floor, and, finally, my bed.

We never do eat those tacos, and all the ice in the margarita pitcher eventually melts. The Tax Man and I don't care one little bit. We're far too busy, happily collecting on those overdue rainchecks.

TOOTH 30

THAT CRAZY MORNING AFTER

THOSE INITIAL MORNING afters are tough for me. I always go into these adventures with high expectations for a wild ride of passionate romance. Then reality always intrudes. The wild ride is more like a wheelchair excursion around an airport...a slow, rolling trip with unfamiliar faces in which you are expected to reach some type of destination. I've had my share of these types of relationships, plus a few that were such utter disasters I contemplated going into WITSEC afterwards, so I know what I'm talking about. You need to believe me when I say that my night with the Tax Man was not one of those deep disappointments. As a matter of fact, it's been approximately 11 hours and 46 minutes since he first kissed me in my kitchen, and I'm still walking around with a stupid grin on my face; and if I were to look down at my feet, I'm betting my toes still would be curled.

You can take this to the bank: D.P. Fitzpatrick,

Enrolled Agent for the IRS, is skilled in more than just numbers. He was everything I ever could have imagined and more, and if I have any regrets at all, it's that I don't speak enough Gaelic to have understood all the pretty little words he whispered in my ear at all the opportune moments. This could be my one shot at having the perfect fling, the kind of experience old women tell their nursing home girlfriends about, and when it ends, as all good flings must, I'll still have these wonderful memories to take into my dotage.

I also regret that it's Tuesday. I'd much rather spend the entire day in bed with the Tax Man or maybe even let him whisk me away to that lovely mountain spot in the Otherworld so we could do it right next to that stream. *See Mr. Fishy...I can play games with the Tax Man, too!* But I know I have back-to-back appointments today, and calling in sick would make it difficult for everyone in the office. In addition, now that Mel is aware I have issues involving the Black Knight, she'd instantly think I was in some kind of trouble and she'd needlessly worry. No, as much as I wish I could stay home, it isn't possible. I'll just have to wait until this evening to have the Tax Man balance my sheets again.

Anyway this day goes, I will consider it perfect. Unless, perhaps, D.P. wakes up and gives me something along the lines of 'last night was wonderful, Rosie, but let's just be friends.' Then I'll probably just dig myself a deep hole and fall into it. I'm not looking for a lifetime commitment or anything of that sort. I like my life just as it is. I like the freedom of calling my own shots. But one night with Declan Fitzpatrick surely was not enough, and if that makes me greedy, I refuse to apologize. Wildly romantic affairs like this one only come around once in a lifetime, and I would like this one to last just a little bit longer.

I have left said Tax Man upstairs, sleeping peacefully in my bed, while I've slipped downstairs to make a fabulous breakfast. We never did eat dinner last night, and since I otherwise was engaged, I never took the time to put anything away, resulting in my having to toss all the food in the garbage and pour the pitcher of margaritas down the sink. I am in the middle of frying bacon when I hear D.P. let out an excited whoop. It's a rather strange reaction for a grown man waking up in a woman's bed, so I call up the stairs. "Declan…are you alright up there?"

The Tax Man comes bounding down the stairs wearing nothing but a smile. He's obviously happy. Very, very happy. If having a shirtless man in my kitchen was distracting, having a very happy naked one in there blows my mind. He's speaking rapidly in Gaelic, and I can't understand a single word. "Declan, slow down and speak English. I don't understand a word you're saying," I profess.

He runs a hand through his ginger hair while he paces back and forth; then he takes a deep breath and says, "I'm sorry. It's just that this is so unbelievable…and so long in coming that I'm being over…emotional." I don't expect his next words. "Rosie, Love, take off your robe."

Never let it be said that Rosie Parker isn't a fun-loving girl. I would have no regrets about a morning tumble with the Tax Man, right here in my kitchen, but getting naked while I'm frying bacon just seems like a terrible idea.

"That's a lovely request, Hon, but can you give me like five minutes to finish frying this bacon? Then I'm all yours."

He appears exasperated with my insistence on a delay. "The bacon can wait, Lass. This is important! Please, take off your robe for me!"

I said I wanted an adventure, and here it is, naked and demanding in my kitchen. I turn off the stove and stand in front of the Tax Man while I untie the belt to my robe and let it drop to the floor. I have some serious body confidence issues, and standing here like this in the harsh morning light is not easy for me, but I am determined to have great stories to tell in my golden years. I wait for something sexy to happen, but my lover seems more intent on examining my body as if he's looking for a spot on a roadmap. It's decidedly not very romantic. Then he turns me around, and I hear him suck in his breath. I feel his finger trace something on my back.

Suddenly, he turns me around again and hugs me so tightly he lifts me off the floor. He's kissing my face and my hair and all the parts he can reach, which is more like what I expected in the first place. He's babbling in Gaelic again, and I really hate not knowing what the hell he's saying. "Again, Declan, please speak in English! I feel like I'm missing out on something important."

He steps away and puts both hands on my cheeks. That would be my face cheeks. Not the others. "Rosie, my love, it's you! It's really you!"

Even in English he doesn't make any sense. "What, Hon? I'm sorry, but I'm clueless here."

The Tax Man grabs my hand and leads me through my house, both of us still buck naked, to the guest bathroom down the hall. He turns me so my back is facing the mirror and suddenly out of nowhere, there is a mirror in my hand which he angles toward the sink mirror. He obviously wants me to see something on my back. At first, all I notice is my fat ass staring straight at me. Then I look higher. I can't make sense of what I'm seeing. As I peer closer, I realize that on my right shoulder blade there is a dark ink tattoo that I know categorically was not there 24 hours ago. And if that's not shocking enough, it looks vaguely familiar. I know I've seen it before. That's when Declan turns and shows me his right bicep, the arm with the ink. The band of Celtic knotwork is still there, but the center piece, the design with the wolf, is gone from his arm and now is sitting plainly on my right shoulder blade.

The expression on his face is hard to describe. It's one of wonder and astonishment with an underlying sense of shyness. The Tax Man draws me in closer and kisses me, ever so gently. "I'd given up hope, Love," he says, "of ever finding you. No one in my family has ever waited this long. I just assumed the Universe had turned its back on me. But I was wrong. You are my *Mo Shíorghra*, Rosalinda Parker...my eternal love...my soulmate. I've waited more than 20 years to find you."

TOOTH 31

HOW TO RUIN A PERFECTLY GOOD FLING

THE TAX MAN has his unclothed body firmly pressed against my similarly unclothed self. All of him. It's very distracting. And just what is one supposed to say in response to such crazy, ridiculous words which have just tumbled from my fling's mouth. I stand there with my mouth open.

"I know this is quite the shock for you, Love, but it's true! The Universe does not make mistakes. You, Rosalinda Parker, are my one and only, my *Mo Shíorghra*. The tattoo on your shoulder blade is proof." He's rolling the Rs in my name like crazy, which still gives me butterflies. Then, out of nowhere, a velvet box appears in his hand, and I think I'm going to be sick. He flips open the box and pulls out a ring with the biggest blue stone I have ever seen. He tries to slip it on my left finger, but I pull my hand away before he can accomplish his goal. He seems confused by my reaction.

I take a step back and he takes one forward. I put up a hand to stop him. "Whoa there, cowboy! I need me some space! This is all too...too crazy. I've known you for... what? Ten days?"

He corrects me. "It's actually been twelve days."

"Ten...Twelve...neither is long enough!" I say, a bit louder than I intended. "Not to accept a marriage proposal from you!"

He shakes his head as if he's trying to explain a concept to someone who has trouble understanding the simplest of things. "This is not a Mundane marriage proposal, Lass. I'm asking that we handfast."

"Same thing," I respond.

"Not quite," the Tax Man says. "Not in the Fae tradition. Do you not know what a handfast entails, Love? I will explain it all to you. It will be fine. You'll see." He again attempts to set the ring on my hand, but I duck and evade his reach. My reluctance seems to hurt his feelings, and I can see he's not quite as happy as he was when he first came downstairs.

Look," I explain. "I can't have this conversation this way. Not with us both naked in my powder room and certainly not without my morning coffee. Can we at least put on a robe or something, sit down over a cup of coffee, and discuss this like sane adults?"

"Aye, as you wish, Rosie, Love," he says. I can tell I've sucked some of the joy out of his moment, and I feel guilty, though it seems to me that one of us needs to be rational about this.

I pick my robe off the kitchen floor and hand him a towel I've grabbed from the guest bathroom to wrap around himself. He seems amused that his nakedness distracts me. The Tax Man sits at my kitchen table, and I pour us both a cup of coffee and look sadly at the bacon getting cold in the pan. Settling myself down, I try to appear like all of this hasn't shaken me to my very core. I start the conversation. "Declan...Sweetie...do you not understand why this 'handfast' thing is rather absurd? I mean...we hardly know each other. How do we know at this point whether we even like each other?"

He grins, and obviously sensing I like the whole brogue thing, lays it on thick. "From my perspective, Lass, we seemed to 'like each other' vera much last night. Several times, in fact. We could be doin' a lot more 'likin' if ya weren' so set on wastin' time discussin' what is already fact."

I blush, which I'm pretty sure is exactly what he was aiming for. "I will admit...last night was amazing. Truly it was," I profess.

"Tis the way it is between those who are *leannain siorai* (eternal lovers)," the Tax Man offers, as if he's selling the concept.

"But beyond last night, Declan, we don't know anything about each other. Hell, I don't even know what the 'P' stands for in your middle name. What do you like to do in your free time? For Pete's sake...where do you even live?"

"Phineas," D.P. replies.

"What?"

"My middle name is Phineas. Which means, by the way, that all those terrible names you called me in those emails were the wrong alliteration," he states.

It's hard to believe I wrote those nasty emails only a week or so ago. It seems like that nonsense was further in the past; so much has happened since then. "Do you see what I mean? We are basically complete strangers, Declan! We have no business making serious commitments to each other. At least not until we see where all of this is going."

The Tax Man gets up from his chair and begins to pace the room, his frustration showing. While he moves back and forth, the towel slips from his ass, and I am treated to a fine view. Part of me wishes I hadn't hopped out of bed so early to make a damn breakfast that never got made. My time could have been better spent before all this soul-mate stuff came crashing down on us. He puts a hand on the back of a chair and leans across the table to take my hand with his free one. "We will have plenty of time to learn about each other, Love. After the handfast. Why is it necessary to know everything right this very minute? We have been brought together by the will of the Universe through Sacred Magic. Why is that not enough for you? You claim to be a follower of the Sacred Tenets but you refuse to believe what you can see with your very eyes! You wear the sigil of House *Nuada* on your own shoulder! How can you refute our connection?"

My Tax Man is talking so fast and with such a heavy accent I can barely keep up with his words. I don't think I've ever seen him this agitated, not once since we've met. During this past week he's appeared annoyed, exasper-ated, frustrated, and cranky. This is different. There is an intensity here that's new, with a surprising touch of what seems like uncertainty. I don't feel great about causing these feelings in him. I need to slow this conversation down and get some facts.

"Declan, Hon, I'm not refuting anything. I just need clarification. Please, just sit down so I can get a better understanding of everything. You can start by explaining the tattoo. What does it all mean, and why is a part of your tattoo now on my body?"

Declan Phineas Fitzpatrick puts a hand to his forehead in exasperation and sighs before sitting down. He's completely lost the towel he was wearing, but I decide this isn't the time to mention it. Picking up the ring box, he moves it back and forth between his hands while he tells his story. "It's the way it's always been done with my line. We trace our roots back to King *Nuada*, the first King of the *Tuatha De Danann,* he who lost his hand in the Battle of *Mag Turied* and replaced it with a hand made of silver. His blood passes through every generation by the offspring of the eldest sons."

I know the story he's talking about. It's a classic in human mythological literature and considered factual history by the Fae of the Otherworld. A shiver runs down my back as I consider the consequences of what he's saying. I've just spent the night with a living descendant of *Tuatha de Danann* royalty. This reality takes away a bit of the lightheartedness of last night's adventures. I try instead to focus on him being regular Declan, my hottie Tax Man.

D.P. continues. "I am my father's only son, though I have five sisters. As is our tradition, I had the tattoo inked on my bicep on the night of my fourteenth birthday. It is the age accepted as *Sidhe* passageway into manhood, and of course, also the age of heightened Fae puberty. So as not to blemish the line with unsuitable... offspring, the tattoo is deeply imbued with magic, ensuring that the male's true mate will be selected solely by the will of the Universe, and guaranteeing that the true blood line will be as it should and not a product of wanton seduction."

What Declan is telling me sounds so archaic and misogynistic, I want to rail against every part of it. But because my Tax Man looks absolutely miserable right now, I have a strange feeling he's leaving out large parts of the story. My heart hurts for him, which tells me my feelings for D.P. Fitzpatrick might go beyond a night of fun.

This is dangerous territory for me. I've been burned before by feelings like this. Still, I can't help but reach across the table and take both of Declan's hands in mine. "No offense to Fae tradition," I say, "but that's a lot of pressure and responsibility to put on a kid. It couldn't have been easy for you, waiting around to live up to your family's expectations."

I read weariness in his expression, so unlike the Tax Man I've come to know over the past week or so. "Aye. And when you are the only male in your line to reach such an advanced age as I have without your *Mo Shíorghra* being revealed, it tends to shame your family."

This is another ridiculous concept I don't agree with. "You're not that old, Declan. 35 is not old. Surely your family understands that you've been busy building a successful life and career."

The Tax Man snorts. "According to my father, my one and only responsibility is to ensure an heir after me. I doubt I will change his mind on that tenet anytime soon.

Before me, the oldest male to wait for the Universe's decision was 26 years old. That was four hundred years ago. And even then, there were whispers that his family had been seeing powerful mages to beg the Universe for an answer. My being 35 and childless is a huge embarrassment for my parents."

All this talk about children and family lines makes me nervous. It's not that I don't want kids of my own. I love children. It's why I became a pediatric dentist. But some of D.P.'s anxiety is floating over to my side of the table. "So, I'm guessing that because I have the centerpiece of your tattoo on my back, you're convinced that I am...this soulmate...you've been waiting for?"

"Aye, my Love. You are the one I've been waiting for. I think I may have known this since the day we first met. I felt...something 'different' when you walked into the room, looking so beautiful like *Danu* herself."

I'm pretty sure my Tax Man is laying it on thick. *Danu* is the Celtic Mother Goddess. Never in my entire life has chubby, wild-haired Rosalinda Parker ever been mistaken for a goddess of any kind, especially not one as notable as *Danu*. "I think you are confused, Mr. Fitzpatrick. As I recall, I was wearing purple scrubs two sizes too small because I spilled iced tea all over myself. Then my fat ass proceeded to knock hot coffee into your lap. Which, by the way, I am happy to note did not cause any lasting harm to the family jewels. Not from what I could tell."

My irreverence in such a stress-induced situation makes my Tax Man laugh, and I am thrilled to see happy Declan back, even for a few moments. Suddenly, he stands up so quickly that he knocks over the kitchen chair and startles me enough to slosh my coffee. "What's wrong?" I ask.

D.P. looks toward the living room. "We have uninvited guests at the door," he says. His face, as well as his lower regions, indicates that he no longer is a happy camper.

I stand up alarmed as well. "Is it the Chechen bad guys?"

The Tax Man shakes his head. "No. It's worse than that, Lass. My parents are at your front door."

TOOTH 32

DON'T BE CRUEL...

I HEAR THE WORDS, but it takes a long while for them to sink in. **Declan. Parents. Front Door.** It's hard to say which of us has the more panicked expression. "If we stay quiet and don't answer, do you think they'll just...go away?" I ask.

The Tax Man looks at me as if I've lost my mind. "Nay," he says, as he shakes his head. "They know we are here in the kitchen." He taps his head. "They already are busy scolding me as if I were a wee boy and not a grown man." He sighs and adds, "I'm afraid you'll have to give them permission to enter. There are no greater authorities on proper Fae protocol than Lord and Lady *Nuada*."

At this point, I am wishing I had enough magical wherewithal to make myself disappear. I wonder whether Declan's parents can see us in the kitchen? Do they have any idea that their son is bare ass naked and that I am wearing only a very clingy satin robe with two Chinese dragons embroidered over my boobs? As I am having these thoughts, I find myself suddenly wearing my sage green shift and sandals, and my hair, which seconds ago was a nest of tangled curls, now is plaited neatly in a single braid down my back.

The Tax Man is back to wearing his hot surfer boy jeans and the now dry white T-shirt he wore last night which instantly causes me to recall the activities of our night together. D.P. grins, then points to his head and says, "You best try to put up the tightest shield ya can, Lass. You surely are leaking your thoughts all over the place, and while I find them most enchanting, I'd guess you might not want to share those images with my mother."

We head together toward the parlor and the front door. I am shaking so much I swear I can hear my teeth chattering. Though I'm glad to be wearing more than a robe, I heartily wish the Tax Man had thought to include underwear in his magic. It is disconcerting to be meeting your lover's parents commando style, and I'm pretty sure my dress keeps sticking into the crack of my ass in a highly unflattering way.

The Tax Man stops and kisses me before we reach the door. "It will be fine, my Love. They have done nothing but harp at me for the last twenty years over the fact that I hadn't found my *Mo Shiorghra*. They will be overjoyed at the prospect of meeting you, although I do apologize in advance for anything rude and inappropriate they are sure to say."

This statement does not fill me with confidence. On the other hand, I've met my share of rude people. The Fae certainly don't corner the market on that attribute. I've come across plenty of asshole human types as well. I take a deep breath, pull my dress from my butt crack, and open the door. I give my little welcome speech in one long breath so it sounds as though I've just finished running a marathon. "Lord and Lady *Nuada*…how nice of you to visit my home. Won't you please come in."

They step through my front door, and I can feel their magical energy humming under my feet. I point to my parlor. "Please… make yourselves comfortable." Instead of moving, everyone just stands there, sizing each other up. Even if I didn't know who they were, it would be easy to recognize them as the Tax Man's folks. Declan is the perfect combination of them both. My Tax Man has his mother's jade green eyes, with the same angled, expressive eyebrows, and he has his father's strong jawline and high forehead. Both parents are ginger haired, with the same pale complexions that are so prized among the Fae elite, and both are tall with an athletic, lithe build. Say what you want about the elitist attitudes of the *Tuatha De Danann,* but they truly are the most physically beautiful people. I can just imagine what they think of the well-rounded, mostly human tooth fairy standing in front of them.

D.P. 's father speaks first, while his mother continues to study me as if I were a piece of art she was looking to add to her collection. Lord *Nuada* raises his hand and says, *"Beannaich an Cruinne-cè thu le aonadh torrach.* (May the Universe bless you with a fruitful union)." Then he slaps his son on the back and hugs him.

I understand only a few of the words; "Universe, fruitful, and union," but I get the gist of his blessing, and I can't help but to blush. I don't know how I could even have thought that they might not know what the Tax Man and I have been up to these past twelve hours. It was pretty naive of me to think that, considering that part of their son's tattoo now is residing on my back.

As congenial as his father looks, his mother still is eyeing me with a less than enthusiastic appraisal. "No greeting for your dear mother, Declan?" she asks. The Tax Man leans in and kisses his mother on the cheek. "It is good to see you, *Mathair*. You look well."

"Not nearly as well as you, my son. You positively are glowing. It appears that you've been well...satisfied with the Universe's choice for you," Lady *Nuada* comments. She raises her one eyebrow in the same manner I've seen my Tax Man do when he's being...cheeky.

"I am feeling undoubtedly blessed this morning, *Mathair*," Declan says. "Thank you so much for noticing."

Yup. It's pretty apparent from whom my Tax Man gets his dry sarcasm. I decide to put my two cents in. "It's so very nice to meet you, Lord and Lady *Nuada*," I say.

"But that's just the point, dear girl. We have not met you. In fact, our Declan has not said a single word about you to us. No warning at all. We were shocked when the Master Druid informed us this morning that our son was finally mated. Surely, Declan, you had some inkling that this woman might be your *Mo Shíorghra*? Both your father and his father before him had physical signs. Are you telling me you did not? I hope that this is not the case. There are enough concerns already about your role as the future of House *Nuada*."

I can tell that D.P. is very embarrassed by his mother's

comments, and I've already decided that I don't like her much. The jury is still out on his Father. I jump to my Tax Man's defense. "Well of course he did Lady *Nuada*. His arm, the one with the ink, has been itching like crazy for days. But I think Declan was waiting for it all to be…'official' before he told you. Wouldn't want to get your hopes up too soon, would we?" After I say it, I realize that it not only sounds sarcastic, but it also implies that Declan had concerns about me, but now it's too late. I've already said what I said.

Thankfully, his father jumps in before his mother can say something rude. "Then you take after your Sire, my boy! I thought I would rip my skin right off that arm when I met your mother. 'Tis a joy to find that the apple does not fall far from the tree."

The Lady *Nuada* gives her husband a sour look. Then, she stares straight at me like she wants to drill a hole right between my eyes. "Then if this is all as 'official' as you so creatively imply, girl, why are you not wearing the ring?" she asks.

"Her name is Rosalinda, *Mathair*…not 'girl.' As to the matter of the ring, your arrival so early in the Mundane world's morning hours has not allowed me enough time or privacy to present it to my *Mo Shíorghra* in a manner befitting House *Nuada*."

This obviously is a lie on Declan's part. I've already seen the ring and have been avoiding it like a form of the plague. But I feel my Tax Man's panic at being embarrassed in front of his parents, especially his bitchy mother, so I decide for appearance's sake I will lovingly accept it when it's offered. I can always give it back after they are gone.

In hindsight, I wish that this had been the way the scenario had actually gone down, with Declan giving me the ring and me accepting it. What happened next was by far one of the most humiliating and hurtful moments of my life. Declan's mother smiles, but it doesn't reach her eyes. "Then it is not as 'official' yet as …Rosalinda…says." Lady *Nuada* stresses the first syllable of my name, as if she might choke on it. "Despite your thinking differently, Declan, it is a good thing that your father and I arrived when we did. We still have time to discuss some important…matters. I do believe the Americans call this 'the elephant in the room.' I don't wish to be cruel to my own child, Declan. But the Universe has chosen a lowly tooth fairy as your mate! Yet another unfortunate sign that you've been cursed from birth."

TOOTH 33

...TO A HEART SO TRUE

AFTER HIS MOTHER'S devastating comment, Declan's father finally seems to come to life. "Perhaps this is not the proper time to bring that up, Siobhan. This is an important day for our son."

His mother swivels around to face her husband. She does it so quickly, she reminds me of the crazy, possessed green girl in the old movie *The Exorcist.* "What better time to bring it up, my Lord? This is just another misstep in Declan's complicated life. This...this tooth fairy needs to understand that our son is not the 'golden goose' she believes she's just stolen."

What the hell does Mommy Dearest mean by that? Is she implying that I set out to seduce her son just so I could rise through the ranks of *Sidhe* bullshit? This is so far from the truth that I want to give her a good piece of my mind. Before I can contemplate how even to begin doing that, Lady *Nuada* turns her wrath toward me. "He's told you, right? The reason why the Universe continues to shadow his life with negative energy?"

I don't believe I'm leaking any thoughts from my head, so it must be either my face or body language that she's reading to deduce that I don't have a friggin' clue as to what she's talking about. She shifts her attention and wags a manicured finger at her son. "You haven't told her yet, Declan, have you? She's far too calm to have been told the truth."

The new ink on my back must be like a conduit between the Tax Man and me. I can feel his angst, his shame, and yes, his hurt. Lots and lots of hurt. It over-whelms me, and I have to fight the urge to get up and physically throw Mommy Dearest out my front door. Unfortunately, it is forbidden to put one's hands on *Sidhe* of Lady *Nuada*'s standing. Besides her own personal magic, of which I have no idea the strength, Otherworld protocol is clear regarding guests in one's home. My only hope is that Declan's father will put a stop to her abuse of my hospitality.

The Tax Man doesn't look up at his mother. "No, *Mathair*, I have not told Rosie the whole sordid story. We were interrupted this morning by 'uninvited guests.' Perhaps you should do the honors. You've told this story so many times, you are the expert now."

I feel heartache in each word D.P. utters. I've gone from merely disliking this despicable woman to wanting to cause her actual, physical harm. I call upon every goddess I know to help me keep these thoughts from leaking out of my head, and more importantly, to keep me from following through on my desire to slap this woman silly. It's then that I'm sure one of the goddesses delivers. Suddenly I develop a perfectly evil idea.

Before his mother can open her nasty mouth, I jump up from my chair. "With all due respect, Lady *Nuada,* can you please hold that thought just one teensy, weensy moment. There's something important I have to do before you tell me the horrid truth."

The Lady *Nuada* looks at me with utter annoyance, and in that expression, I see my Tax Man, whose eyebrows also arch up like that and whose lips shift to the right when he's annoyed. I hope he hasn't inherited anything else from this she devil. Not waiting for her snarky reply, I go over to D.P. and plop myself directly into his lap, positioning myself so that I don't inadvertently flash Declan's parents with my uncovered lady parts. I can tell he's a bit shocked, but he doesn't try to dislodge me. I whisper into his ear, "Do you still have that ring on you?"

Declan nods his head in the affirmative. I put out my left hand. He looks at me questioningly, and I hear his thoughts in my head. *"Are you sure this is what you want to do, Lass?"*

It's my turn to nod. *"Absolutely, Tax Man! Slide that baby right on my finger. But do it fast...before she figures out what we're up to."* D.P. somehow manages to pull the ring out of the box unseen, perhaps magically, and slides it on the ring finger of my left hand. I feel a current of electricity run from that finger straight to my brain and then slowly head south. It's a pretty weird feeling, especially considering where I'm sitting. It takes the Lady *Nuada* only a few seconds to figure out what has just happened, and I can see her face blossoming into a full scowl. I kiss my Tax Man with extra enthusiasm, then slide out of his lap and calmly flounce back to my chair.

Across the way, I hear Lord *Nuada* laugh quietly under his breath and say "Well played, girl."

Mommy Dearest is now in full anger mode. "I do not know what you think you have accomplished, foolish tooth fairy. You should have waited until I told you just what you've chosen for yourself."

I smile at her serenely. "But that's exactly why I've done what I've done, Lady *Nuada*. Nothing you can say to me will change the fact that the Universe has deemed me to be your son's *Mo Shíorghra.* I trust in the wisdom and magic of the Universe, so old family stories are meaningless to me. I must admit, however, at being shocked to witness the opposite in someone with such an ancient *Sidhe* bloodline." Truthfully, I'm not sure whether I one hundred percent believe any of that shit myself. All of this talk about soulmates and eternal love seems a little naive to me. But I will be damned before I let that evil tongued woman hurt my Tax Man without giving her a taste of her own medicine.

If looks could kill, and they actually can among powerful *Sidhe*, then I would be dead where I sit. Declan's mother is super pissed at me, which is why I start to worry when she calmly sits back down, steeples her finger tips, and smiles at me in the same serene manner I'd shown her a few minutes ago. "Very well, little tooth fairy...well...maybe not so little."

I can't believe that his mother has stooped to body shaming. *Go ahead, sister! Give it your best shot. I've heard it all before. It doesn't change a single damn thing.* "Yes, Lady *Nuada*. You are correct. There is plenty of me for your son to…hang on to."

I can hear D.P. snort next to me, and his father even grins a bit. If Mommy Dearest is embarrassed, she doesn't show it. Rather, she just gives a sniff and continues on with her story. "I'm sure you're not aware that our Declan is actually a twin."

I did not know this. She reads my surprised expression and looks triumphant. "I probably should say 'was a twin' instead," the Lady *Nuada* relates. "It's a very tragic story, tooth fairy. You see his older brother, Dylan, was born dead. Born blue, with Declan's cord wrapped around his neck. I assume you are aware that twins are a sign of prosperity and luck to the Fae. A dead one is quite the opposite."

My heart drops to my stomach and I don't dare look at my Tax Man, lest I throw myself at him in sympathy. I get the distinct feeling he would be humiliated if I did so. Instead, I say, "Surely, Lady *Nuada*, you cannot blame an infant in the womb…"

She holds up a hand to silence me. "If that wasn't enough, on the day of Dylan's death and Declan's birth, there was the most powerful storm the Otherworld had seen in centuries. It rained non-stop for twenty-six hours, and wicked winds tore through the countryside. When it finally was over, most of the fields were underwater, buildings and houses were destroyed, and more than forty Fae residents were dead of drowning or broken necks. It was a day few of us can forget. Since then, our son's life has been marked with disasters of all sizes and shapes." She paused and turned to look at her son. "How many souls have ended their life in your presence, Declan?"

He doesn't answer, so she answers instead. "Five. Five innocent souls gone from their rightful place in the Otherworld. Declan was there for all of them. Surely, if you believe in the Sacred Tenets as you say you do, then you can see the implications as plain as the nose on your face, tooth fairy. Declan is not your ticket to the good life."

The dark silence in the room is like a heavy woolen blanket covering all four of us. I want to say something, anything, to break the hold her awful words have on us. But my mind is entirely blank. On my left hand, I swear the ring is pulsating, and I wonder if anyone else in the room notices it. Declan is looking at his hands, folded in his lap. His hurt physically hurts me as well.

D.P.'s mother starts to speak again. "What? You have nothing to say, girl?"

The Lord *Nuada* stands up. "That is quite enough, Siobhan. I've had all I can stomach of your tirade. We will be leaving now."

Next to him, Siobhan obviously doesn't agree. "I am not finished yet, my Lord. It is best to get this handled…"

She doesn't finish her statement. He hauls her up by her arm and his voice is cold. "I said enough, Siobhan. You will be well advised to remember I am still Lord of House *Nuada*."

Declan's mother goes a shade paler but keeps quiet. She seems to have shrunk a few inches in his presence. Declan also stands and I follow his lead. The Lord *Nuada* takes my left hand in his and pats the ring on it. "You have fire, Rosalinda Parker, and you surely will need it as we go forward. Trust the Universe." He pats his son on his back. "Put an heir in her belly, son. As soon as possible." Then, with absolutely no additional warning, they both disappear from sight.

TOOTH 34

AFTERSHOCK

THE SUDDEN DEPARTURE of Declan's parents...more like one second they were here, then *POOF* they were gone... catches me completely off guard. I expected them to leave in the same manner they arrived: politely, through the front door. Having them simply evaporate before my eyes reminds me of just how little experience, other than my personal experiences as a tooth fairy, I have with living, breathing magic. "Where the hell did they go?" I ask D.P.

"Hell would be a fine place for my *Mathair*, although since they've used magic to travel, I am sure my parents have returned to the Otherworld," Declan explains.

"I thought you were from Ireland?" I question.

"I am. We have homes in both places. When my sisters and I were children, we spent our lives going back and forth. Now that we are all grown, my parents prefer to spend most of their days in *I Idir* with my sisters and their families."

"Can you do that?"

"Do what?" the Tax Man asks.

"Pop in and out like that?"

"Aye," D.P. says. "But only if I'm going between the two worlds. The physics of the Mundane world requires that I move long distances like everyone else here. Only tooth fairies can easily move magically in this world. It is why they have roles as tooth fairies."

I suppose this gives me one up on Lady *Nuada* and her kind, though if given a choice, I'd prefer not to have magic at all. Plus, my magic only works between sundown and sunup, which is rather inconvenient. It makes me feel vampire-ish.

"I am truly sorry, Rosie, Love, for all the spite my *Mathair* brought into your home. When I am her focus, she loses all sense of proper boundaries. But nothing she said is a falsehood. It is all true as Lady *Nuada* has stated. It is clear that the Universe has not looked kindly on my life. When the signs indicated that you might be my *Mo Shíorghra* I should have told you all of this up front, Lass. I got swept up in the moment, but that is not a proper excuse."

My Tax Man seems so sad that I go to hug him, but he stiffens in my arms. "What's wrong?" I ask. "Why are you pulling away?"

The Tax Man extends his arms and pushes me away. "I don't need your pity, Lass. 'Tis the last thing I want to see on your face when you are in my arms."

His pushing me away hurts more than anything his Mommy Dearest spewed. I feel a burning in my throat that usually signals tears are on their way, but I will be damned if I will start boo-hooing now. I answer the only way I can to prevent this. "Whatever."

I expect him to apologize for being so hurtful; instead, he just looks like cranky Declan. I've seen this face plenty of times within the past twelve days. "I need to know something, Rosie," D.P. says. "Something important. Did you take that ring from me because you truly want what it represents, or did you accept it only to anger my mother?"

For a split second, I think about lying, but it seems like a bad way to start off our relationship. I open my mouth to speak, but the Tax Man jumps in before I can answer. "I can see the answer on your face, Rosie. I think it best you return the ring to me until you truthfully can accept my proposal to handfast. Until then, we shall just pretend our relationship is nothing more than…a fling."

Now I am both hurt and angry. I'm hurt because the Tax Man doesn't understand that I did what I did to show my support of him against his mother's awful badgering, and I'm hurt because he does nothing to try and change my mind. I'm angry because this is not how I wanted this morning to go, and I'm going to be late to work for no good reason. Finally, I'm most angry because he stole the word fling from my own frickin' mind. "If that's what you want, Fitzpatrick, then here…take your damn ugly ring back." I tug at the wretched thing, but it doesn't want to move. I try twisting it around and pulling some more, but if anything, it feels even tighter on my finger than it did before.

Declan's left eyebrow is raised, and I can see from his expression that he thinks I'm just adding drama to the situation. At that moment, he looks like his awful mother, and I just want to give him a good punch in the arm. He rubs a hand over his face as if he's embarrassed for me and says, "Give me your hand. I'll do it."

I stick out my hand, and there's no way he can miss the evil eye I'm giving him along with it. He ignores me and pulls at the heavy platinum ring on my finger. None of his wrenching and maneuvering moves it at all. At one point, he tugs so hard it feels as though he's going to dislocate my knuckle, and I yell, "Ouch! Stop! You're hurting me now!"

He instantly drops my hand, horrified that he's causing me harm. "I'm not trying to hurt you, Rosie. Truly, I'm not!"

I'm still too pissed at him to worry about his feelings. "This pulling at it clearly is not working. Let me try some other tricks I know." We spend the next twenty minutes trying to get the ring off my finger. I try using dish soap to lubricate it. That's a no go. I then try using olive oil and butter. I even try using my $84 a jar moisturizing cream to loosen the damn thing over my knuckle. Nothing works. The ring stays firmly in place on my left hand. As I sit at the kitchen table with my hand going numb in a bowl of ice, the Tax Man asks me sheepishly, "Is it possible that you don't really want to give the ring back to me, Lass?"

I am still angry with him, so I just make a face. I don't understand why the ring won't come off. Maybe my finger has become swollen from all of the abuse it has taken and just needs time to return to normal. Or maybe D.P.'s right. I don't really know the answer, but I've grown weary of the drama and wish desperately that I could start the morning all over again. Then, a thought suddenly comes to me. "Maybe it's a sign from the Universe telling us that things will be as they will be, Fitzpatrick, and that all of our fussing won't change any of it."

He looks pensive for a moment. "Aye. It would not be the first time I've felt the Universe's hand in my doings. Perhaps we should leave things as they are and see where it takes us?"

I'm glad to move on. "Good plan, Tax Man. All that I currently am sure about is that it is nearly 7:30 AM, I have not yet showered, and, frankly, I'm starving. We never ate dinner last night, remember?"

This line makes him smile. "Aye. We abandoned yar par tacos to the solitude of the kitchen. Yar quite right, Lass. 'Tis getting' late. You go shower. We shall worry about the plans of the Universe later this evening."

I jump at the chance of a shower and hurry upstairs, working through three Neil Diamond classics before I finish. The ring, by the way, never moves an inch despite all of the water running over it. Afterwards, I check to see where D.P. has gone, only to find him still in the kitchen. A place is set at the table, complete with some type of omelet, a cup of diced fruit, and two slices of toast. It looks pretty damn good. "What's this?" I ask.

"You said you were hungry, Love, so I made you some breakfast. However, I mus' warn ya...ya'll be eatin' some of my 'magic shet' as ya so love to call it."

The way he says that word is so stinkin' cute that I giggle. He looks at me questioningly. "What is so funny about ma par attempt at breakfast, Lass?"

"It's not the breakfast itself that's funny. It's the way you say the word 'shit,' Declan."

"Shet is shet, anyway you call it. Or *Cac* if you prefer."

I laugh. "See! You did it again! The word is 'shit,' short vowel 'i,' not short vowel 'e.'"

He pretends to look angry. "Are ya makin' fun of the way I speak, Lassie?"

"Heavens, no! I love the way you speak. I think it's adorable. It does 'funny' things to my insides."

The Tax Man laughs and heads for upstairs. "I'm glad you kin' still find something about me 'adorable,' Love. I'm off to take my own shower." He takes two stairs at a time, then suddenly turns around. "Unless, perhaps you'd care to join me?"

"I just finished taking a shower," I say.

"I've heard it said that ya ken't be too rich or too clean, Love," the Tax Man offers.

"I don't think that's the way that saying goes, Declan," I counter.

"I'm not sure of old sayings, Rosie, but I am sure I ken be mighty adorable in the shower."

I look at the delicious breakfast in front of me and push myself away from the table to join the Tax Man on the stairs. If this keeps up, me missing meals, plus the addition of all of this extra exercise, I'm gonna be Fae svelte in no time!

TOOTH 35

SPILLING THE BEANS

IT'S no surprise that I am late to work. Very late. I call Mel from the car and feed her some convoluted story about my car not starting. She asks me if I'm alright and I hear worry in her voice, which in turn makes me feel guilty. On the drive in, I ask D.P. for permission to tell Mel about the two of us. He counters that I can tell anyone I damn well please because it is likely that everyone in *I Idir* already knows and that if I should change my mind and decide to back out, it will be me who will look like an idiot and not him. Did I happen to mention that my Tax Man has a tendency to be painfully blunt?

I insist we do not walk in together today. The fact that we are late does not help the situation and I don't care to have my staff winking and giggling at me, especially if there are patients in the waiting room. Declan rolls his eyes and tisks loudly but agrees, though only if he can follow behind me unseen and then circle back once I am safely inside. I don't ask how he intends to do that. If he can make himself unseen, I don't want to know about that creepy skill.

I float through the door alone, trying to appear stressed out over the fact that I am so late. I fool no one. When the Tax Man walks in five minutes later, looking like the Catch of the Day, I see my hygienists nudging one another and hear them whispering behind my back. I want to check in a mirror to see whether *just did it with the tax guy* is written on my forehead. Strangely, Mel doesn't say a word. She just looks at me with big, wide eyes. But because I'm already a half an hour behind schedule, there is no time to speak to her personally. However, while I'm on my way to see my second patient, she grabs my arm and roughly pulls me into the supply closet again. Even in the dark I can tell she's perturbed.

Mel jumps all over me before I can get a single word out. "How could you, Rosalinda Parker? I'm the best friend you've ever had, and you don't tell me about you and the tax guy?"

I'd planned on telling her the truth, but now faced with it, I'm having second thoughts. She knows very well the date I first met D.P, and it wasn't that long ago. Plus, she knows we spent the first few days at war with each other or sick in bed with the flu. How can I tell her I went from disliking the man to jumping at any excuse to engage in a little mattress mambo? All in less than a week? Worse yet, how do I explain that I think I've gone and accepted some kind of crazy Fae marriage proposal from him?

I stumble over another lie, "It's not what you think, Mel. We're just…"

"Bullshit, Rosie! Your aura gives you away, girlfriend! You're positively glowing red! As is your hottie tax guy! Did you forget that I'm *Sidhe*? I can see that shit as plain as the nose on your face. When did 'it' happen?"

"Last night," I admit, then also add, "and this morning. That's why I'm late. I'm sorry I lied to you."

She socks me in the arm. "As you should be." Then she squeals and hugs me. "Spill it, Rosie! How was it? Is the tax guy any good?"

I try and imitate Declan's brogue, "I would say vera,' vera' good, Lass. Mayba betta' than just good."

She squeals and does a little dance in the small space of the closet. "I'm so happy for you, Rosie! I truly am! And all these years of saying you didn't want anything to do with Fae men. See what you've been missing?"

"Apparently, when I change my mind, I do it in a big way, Mel." I hesitate, but then I ask, "If I tell you something, do you promise not to lose your mind."

"There's more?" she asks in disbelief.

My friend watches me unbutton my blouse with a questioning look. I slip the blouse off the shoulder with the ink, and turn around so Mel can get a good look. She still seems puzzled. "What is that Rosie? Did you go and get a tattoo without me?"

"Use the light on your phone, Mel, so you actually can see it," I suggest.

Mel pulls her cell phone out of her pocket and points the flashlight at my back. I can hear the intake of breath when she realizes what she's looking at. "Sandals to

Samosas, Rosie Parker! Do you have any idea what this is? It's the frickin' sigil for House *Nuada!* How the hell did this ink get on your shoulder, already healed, in fact?"

I explain the story as expediently as I can: who Declan really is, what the tattoo signifies, and the decision I have to make. Then I take off my latex gloves and show her the ring. I leave out all the shit about the Chechens and the tooth fairy plot. I'm still not sure I'm allowed to talk about that. This is the first time I've ever seen my BFF at a loss for words. She shakes her head back and forth. "OMG, Rosie! It's just like the Cinderella story! You're going to be Fae royalty."

I grimace. Being Fae royalty definitely was not on my list of things to accomplish. Plus, I haven't made up my mind yet. At least that's what I keep telling myself. Honestly, everything has been happening so fast that I haven't had time to sit down and process it all in its entirety. In the back of my mind, I keep hearing my mother's words of warning about the true nature of Fae men, and I know next to nothing about the one who says I'm his one and only. When I convey these thoughts to Mel, she's impatient with me.

"Hairy Bullocks, Dr. Parker! You get handed an amazing gift from the Universe Itself, and you stand here complaining about how you're not convinced it's a blessing," Mel argues. "I've known you since you were eight years old, Rosalinda Ann, and you are your own worst enemy. I can tell simply from your aura that you're head over heels crazy about this man. Why can't you just accept it and be grateful? I sure as hell know I would be if I were in your place. I'm still desperately seeking someone to call my 'one and only.'"

We've been in this closet for nearly five minutes, and I can hear people in the hall looking for the both of us. "I gotta get back to my patients, Mel. We'll talk more later. I promise. But for now, can you please not say anything to the staff about Declan and me? I realize they're abuzz with interest, but I want to be absolutely sure before I go spreading the news around." D.P.'s words from earlier this morning bounce around in my head, and I add, "I don't want to look like an idiot if this doesn't work out."

"I won't say a word, Rose. I promise. But it's all gonna work out. You'll see. Just don't pick out some ugly color for my Maiden dress. Keep in mind that I look positively putrid in yellow and sickly in green." She gives me another squeeze, then slips out of the closet.

I take a minute to compose myself. I hadn't even thought about a public ceremony, but now that Mel has brought it up, I reason that of course there would be. As Declan is House *Nuada's* heir, one can be assured it will be held with all conscripted trappings of Fae protocol in regards to handfasting, whatever that fully entails, of which I haven't the faintest idea. It also means having to interact on a personal level with his Mommy Dearest. That's a detail I'm definitely not ready to think about. I open the closet door a crack and peek into the hall. No one is around. I make sure my blouse is buttoned up correctly and that I'm put back together. All I need is for a member of my staff to see me come out of the broom closet disheveled. I slip out and quietly shut the door. All the while, the ring on my left hand vibrates with a renewed sense of urgency.

TOOTH 36

A WEE ADVENTURE

Work proves beneficial for us both. My patients ground me here in the present, within my Mundane world, and leave little time for thoughts of fated mates and handfasting. When I pass my office, I see the Tax Man bent over yet more boxes of unfiled receipts, and I hear him muttering what I am sure are Gaelic obscenities under his breath. When I stop in the office to take a call from an oral surgeon regarding a consult, Declan points to a stack of now organized paperwork and growls, "Never again, Lass. There will be no more nonsense like this goin' on with your finances. Not anymore." I try to evoke some feminist indignation over his bossiness, but part of me is relieved that someone wants to look after me for a change. I feel like I've been on my own for far too long.

When lunch time rolls around, I decide that the Tax Man and I will eat alone in my office. I don't have enough energy to ward off the sly smiles or amusing innuendos of my staff or to field Mel's probing questions. However, I reluctantly nix D.P. 's suggestion that I lock my office door. I'm not yet ready for a tumble in my office with an entire audience outside listening, though I admit to being thoroughly tempted by the idea. I seem to have lost proper perspective where Declan and sex are concerned. It might be the *Mo Shíorghra* thing or because I've just come out of a really long dry spell, but damn, I can't seem to keep my hands off the man. Unfortunately, the departing words Declan's father said to him about producing an heir linger in my head like an unwelcome visitor. I honestly want to believe the Tax Man's passion for me is real and not just a ploy to knock me up with an heir, but I've always been a realist. So far we've been taking precautions to avoid parenthood, but this is definitely an issue we need to discuss and I'm not looking forward to doing so.

D.P. spends the rest of the afternoon working hard to make me regret my decision not to play "lunchtime lollapalooza" with him. By the time five o'clock rolls around, we are the first ones out the door, and to hell with what anyone might infer over that. I turn the tables on the teasing for the entire ride home until the Tax Man warns that if I don't wish for him to stop the damn car and make the two of us a public spectacle, then I probably should cease and desist.

We barely make it through my front door when all bets are off. The couch would have been fine for me, but D.P. has other ideas; he grabs my hand and leads me upstairs, though I am surprised when he pulls me into the loft. The Murphy bed is still down, so I assume that is his destination, but I've guessed wrong. The Tax Man takes both of my hands in his and asks me not for the first time, "Do ya trust me, Love?"

"You seem to really enjoy asking me that, Declan," I joke.

"That is not an answer, Lass. Do ya trust me? Be it a yay or nay?" he asks again with a grin on his face the size of Texas.

I pretend to sigh dramatically, "Yes, Declan. Of course I trust you."

In the blink of an eye, we are both small and standing inside the Master Suite of my largest dollhouse. I remain confused for only the tiniest moment before the Tax Man plops on the bed and bounces a few times before pulling me down as well. "I've been vera' much curious to test out this wee little bed, Lass, if that is fine with its maker?"

How can I possibly say nay to an invitation like that? I kiss my Tax Man and think to myself how I am so happy that I did not glue down the linens on this bed like I originally had planned.

I wake from a blissful, coitus-induced nap with Declan sitting on the edge of the miniature bed, shaking my shoulder with a look I immediately register as concern. I am instantly one hundred percent awake. "What's wrong?" I ask.

"I'm sorry to wake you, Love. You looked so peaceful. But I'm afraid I've received some disturbing news." It's only then I notice he's holding a rolled parchment consistent with those used for raven-grams, and I see from the dollhouse that the loft window is open.

"What's the news?" I question. I'm suddenly concerned that there may be movement in the case involving the Chechens and here I sit, naked in my Victorian dollhouse. However, once again, my thoughts are on the wrong track entirely.

"Apparently my father suddenly has been taken ill with an unknown ailment that has his doctor both concerned and puzzled. My mother requests me to return home as soon as possible," Declan explains.

The timing of this is suspicious to me. His father looked perfectly fine this morning, and I smell a Mama Rat somehow involved in creating this so-called emergency.

I obviously am not shielding my thoughts because the Tax Man responds without delay. "I agree, Love. It does sound like something my *Maithair* would involve herself in. Still, I am my father's only son and his heir, and if it be true that he is in dire straits, then I must return to *I Idir*." He is silent for a moment and then hesitantly adds, "You are most welcome to join me, Love."

I can't imagine dealing with Mommy Dearest again so soon; plus, it would necessitate rescheduling patients for an unknown number of days. On the other hand, I don't want to seem unsupportive. Before I can respond, Declan takes the decision out of my hands.

"Frankly, because I am unsure of what truly is going on, I think it best if I go alone," he says. "If it appears I need a more lengthy stay, then I will return and we can discuss it further. In the meantime, I will ask Duncan to come take over your security detail."

His icky cousin is the last person I want in my house, especially after what I heard him say to D.P. after Sunday's meeting. "Duncan? The cousin who came to your meeting? Jeez...I can't say I am crazy about that idea, Declan. I'm sorry, but I'm not a big fan of the guy, and it was more than obvious you aren't too fond of him, either."

"Aye. Duncan and I don't see eye to eye on most things, but he is exceptionally capable in providing for your safety," Declan explains. "I will rest easier knowing he is here with you while I am not. And because he is now aware that you are my *Mo Shíorghra*, he will be forced to treat you with the respect he hasn't shown so far. I would prefer not to leave you at all in the midst of this trouble, my Love, but my family duty requires this of me and I ask for your patience and understanding of it."

TOOTH 37

BAD CLAMS

WE HAVE neither the time nor the privacy for a long goodbye. After I finish taking a quick shower, I head downstairs and find both Declan and his cousin, Duncan, standing in my parlor. Duncan looks less carefree and confident than he did on Sunday, and it might be just my wishful thinking, but he appears to be a bit sheepish as well. Furthermore, he also looks a bit less Otherworldly than he did a few days before, now dressed in ordinary faded jeans and a washed-out Green Day concert T-shirt, with a pair of beat-up Nikes on his feet. The two of them are speaking Gaelic when I enter, but switch to English when they see me.

"Duncan has something he wishes to say to you, Rosie," my Tax Man says.

Duncan steps forward. "I am most apologetic for my behavior on Sunday, Lady Rosalinda. I am ashamed that you heard my disrespectful comments. Even though I did not realize that you were Declan's *Mo Shíorghra*, my words were inappropriate and degrading, and I humbly ask for your forgiveness."

He almost loses me with his use of the term *Lady Rosalinda*; it sounds so strange to my ears, and I fervently hope this will not be the way other Fae address me from now on. I stick my hand out to shake on his apology then instantly pull it back, remembering that the Fae shun skin to skin contact with strangers. Plus, he's a *Gancanagh Sidhe*, an incubus type of Fae, and in my current sexed-up state of mind, I have no desire to touch him. "I accept your apology, Duncan. I look forward to a fresh start between us." Duncan smiles, and I can see how any woman with a pulse, Fae or otherwise, might instantly be smitten. He is very, very appealing, and though his apology feels sincere, I have a nagging suspicion that it's directed more toward Declan than it is to me.

My Tax Man steps between us and embraces me. "I will miss you every second I am gone, *Mo Shíorghra.* I have every confidence that Duncan will keep you safe, but I ask that you do not make his job more difficult by taking any unnecessary risks. If I am not able to return before you go to work tomorrow, then Duncan will accompany you under the guise of being my partner."

I'm not happy with this potential scenario at all. My entire staff is female. I can't foresee anyone in the office getting any work done with Duncan present. I start to protest, but D.P. stops me. "I understand your concerns. My cousin knows how to tone down his 'glamour' when it's necessary. I realize this is not the best of plans, but hopefully this 'emergency' is all nonsense and I will be able to return to you in no time at all." Then, my Tax Man kisses me and it is not a kiss of the type one usually shares in front of an audience. I wonder how much of it is meant to show Duncan the truth regarding our affections. Declan releases me and then vanishes, empty space existing where he stood just a second before.

Duncan and I remain standing for nearly a minute in awkward silence until my stomach grumbles. Loudly. It's almost 8:00 PM, and I haven't had anything to eat since noon. I do what I always do when I don't know what to do. I head for the kitchen, while I ask Duncan whether he's had his dinner yet.

He shrugs. "If two glasses of stout and bar peanuts count, then yes, I've had my dinner."

"Well, I'm starving," I explain. "I'm going to fix myself something to eat. Will you join me?" I ask.

"I do not wish to put you to any trouble, Lady Rosalinda. I have been warned by my Superior Officer not to cause you a speck of imposition or grief," D.P.'s cousin states.

"Stop with the 'Lady Rosalinda' shit. It's just too… weird and elitist. Please just call me Rosie, and if I'm cooking for myself, you might as well join me," I say.

The *Gancanagh Sidhe* gives me a slight bow to the head, "As you wish, La…I mean…Rosie. I would be most honored to share your meal."

Duncan follows me into the kitchen. I ponder whether I should make linguini with clam sauce or create something with the veal chops. When I open the fridge, I have my answer. The prevailing odor of over-ripe shellfish smacks me in the face, and I realize that the clams I purchased Sunday afternoon are no longer fresh enough to use on Tuesday night. I bundle up the Littlenecks for the trash and pull out the veal chops. "You're not, by chance, a vegetarian, are you?" I ask my guest.

He answers in the negative, so I get to work on chopping thyme and garlic. The echoing silence in the room gets to me after a few moments, and I decide to use this opportunity to gather info on the odd relationship between my Tax Man and his cousin. I try to sound casual as I ask, "So, you're Declan's cousin? How exactly are you related?"

Duncan looks up from his phone. "Our fathers are cousins on the Fitzpatrick side, and our mothers are long-time childhood friends."

I was hoping for more of a two-way conversation, but Duncan goes quiet and back to whatever he was pursuing on his cell phone. I try again. "So…are your families close?"

The *Sidhe* places his phone down on the table, and his voice sounds terse. "Is it a full family history you want, Rosie, or is there something more specific you're looking to uncover?"

My face turns hot at his sharp reply. "You don't have to be so rude, Mr. Fitzpatrick. Despite Declan's insistence that I am his *Mo Shíorghra*, I know next to nothing about his family. I'm just looking for a little background, is all. If my questions are annoying you to such an extreme, then I guess we can just not talk at all."

It's Duncan's turn to look embarrassed. "I am sorry, Rosie. 'Tis just that my cousin does not hide his animosity towards me, but then gives me watch over his most prized possession. I tire of Declan's disregard for my feelings. But you are correct. There is no reason to take my annoyance out on you. In answer to your question, no, our families are not close. Declan's father is Lord of House *Nuada.* My father is *Gancanagh Sidhe.* We do not move in the same social circles."

I don't much like being referred to as a possession, even a prized one, but pointing that out will not help further this already strained conversation. I'm more concerned about what Duncan has just inferred regarding my Tax Man. "Are you saying Declan dislikes you because of your heritage?" I'm praying to all the goddesses I can think of that this is not the case. I don't want to think I'm falling for a person who judges others using such ridiculous and petty social criteria.

"Oh, no. You have the wrong idea," Duncan corrects me. "Declan is angry at me personally. It has nothing to do with my sire." My guest must see the relief on my face because he quickly adds, "Declan is unlike many of the *Tuatha De Danann* who consider themselves better than other Fae. He is known to judge a man on the work of his life, not his family line. My cousin is the only one in his family ever to have treated me with any type of consideration or courtesy. I am honored to be part of his team."

I am more than a little relieved, but his admission makes me curious to know more. "So, if you don't mind me prying, what happened to make my *Mo Shíorghra* so 'personally' angry with you?"

At first he doesn't answer, and I figure I've probably crossed the personal information boundary line. Then he scowls, which, frankly, doesn't do a single thing to mar the beauty of his face, and confesses. "I suppose its best if you hear it directly from me and not the shet ya are bound ta hear in *I Idir*," Duncan admits. He folds his arms across his chest and puts his feet up on the chair across from him. "There are a series of athletic and ancient arts competitions held in *I Idir* every year to celebrate Beltane. Are you familiar with them?"

"My mother would take me when I was younger; though honestly, I found them boring. I found the fair to be more to my liking. But I know of what you are speaking," I say.

"Good. Then you understand what a big deal these races are. Last year, we both entered the *Stiopal*," Duncan explained. "'Tis a race on horseback that requires jumping over hurdles and water elements. It was an extremely close race, and near the final jump, Declan's horse was spooked and it threw him. This cost my cousin his standing in the final round of competition. Like all of the *Tuatha De Danann*, Declan is very competitive, and he was quite angry about losing his top ranking."

"But why be angry at you?" I ask before the thought comes to me. "Unless, perhaps, you were the reason his horse got spooked?"

"I swear to you on the good will of the Universe that it was a complete accident, Rosie! Declan and I were neck and neck on the last length when the leather toggle of my crop loosened and flew off. It happened to hit *Mo Mhuirnin* (My Darling), his horse, on the side of her right ear and caused her to throw him. Believe me, Rosie, I would never take a risk with my cousin's life. Getting thrown is very dangerous, and many a Fae have broken their neck in just this manner."

"And you explained all this to him?" I ask.

"Aye. A million times. But he will not accept my explanation nor my apology. We have been at odds ever since, but I do admit that me making love to his baby sister did not help the situation much."

This was more family dysfunction than I expected in one story. I wipe my hands on a paper towel. "Hold that story, Duncan. I want to hear all the dirty details, but those spoiled clams are really stinking up the kitchen. The gross smell actually is making me queasy. I'm gonna run them out to the garbage. Be right back."

I grab the bag and head out the kitchen door to the back of my yard, where I store the trash cans. I am just about to turn around and go back inside when someone steps out of the shadows, startling me so much I drop the lid with a loud bang. I recognize the intruder's face in the light streaming from my neighbor's patio. "For Pete's sake! You scared the shit out of me!" I say. "What the hell are you doing here?"

TOOTH 38

TROUBLE PAYS A VISIT

ERIK ASHTON LEANS against my trash can and sneers. "How ya doin', Parker? Long time no see. Still living... uhmm...large I see."

Seriously? That's the best he's got in the way of insults? Just another worn out dig about my weight? I can't decide whether I'm shocked, confused, or just plain annoyed with him. There is absolutely no reason I can think of for this asshole to be standing here in my back-yard. I look toward the kitchen door to see if perhaps Duncan is watching, but no one is standing there. "What do you want, Erik? I can't for the life of me figure out why you're here, lurking around my trash cans."

"Haven't seen your name on the rotation, Jumbo. Did you maybe forget you had responsibilities to the Corps? To me and the rest of the team?"

There's something creepy and suspicious regarding his tone and attitude. He's never treated me very well, but tonight I feel an especially virulent sense of hostility from him. I suddenly wish I had sent Duncan to throw away the bad clams instead of taking them out myself. Being out here alone with Erik is making me very uncomfortable. "I'm on a leave of absence, Erik."

"And why is that, Parker? Under whose authority are you off the rotation?" my Corps Supervisor asks. "Because it's certainly not under my authority, that's for sure."

I take a step backward, increasing the space between us. "I'm sorry, Erik, but I'm not at liberty to say." The last thing I want to do is to give Erik Ashton any information about the Chechen tooth plot.

"Not at liberty to say, Parker? We'll see about that." From the dark expanse surrounding him, Ashton pulls out a gun and points it directly at me. "I'm guessing my little friend here can be a great persuader, especially now that your fucking watchdog is no longer at your side." He pokes the gun into my back. "Start walking toward the house, nice and easy. Don't you dare make a sound unless you want a rather large hole in your spine? You'd bleed out before you'd heal up; one of the drawbacks of being a lowly tooth fairy, eh?"

I don't know whether his reference to my watchdog is Declan or Duncan, and I consider the horrid possibility that maybe Erik is the reason behind my Tax Man's emergency in *I Idir*. If that's the case, does he know that my watchdog has left another in his place? There's little more I can do right now except concede to the asshole's demands. I start to put my hands in the air, but my supervisor growls at me. "Knock it off, Parker. I can't have your neighbors thinking something funny is going on here. In fact, let's make this look a little cozier." He steps to my side and puts an arm around my waist, the gun now pointed toward my rib cage. My next-door neighbor steps out on his patio to have his usual evening smoke, and Erik waves to him. To Mr. Storks next door, we must look like a young couple enjoying the evening air.

As we climb the few stairs to my deck, Erik grabs the skin at my waistline and gives it a hard squeeze. I can't help but gasp. The jerk whispers into my ear, "You know what they say about being able to pinch more than an inch, Jumbo…and I gotta say, sweetheart…you got about half a foot of excess here." He pushes me through the kitchen door and locks it behind us.

I don't see Duncan anywhere, but I notice that the chair he was sitting in has been pushed in and his cell-phone is gone. Instead, my phone, which I know for a fact was still in my purse from when Declan and I came home, now is sitting on the kitchen island. I hear it ding, noti-fying me of an incoming text message. Erik hears it too and picks up my phone. He reads the message and laughs. "Looks like it's just gonna be me and you, Tubby. Your friend Duana is canceling out for tonight, but she says she'll be by next week to help you paint your hall closet."

The message makes absolutely no sense. I don't know anyone named Duana and have no plans to paint the hall closet. Then, somewhere from the far reaches of my mind, I recall that the name Duana is Gaelic and means small, dark one, a description befitting D.P.'s cousin, Duncan. Since Erik is also Fae, sending mental messages is risky, as my shielding ability is tentative at best. It makes sense that Duncan would try a more human way of cluing me into the fact that he's in the front hall closet. I'm not yet clear how I'm going to get this bastard holding a gun out of my kitchen and into the parlor, but the dickhead eventually makes it easy for me.

"First things first, Porky. I know you have a whole load of baby teeth here at home. I've checked. You haven't made a drop off in six weeks. I want you to hand over all those precious little pearls to me. Right now."

I don't have the teeth anymore, as the Black Knight took possession of all of them on Saturday. It feels like a lifetime ago. It's also odd that Erik knows about my Tax Man but not about any of these other details, like Duncan being here or the fact that I no longer have the teeth. I try to piece together his role in everything but I am short on information, so I try to probe him a bit. "I don't have any teeth, Erik. I swear I don't. What do you need the teeth for anyway?"

My Corps boss turns and slaps me hard across the face. I taste blood, so I figure he must have split my lip in the process. "Don't lie to me, you fat bitch! I know you have them. I also know about all of the missing tooth fairies. Who the hell do you think outed them to the Chechens? Those teeth and their retrieval process are worth big money to certain people, Parker. And when we're done here, I'm gonna turn you over to them. Then you can decide for yourself whether you want to play nice with my friends or end up like the others who refused to cooperate. And believe me, there's enough of you to be sending parts to the fucking Queen for months!"

My face is throbbing, and I'm pretty sure the bastard has dislocated my jaw with his slap. But the knowledge that he's sold out his fellow tooth fairies, and all of his Fae brothers and sisters, for that matter, hurts more than my injury. I hope I'm around to see what happens when justice is served. But first, I need to survive the evening. I know I'm as good as dead if I let Erik take me out of this house, so I make him the following offer, trying not to seem too anxious to get him into the parlor: "Let me put some ice on this cheek, Erik, and then I'll show you where the teeth are."

"Teeth first, bitch. And if I like what I see, then I may let you ice that fat face of yours."

Even better. The quicker I get him towards the closet, the quicker Duncan can take care of him. I walk in front of Ashton, his gun still pressing against my back. "The teeth are in a hidden compartment in the front hall closet. The latch is behind the winter coats," I lie. I pray that the dickhead is so focused on the money he'll earn for me and the teeth that he doesn't remember the bogus text message I received ten minutes earlier about painting the closet and then somehow put two and two together.

Apparently, that thought never crosses his mind. He turns the knob and flings open the door. Duncan instantly leaps out, left leg in front of him and knocks Erik off balance with some kind of ninja kick. Erik's gun fires and a bullet catches Duncan in the upper thigh. I see the *Gancanagh* suck in his breath, but it doesn't slow him down. Duncan wrestles the male tooth fairy to the floor and with one solid punch to the side of his head, knocks him out cold.

Erik lies unmoving on my living room floor. Out of nowhere, a pair of gloves materialize on Duncan's hands and he removes a set of what appears to be some type of handcuffs from his back pocket, though they are golden in color and etched with several magical style sigils. He notes my curiosity and explains, "These are specially made by the Merlin for restraining Fae perps. They're brass with special wards."

I nod my head in understanding. Though most stories and myths have fairies being brought down by iron, that conjecture is pure fiction, probably fed to humans by the Fae themselves. Brass has been around since 500 BC, and the combination of zinc and copper is the best-known magic repellant ever invented. The elements of zinc and copper are safe when used alone, but when mixed together, they are highly toxic to any kind of magical energy. Wearing the brass handcuffs will render Ashton harmless and will be rather uncomfortable for him to boot. I try to drum up some small amount of sympathy, but the truth is, I won't shed a single tear for this asshole.

Unfortunately, Duncan has his own problems. The bullet wound caused by Erik's gun is not healing as quickly as it should for someone of Duncan's almost pure Fae ancestry. Something definitely is wrong. His beautiful face is contorted in pain. "The fucking thing is burning like hell fire," he says. "I think the dirty prick used brass bullets made especially for Fae targets." D.P.'s cousin looks up at me in anguish. "You gotta take this damn thing out, Rosie. As soon as possible."

TOOTH 39

KISS MY BRASS GOODBYE

The left pant leg of Duncan's jeans has become soaked through with his blood, and he's gone a definite shade paler. Most *Sidhe* can heal themselves easily from injuries similar to his, but Erik's use of brass bullets complicates the *Gancanagh's* recovery. Fae physiology is similar to humans, but typically injuries and disease that often kill residents born of the Mundane World don't affect the *Sidhe*, except, apparently, in cases in which one has a few ounces of Otherworldly toxic brass embedded in one's upper thigh.

"The feckin' thing is killin' me, Rosie! 'Tis like a burning knife twisting away! You have to do something to help," he pleads. "You're a doctor, right?"

"I'm a dentist, Duncan! Not a medical doctor," I explain.

"Ya still have ta pull teeth sometimes, is that not right? It canna' be too much different, I wouldn't think."

He's right about that. I am an oral surgeon, and an extraction is an extraction. Dentists take the same two years of basic biology and physiology as med students, so I do know enough to remove the brass bullet safely without nicking a major artery. If I can dig the damn thing out, then he probably will be able to undertake the rest of the healing on his own. I contemplate putting him on the kitchen table for the procedure, but frankly, I don't think he can walk even the few feet it would require to get to the kitchen, and I definitely can't carry him. He's starting to go into shock; his forehead is moist and clammy, and his breathing suddenly seems a lot shallower. I need to get the damn bullet out, pronto.

"Okay, Duncan. I'm going to try to remove the bullet. Let's get you situated on the sofa." I put my arm around him and literally drag him over to it. He's got his eyes closed, and, no lie, I'm really beginning to worry. Calling 911 is out of the question. One blood test and he'd be outed for good. He's far too Fae, and there are too many discrepancies in his genetic make-up for a medical facility to ignore. I literally run into the kitchen to look for my sharpest filet knife, my utility scissors, a large deep bowl, every clean dish towel I own, plus the bottle of French cognac I was going to use on the veal chops. Once gathered, I stack everything on a clean baking sheet.

Then, I scrub up to my elbows using the bacterial soap I keep next to the sink. I know that somewhere upstairs I have latex gloves I use for crafting, but there isn't enough time to look for such niceties. I catch a quick look at my reflection in the stainless steel of my refrigerator door. The side of my face where Erik slapped me is swollen and beginning to show one doozy of a bruise, but there's no time to ice it now.

I wrap each of my hands in dish towels to keep them clean and hurry back to the parlor with all of the things I gathered on the baking sheet. By the time I return, Duncan is panting, both from pain and blood loss. "Hang in there, my friend. I'm going to get that damn thing out, and then I'm sure you're gonna feel much better right away," I try to assure him. Any effort to remove his pants in the traditional way would be impossible, so I use my utility scissors to start cutting away the left pant leg. The wound is high on his upper thigh, practically near the spot where leg meets groin; when I finish cutting to that point, it becomes obvious that Declan's cousin is not wearing any underwear. "Shit, Duncan, are you free balling it?"

He manages the weakest of smiles and then grimaces. "Aye. I'm no fan of tyin' up the lads," he admits.

Well, I can't let this stop me, so I keep cutting away. It's not like I've never seen a dick before, and I've got more pressing issues at the moment. The wound is ugly: irregularly jagged and torn; I can see exposed muscle, cluing me in that the bullet is lodged deeper than I had hoped. Getting it out will involve serious maneuvering through multiple layers of tissue and undoubtedly will be painful. "I'm sorry, Dunc, but this is gonna hurt…a lot…and I have nothing to give you for pain, particularly because your pulse is so erratic. I'll try to be quick." I get only the slightest of nods in return, which encourages me to move even more quickly. I hold the knife over the bowl and pour the cognac over the blade to sterilize it as best I can. Then I bend over Duncan's wound and begin pulling away torn tissue from around its entrance with the tip of the knife's blade. Duncan flinches, so I have to put some of my weight on his leg to keep him from jerking it away.

It seems like an eternity passes before I clean away enough tissue to see the gold color of the brass. At some point, the *Gancanagh* slips into unconsciousness, but I proceed. All I need now is to wedge the knife under the bullet and maneuver it upward. Suddenly I feel a whoosh of air behind me and hear Declan's familiar voice. "What the feckin' hell is goin' on here?"

I realize that from where he's standing the armchair is blocking his complete view, and from his vantage point all he can see is his cousin lying on the sofa with his package completely exposed and me bent over him. I almost laugh at the absurdity of it, but I'm too damn involved in the surgery to bother. I turn my head as best I can to face him, and he gasps. Obviously, my cheek looks worse than I thought. "We have big trouble, Declan. Come here quickly and help me keep Duncan from moving."

He immediately responds and takes in the entire scene for the first time: his cousin pale and unmoving; blood soaking the sofa and puddling on the hardwood floor; the gaping wound in Duncan's thigh; my battered and swollen face, complete with split lip; and Erik Ashton, handcuffed and still out cold in my foyer. At first, his handsome face contorts with shock and worry and then darkens with what obviously is rage. He spits out every dirty, curse word he knows in English, Gaelic, and some other strange language I don't recognize. Unfortunately, his fury isn't helping me. "Be angry later, sweetie. I need you to concentrate on holding him down. This last part's going to really hurt him."

Declan nods and sits on the floor, ignoring the pooled blood, so he can keep one arm on his cousin's chest and the other on his lower legs. He looks at me and asks, "Will the lad be alright?" He looks so earnest and worried that I want to lie, but I don't. It wouldn't be fair. Frankly, I'm not sure what will happen. I have no background in Fae medicine, and if he were human, I'd say his prognosis was poor. Duncan has lost a lot of blood, and he's been in and out of consciousness for nearly forty minutes. The best I can offer my Tax Man is a quiet, "I'm not sure."

I take a deep breath and wedge the knife tip under the bottom of the bullet, then push down on the blade handle. The bullet releases with a wet, slooshing sound and pops out, rolling off the sofa and hitting the hardwood floor with a ping. I pick it up with a dish towel and drop it into the bowl. Not knowing whether Fae physiology can circumvent infection, I have no choice but to grab the bottle of cognac and pour some of it over the wound, causing Duncan to jerk and moan when the stinging alcohol makes contact. Then, I fold the last remaining clean dish towel into a square, place it over the open wound, and pray that the Universe and Duncan's own body will take over from here.

TOOTH 40

FEELING LIKE ALICE

DECLAN GRABS the afghan that's laying across the arm of the chair and throws it over his cousin. I assume this is more in deference to my supposed modesty rather than to preserve the man's body heat. I find this ridiculously ironic, since my face was just mere inches from Duncan's family jewels. Add to that the fact that Declan himself has wandered casually around my house naked more times than I can count since Monday. I decide to keep these thoughts to myself because my *Mo Shiorghra* already is wearing his cranky Declan face, and I have learned in our short time together that this means it would not be a good time to have any meaningful discussion with him.

My patient still is not fully conscious, but his color is starting to pink up and his breathing is less labored, both of which are good signs for recovery. The Tax Man now turns his attention to me, insisting my face needs to be iced. In his mind, this means I must sit in his lap while he holds ice to my face and swears about how stupid he was not to see that the emergency in *I Idir* was a ploy to distract him from the mission at hand. I know he means well by personally attending to my face, but the negative energy rolling off of him is not helping me to relax as he must have intended. Plus, I can't stop thinking about the veal chops still marinating in my fridge that need to be cooked.

I mention the veal chops to Declan, but he ignores my offer of dinner. Instead, he asks me to relate the entire story regarding Erik's capture. I hesitate to tell him, figuring that in his current mood my Tax Man will determine that Duncan handled the evening incorrectly and is completely at fault, which absolutely is untrue. When I explain that the clams had gone bad and that I'd decided to take them out to the garbage, I can tell from D.P.'s expression that he's already annoyed with his cousin for letting me go out of the house alone; yet I feel like I owe the younger Fae my loyalty for saving my life. "It's a good thing Duncan didn't come out to the yard with me, Declan, otherwise that asshole would have had us both under his gun," I reason. "And if Duncan had gone out instead of me, it would have clued Erik to the fact that someone else was acting as my 'watchdog' as he put it, and he might have slipped away again without being caught. Now you have him in custody, and we finally can be done with this whole mess."

The Tax Man shakes his head. "I'm afraid not, Lass. That Corps bastard is part of it, no doubt. But he's far too stupid to have put the whole plan into motion. He's definitely not the head of the snake, that's for certain."

"Well," I counter, "I'm sure the Black Knight will get the information out of him that he needs to find the rest, one way or the other."

"Aye. Of that I am certain," Declan says. "And he is welcome to the bastard…once I'm done with him myself."

I'm pretty sure I don't want to know what my *Mo Shiorghra* means by that. It's not that I don't absolutely hate what this creep has done to my fellow tooth fairies. It's just that I believe strongly that violence is not the way that civil, intelligent people should handle things. Then I remember that as tooth fairies, Ashton and I are subject to the laws of *I Idir,* even if we spend most of our lives in the Mundane World, which has proven no better at handling aggression than its Otherworldly counterpart. D.P. asks me, "Do you know whether Duncan already has sent for the Black Knight?"

A weak, hoarse voice answers from the sofa, a further sign that Declan's cousin slowly is improving. "I have not, my Lord. There was simply no time to do so before the effects of the brass bullet put me down. Do you wish for me to contact him now?"

"Nay, cousin," Declan says. "You must concern yourself with gathering your strength and healing mind and body. I will send for the *Ridre Dubh* when I have finished 'interviewing' the prisoner myself." He helps me gently off his lap. "I am thinking, my Love, that veal chops sound vera, vera tasty to me. I will leave you to the culinary activities you so enjoy."

Declan's sudden interest in my veal chops makes me suspicious. I have no doubt the Tax Man doesn't want me observing his interview. I narrow my eyes and say, "If I didn't know you better, Mr. Fitzpatrick, I'd say you're looking for an excuse to get me out of your way. Here's a word to the wise: you'd better not be planning to lock me in my kitchen like you did on Sunday! This is my house, and I will not be locked away in its rooms like a small child."

The Tax Man looks at me directly and says, "I won't need to set up wards to keep you in the kitchen, Love, because if you truly care for me as I believe you do, then you will stay out of this business in the parlor simply because I have asked you to do so."

Damn. This is a statement that's hard to circumvent, and, in effect, it's a very public challenge regarding my feelings for him. It's also a question I haven't quite answered for myself. I know for a fact that I am very much physically attracted to Declan Fitzpatrick. There's absolutely no doubt about that. I'm drawn to him like a hummingbird to nectar. But how much of that is lust and how much is something more? I feel like there hasn't been enough time for me to answer that question honestly, despite all of the signs indicating that we are fated soul-mates. I feel this is an important turning point for the two of us, so I try not to overthink it. My heart simply leads me to turn around and head for the kitchen without another word.

Once in the kitchen, I ask Alexa to play the soundtrack from 'A Chorus Line' loud enough to block out some of the sounds coming from the parlor, but not so loud as to bother my elderly neighbors this late at night. I am in the middle of the last rousing 'Singular Sensation' when Duncan hobbles into the room. He is still white as a sheet and wobbly on his feet, but he's in an upright position and looks a whole helluva lot better than he did an hour ago. If he thinks my leg-kick dancing around the island with a pan of potatoes is odd, he keeps his opinion to himself.

D.P.'s cousin slides into a kitchen chair, and it's obvious the walk from the parlor to the kitchen has sapped a lot of his strength. "Why the hell aren't you still lying down, Duncan?" I ask. "You're not ready for treks around the house yet."

"I was asked by my Lord to join you in the kitchen if I was able to do so. I did not wish to look weak in front of my cousin," the *Gancanagh* explains.

"Weak, my ass! You're lucky to be alive! Do you realize how close you came to...?" I don't finish. I don't know enough about Fae medicine to determine whether Duncan truly would have died in the sense humans understand it. There's a confusing concept about mind versus body for Fae with higher levels of magical energy that I don't know much about. Tooth Fairies don't have that genetic make-up, so it isn't a subject I looked into. Thus, I offer the best advice I can: "You need to take it slow, Duncan. Your body just suffered a very intense physical event."

He nods his head in agreement. "I understand, Rosie. And I thank you from the bottom of my heart for helping me as you did. You are a brave and compassionate woman."

His words are humbling, and I blush; then I change the subject to one that's even more difficult for me to talk about. "How's it going in there?"

The Fae shrugs. "I believe my cousin is showing great

restraint. He is quite angry over the bastard's assault on you. According to ancient Otherworld law, it is Declan's natural right to end the fairy's life for putting hands on his *Mo Shiorghra.* But he understands how important the asshole is to our intelligence work, so my Lord will sacrifice his right for the common good of *I Idir."*

"Gee," I say, "it's good to know that my lover draws the line at murder in my parlor." I say this with sarcasm, but it hits me that I am playing in an entirely different ballgame than I ever have before. The players are unknown and the rules are completely different. I am now deeply regretting that I have stubbornly avoided learning more about my magical heritage. It's definitely a disadvantage to me now in my current situation. I wonder whether all of the Fae classes Mel tried to get me to attend these past few years wasn't the Universe's attempt to help prepare me for what was to come? Despite all my studies in Druid spiritualism, I stupidly ignored everything set along my path. Label me a genuine dumbass.

Alexa has finished playing the complete musical's track and has turned itself off. Duncan and I now hear a third male voice in the other room and assume that the Black Knight has come to take custody of Erik. I'm glad about that. At least my conscience is clear knowing that the asshole tooth fairy is alive when he leaves my house.

Declan makes his way into the kitchen, and I put out our dinner even though it is nearly 11:00 PM. I serve the two veal chops to the men, and I scramble a couple of eggs for myself; my jaw isn't up to chewing red meat anyway. Except for a few compliments on my cooking, there is no conversation. The events of the evening speak for themselves.

Finished with his food, Duncan rises from the table. "I think I will head home now. I'm dead on my feet." He realizes the irony of what he just said and laughs, but I can see he's still not completely healed.

"Do you live by yourself, Duncan?" I question. He nods in the affirmative. "I think it's a bad idea for you to be alone while you're still not feeling one hundred percent yourself," I state. "Why don't you just stay here until morning? We can assess how you feel then."

Declan adds, "My Lady is sound in her thinking, cousin. There is a wee bed in the loft you can use."

For a second, I think the Tax Man is referring to the dollhouse bed we had our tryst in earlier in the day, but then I realize he means the Murphy bed he'd been using until he took up residence in mine. My thoughts must be leaking, because I see the corners of Declan's mouth turn up, and I hear his return comment in my head. *"We shall save that particular 'wee bed' for the two of us, Love."*

Later, as I lay in the Tax Man's arms, I feel as if I am Alice and that I have fallen down the rabbit hole to a place that is full of wonder and strange, new experiences, so very different from my life only two weeks ago. As the heaviness of sleep overtakes me, I close my eyes and hold on to one of my favorite lines from the Wonderland story: "It's no use going back to yesterday, because I was a different person then."

TOOTH 41

HUMP DAY

DESPITE HAVING SLEPT ONLY a few hours, I am wide awake and up at the crack of dawn. I hear the shower running in the bathroom next door and assume Duncan must be in there, as my Tax Man is lying dead to the world next to me. (Truth be told, if Declan Fitzpatrick were still asleep three rooms away one couldn't help but know it since his snoring sounds like a freight train running through the house.) The medical professional in me would have preferred the chance to check the condition of Duncan's wound before he showered, but I am neither his mother nor his physician. He is a grown man despite his youthful looks and thus is entitled to make his own decisions regarding his health and well-being.

I am very glad that today is the third Wednesday of the month. It's my day to work at the free clinic, meaning I have no regular office hours and a slightly later starting time. I became involved with the Open Heart Community

Clinic almost two years ago at the request of a colleague who had been involved in its start but who was moving his practice out of state to be closer to his ailing parents. Fast forward to the present, and now, not only do I volunteer my time at the clinic twice a month, but I also sit on the clinic's Board of Directors. Our clinic enjoys a satisfying rotation of doctors and dentists who share their expertise free of charge to some of Salem's most financially challenged population, and I am proud of the work we do for the local community.

I haven't spoken yet to Declan about my plans for today, but I'm hoping he'll be flexible and allow me to do my clinic rotation without having him glued to my side. I take a few moments of secret pleasure watching my Tax Man sleep, and when the bathroom noise goes silent, I slip out of bed and go into the bathroom to take my turn. Duncan's used towel is hanging neatly up on the bar, and he's taken the time to rinse and wipe down the sink. I will say this about Fae men: they do seem extraordinarily neat. I glimpse Declan's razor and toothbrush on the shelf next to my toiletries and it does weird, funny things to my insides, bringing me back to my Alice perceptions of the night before. The two of us need to find some quiet time to sit down and have a realistic, honest conversation about where our relationship is going. The passion and romance of the past few days have been amazing, but sensible me is not sure whether these are the things upon which a long-term partnership is built.

After washing up, I return to the bedroom and find the Tax Man still comatose. I dress for the clinic and head downstairs to try and conjure up some breakfast for the three of us from the food I have on hand. Duncan is already in my kitchen, leaning over the island as he scribbles on a notepad.

"Good morning, Rosie," Duncan says. "I hope I didn't wake you. I was just going to leave you a note before I left. I want to thank you for your expert care and for the use of your wee, funny wall bed. You are a most kind and generous woman, beautiful inside and out. My cousin is a vera lucky man to be blessed by the Universe with a woman such as yourself."

The *Gancanagh* is a very attractive man, and compliments like these make me blush, though I do feel he honestly means them. "You are most welcome, Duncan. I am so glad I was able to help you. On that note, the doctor in me really wants to check on that wound before you leave. Would you mind?"

"As my Lady wishes," he says, and then he unbuttons and unzips the new pair of jeans he's wearing and slides them down to his knees. Thankfully, this morning he's also wearing a snug fitting pair of boxer briefs underneath them. He must sense my relief when I notice because he laughs and says, "I did not wish to offend my Lady's sensibilities this morning." This makes us both laugh because after last night, I've pretty much seen everything the man has to offer below the waist.

I examine what's left of his bullet wound; it's healed nicely already leaving only a small, puckered indentation. I look closely for any signs of infection just at the very same moment the Tax Man trots into the kitchen wearing nothing but a towel.

"Hell's Bells, Declan! Do you have some type of a damn

alarm that goes off every time I find myself in a compro-
mising situation?" I ask.

He pretends to growl. "Aye, my Love. Warnings go off
in my head whenever my Lady asks another man to drop
his pants." Then he laughs and asks, "How does the patient
fare this morning, Doctor?"

"He looks great," I state. "His color and breathing seem
normal and I think Duncan luckily will end up with only
the tiniest of scars despite all that digging I had to do."

"That is positive news for sure," Declan says. Then he
addresses his cousin. "This is a story you will be able to
use to entertain a lady who someday may ask you to
remove your pants, cousin, though I suggest that she not
be mine in the future." The Tax Man puts his hand out for
Duncan to shake, a sign of true intimacy among Fae types,
and I think that more than a gunshot wound has been
healed in the aftermath of last night's horrid events.

TOOTH 42

A GOOD DEED...

DUNCAN HAS BEEN GONE MERELY seconds when Lover Boy makes his move. He backs me up against the kitchen island and simultaneously loses the towel he's wearing in the process. The man seriously enjoys being naked. "I was vera disappointed to find that you'd left me alone in the bed this morning, Lass. And then I was even more distraught to find you downstairs already washed and dressed." He nuzzles my neck. "Why in such a rush on your day off?"

This close to me, it's blatantly obvious that my being dressed does nothing to dampen the Tax Man's ...enthusiasm. "Yeah, 'bout that, Sweetie... I really don't have the day off like you think I do," I confess. "I volunteer at a free clinic on Loring Avenue on the first and third Wednesday of every month. Today is the third Wednesday of June." As I proceed to explain my involvement with the Open Heart Clinic, his expression goes from disappointment, to annoyance, to something completely different that I can't discern.

Declan picks up the towel and wraps it around himself before plopping into a kitchen chair. "I suppose it is commendable to volunteer as you do. I apologize if I seem less than excited over the news. I was hoping we could spend the whole day together. We haven't had vera much time alone since…" His voice trails off, and I feel both guilty and disappointed.

I try to cheer him up with a promise for the weekend. "We'll have all weekend to ourselves, Declan! I promise! Friday, when that clock hits 5 PM, I'll be completely and utterly at your mercy. Whatever you want to do. Even better…I'll have Mel try to reschedule my later afternoon appointments so we can leave earlier."

The Tax Man smiles, but I can tell something still is bothering him. He shrugs it off and says, "Then I will hold you to your promise, Love. As for now, I better wash and dress so that we aren't late. I am sure there is some way I can be of assistance as well."

I try to envision Jr. Lord *Nuada* at the clinic in his three-piece designer suit, stocking shelves in the supply room or pushing a mop over the bathroom floors, but I just can't picture it, and the clinic sure as hell doesn't need a tax specialist. He gets up to head for the bathroom, but I stop him. "You know, Sweetie, as much as I love having you around, I'm pretty sure you'd find being there incredibly tedious. Our patients don't make appointments; they're all walk-ins. We never know how many will come in or what they'll need help with. Sometimes there will be non-stop patients to see and other times there will be long hours of monotonous paperwork. I know how much you prefer your schedules and routines. This might not be your cup of tea."

His expression is bland. "Tired of me already, Lass?"

Damn it! That's the last impression I was trying to give him. "That's not it at all, Declan. I just don't think you understand what this clinic is really like. I'm afraid you won't be able to find enough things to keep you busy for the whole day, that's all."

He raises an eyebrow and sets his jaw, like he's about to dig his feet in the sand and prepare to battle. "Or perhaps you're just tired of having a constant guard dog and would prefer a lover who is not underfoot twenty-four/seven?"

My face must give me away because he nods and continues, "I see I am correct." He takes my hand in his. "I don't blame you, Rosie. In fact, I heartily sympathize. In the same position, I would not care for it much either. However, I'm sorry to tell you this but though you might think that after last night's capture of Erik Ashton your tooth fairy problems are over, that, Love, is so very far from the truth. There is no doubt the bastard came specifically for you, so when he did not return to his employers with you in tow, they did not simply decide to give up. They inevitably will send someone else to complete the mission. It is the nature of their game. The Black Knight does not think that you are out of danger, and I concur, so until that changes, you are stuck with having a constant watchdog, one who also happens to be your *Mo Shiorghra*. 'Tis not the most romantic of scenarios, I agree, but 'tis the one that has been set before us, and we must see it through."

As the Tax Man heads up to shower, I yell up to him: "Okay, I understand you need to come with me, but can you at least not do the whole 'Brooks Brothers' thing? Please?"

He responds only with a laugh, and I don't have a clue as to what that means. This underscores the hard truth that despite our fairytale style romance of the past few days, the two of us still really are perfect strangers.

It turns out my Tax Man understood my request perfectly. He comes down dressed in a pair of nondescript khakis and a plain white polo shirt. Though I still think he looks drop dead gorgeous, he just might be able to pass as your run-of-the-mill hot guy instead of someone off the cover of a fantasy bodice ripper. He's wearing glasses today, and while we drive, I finally ask him a question that's been bothering me since we first met. "Do you normally wear contact lenses, because I notice you only wear glasses occasionally?"

"The truth is, Lass…I have perfect vision and neither is required," he explains. "But when you ask someone to describe a person, they automatically will note the glasses but will forget specific details such as hair or eye color or the shape of the person's nose. Glasses seem to throw off the brain's capacity to make a complete facial recollection."

He doesn't explain why he feels that disguise is necessary, but I get what he's saying. "Oh, so the glasses are just spy shit?"

He grins. "Aye. Just a little spy shet."

The Tax Man stresses the word shet, which he knows makes me giggle. This seems to break the stress of the morning, so for the rest of our drive we chit chat about general topics, carefully avoiding subjects we ought to be discussing if our relationship is as serious as he claims it is: Things like life goals, children, and in which dimension he expects us to take up residence. You know. Important shet.

Although he seems congenial, it's obvious that Declan is tense. This is evidenced by his jiggling leg and his fingers tapping the steering wheel. I see his jaw clench as we near the clinic. The surrounding neighborhood paints a dismal picture of poverty and hopelessness. At my urging, we have taken my lowly Honda instead of his fancy Mercedes, though the Tax Man insists he still will do the driving. He pulls into the parking lot at the back of the building and parks in a spot designated for volunteer physicians. The residents of the community respect our work, and, for the most part, leave us be, but there is no use tempting them with Declan's expensive car.

Though the staff is composed entirely of volunteers, it usually is the same people on the same day each week. I introduce the Tax Man as my good friend, and if anyone notices the honking big, expensive ring on my left hand, they don't mention it. Since the ring still refuses to budge, I slip a pair of latex gloves over my hands so that it no longer is visible. Today the clinic is fortunate to have, in addition to me, an internist, a podiatrist, and a skin specialist, plus three nurses and a social worker. Since the staff is listed daily on the clinic's website, community residents are aware of the types of doctors and staff on duty. Four different specialists at the same time is a jackpot, so there are quite a few people lined up outside before we even open the doors. I predict correctly that it will be a busy day. The waiting room soon becomes full and more people continue to line up outside, so I am glad for Jimmy, our paid security guard stationed at the front door. Declan notes the Glock at Jimmy's waist and expresses his approval.

The Tax Man intuitively jumps in and helps wherever he is needed. In between patients, I see him filing records, stocking supplies in exam rooms, and signing in patients, remarkably speaking to them in their native languages, which are extremely varied in this part of Salem. I feel guilty for prejudging how he would react to the clinic. I was the one with a Fae prejudice. At this very moment, I find him entertaining a large group of children in the waiting room with magic tricks. I'm pretty sure he's using real magic and not the usual sleight of hand favored by human magicians, but the kids, as well as the adults, are unaware of his true identity and are totally engaged. Noting how comfortable and confident he is around the children makes me think that he'll make a wonderful father someday, which, in turn, makes me feel all ooey gooey inside.

Around noon, D.P. finds me between patients and informs me that the current wait time to see a doctor is approximately two hours and fifteen minutes and that the patients, especially the children, probably are hungry and thirsty. I commend his compassion but explain that there is no extra money in the clinic's budget for refreshments. I suggest that perhaps I could send someone to the local food pantry to pick up some light snacks and bottled water, but the Tax Man, moved by the plight of the patients he's met, wants something better. He offers to order food delivered for them, his treat, and asks how much he should get.

My heart melts at the offer, but I've been working at this clinic long enough to understand its harsh realities. "That's so very kind of you, Declan, but you will be hard pressed to find anyone who will deliver here. Unfortunately, this neighborhood has a notorious reputation for armed robberies."

"What if I offer an extra large tip?" he asks.

I shake my head. "I very much doubt that would be enough. GrubHub and DoorDash drivers don't want to take the risk, and I can't really blame them. They're just people trying to make a living."

The Tax Man thinks for a moment. "I saw a supermarket a few blocks away. Perhaps I can run there myself and pick up some things?" He looks at me and says, "But only if you absolutely swear that you will not leave this building while I am gone, Rosie Lass. You must swear to it!"

He looks so earnest about helping these people that I can't help but kiss him in front of everyone. "I promise, Declan...cross my heart and hope to die."

D.P. goes white at the phrase. "Never say you hope to die, Love! 'Tis bad energy!"

I forgot that the Fae are big on the power of words. "I

just mean I absolutely promise you I won't go anywhere. Jimmy's right out front if anyone tries to do anything funny."

The Tax Man kisses me again and then is off on his quest to feed our patients. Years later, whenever I remember this day, I will also forever remember the old adage about no good deed ever going unpunished.

TOOTH 43

RHONDA'S RELAX ROOM

After I watch Declan leave, I head to the breakroom to grab a bottle of water before seeing my next patient. The layout of the clinic requires me to walk all the way to the front of the building near the reception desk and waiting area to reach the staffroom, then all the way back to the end of the building where the two dental exam rooms are located. While this arrangement is not optimal for efficiency, it did save our charity a substantial amount of investment in remodeling costs, because the building that now houses the Open Heart Clinic was at one time Salem's most notorious massage parlor: a lively, popular spot called Rhonda's Relax Room.

The business offered every type of illicit service one might need: prostitution, drugs, gambling, loan sharking, and even money laundering. For years, the Powers That Be turned a blind eye to the goings on at Rhonda's. It was whispered, but never proven, that the place was run by the Irish mob out of Boston, making its owners confidently untouchable until a Federal indictment in 2019 put several "owners" in jail. This was followed by the Covid pandemic which closed many businesses in the area, and Rhonda's Relax Room eventually was boarded up and offered for sale.

The price was right; the location was easily accessible by public transportatio; and the private massage rooms that already were walled in with working doors saved the need for extensive rehabbing. The four rooms in the front of the clinic are dedicated to the medical doctors and fitted with standard supplies and equipment. The two larger rooms in the back are outfitted with dental chairs, drills, and other equipment necessary for basic dental care that required a little extra space. These two rooms, one on the left of the hallway and one on the right, had the unique feature of an extra exterior exit door that led to a small alley, most likely a throwback to a time when the building's customers required privacy and a quick escape from their illicit activities. It was easier and cheaper for the clinic simply to bolt these doors from the outside rather than to remove them entirely, thus leaving both of the dental exam rooms with an unused second exit.

With my water bottle in hand, I grab the patient file from the rack on the exam room door and peruse it. My patient is a 45-year-old male named John Smith. He's complaining of severe pain on the right side of his mouth, and the nurse signed him in at the front desk as an emergency. The fact that my patient is an adult and obviously using an alias doesn't surprise me. The needs of the free clinic don't offer me the freedom to see only pediatric patients. So many people are in need of help that we try to treat anyone who walks through our door to the very best of our abilities, even if they happen to have shady backgrounds requiring them to use aliases.

I knock once and enter as is my custom, but I'm immediately stopped in my tracks by an eerie sense of *deja vu*. I feel as though I already have experienced this moment, which is ridiculous because I've never had a premonition in my life. The patient looks at me but doesn't speak. "Good Afternoon, Mr. Smith. I'm Dr. Parker," I say. "What seems to be the problem today?" I note he is wearing a jacket despite the summer heat, but even this doesn't seem odd, as the community's homeless often layer their clothes fearing their theft.

Mr. Smith grunts and points to the right side of his mouth, which does appear to be a bit swollen. I wash my hands in the small sink and slip on a clean pair of latex gloves before grabbing a probe and concave mirror from my tray of nearby instruments. "Well, let's just see what's going on in there, shall we? Open wide, please."

The patient opens his mouth and I step closer to look inside. Only a few seconds pass before I feel something hard and cold pressing into my gut. Startled, I step away and see that Mr. Smith now has a large pistol aimed at me. I try to rush to the door to the hall, but the man with the gun is faster. He grabs me around the waist and covers my mouth and nose with a sweet-smelling odor that I guess to be ether or chloroform. I struggle and kick while trying to get loose, but the man's hold on me is too strong. I begin to feel the drug penetrating my nervous system; my knees don't seem to be able to hold me up, and I'm starting to see double.

A second man, much larger in stature than the first, enters from the alley exit door, the one that's supposed to be bolted from the outside. Suddenly, I realize why the scene seems so strangely familiar. It matches the one in my nightmare from only a few nights before in which the Chechens were cutting off my fingers and toes. Instead of a saw, however, the second man has a syringe which he roughly jabs into my right arm. I try to scream but my tongue and lips won't move like I want them to, and the sound gurgles and dies in my throat. My imposter patient removes the drug soaked rag from my mouth, replaces it with duct tape, and zip ties my hands behind my back. I am dizzy and confused, and when the big guy throws me over his shoulder, my weak struggles don't amount to much.

I try to understand why no one is coming to my rescue, but even in my limited capacity note that with the hallway door shut and the exam room so far removed from the waiting area, Jimmy the security guy isn't able to hear anything going on back here. Moreover, although it seems much longer from my perspective, I'm guessing this whole scenario probably has taken less than two minutes.

The men exit the clinic unseen from the alley door. I blink in the harsh, bright sunlight, my head still upside down while I hang over the second man's shoulder. I hear the click of a trunk release, and then I am tipped over and unceremoniously dumped inside. Hitting the bottom of the trunk hard, I smash the same cheek Erik dislocated the night before on the car's wheel well. The pain acts like a shot to my brain, and for the tiniest second, my foggy head clears. I should be using this brief moment of clarity to come up with a viable escape plan, but the only thought that forms is about Declan. *Oh, Tax Man...I think I'm in love with you...and it looks like I'm not going to get the chance to tell you...*

TOOTH 44

LOST AND FOUND

CONSCIOUSNESS SLOWLY CREEPS UP on me; one thought melts completely away, like an ice cube in a bowl, before the next one appears. Everything is black. Inky black. It takes me a long time to realize that this is because I'm blindfolded and not because I've gone blind as I'd originally believed. My hands are still secured behind my back, and the memory of how that occurred scratches at the far reaches of my brain. An image floats to the surface: Me. Kissing someone. Someone taller than me, but I can't see their face. I struggle to make my brain work, but as hard as I try, I remain absolutely confused about people and places. Everything's a blur. Nothing is clear. I don't know who this person in my mind is, but I can feel their grief. And anger. No. Not anger. It's rage. Lots of grief and rage. Then, just as I begin to chip away at the bits and pieces of my melty thoughts, I slip back into the darkness and once again I don't think or feel anything.

In this state, it's impossible for me to measure the passage of time. I'm completely unsure how many seconds, or minutes, or hours have come and gone since my last conscious thought. The next time I reach some level of awareness, I start to feel physical things. Lots of them. In fact, I'm aware of them all in red-hot discomfort: my throbbing cheek, an open and burning cut on my lip, a painful pressure on my ass and tailbone from sitting on something hard and unyielding, and so much pain in my left hand that I barely can stand it. For a brief moment, I worry that the bad guys have cut some fingers off from that hand, but a quick check with my right hand determines that I still have all five digits on both.

My mouth is desert parched underneath the tape covering it, but I have the opposite problem under the seat of my pants. I realize I am damp, and I smell the acrid odor of urine, which means that I've most likely peed myself on top of everything else. I want to cry, but I know that if I do, my nose will get stuffy and runny, and since I'm currently unable to breathe through my mouth, I will end up suffocating on my own snot. This definitely is not the way I want to go out.

The inside of my head is still fuzzy, but now I can remember more of what happened. I remember being at the clinic, seeing patients, and kissing Declan goodbye. This recollection squeezes my heart and hurts more than all of my physical injuries combined. I waited too long to tell the Tax Man how I feel about him, even though I think I knew it from our very first meeting. Even as he stormed out of my office, growling at me with wet pants over his arm, I knew deep down, as sure as anything, that

I'd just experienced love at first sight. I know; it's utterly ridiculous to use such a worn out, fairy tale cliché. But the idea of being someone's soul mate is just as crazy, and since I sincerely doubt I'll make it out of here alive, I need to leave this life knowing that Declan is my *Mo Shiorghra* and I am his. I call out to all the goddesses I know for one single, final request: please let the Tax Man know just how much I love him.

Thinking about Declan reminds me of the ring on my left hand. I poke around again with my right hand and I determine that the ring is still in place, but touching the finger it's on makes me moan in pain. It hurts like a sono-fabitch, and I'm guessing it's broken or dislocated. The sharpness of the pain makes the bile rise up in my throat and I feel as though I will throw up, which is the number one thing I don't want to do. Not with my mouth covered like it is. I sit still and breathe deeply through my nose, willing my stomach to settle down.

I use every deep breathing method I ever learned during my brief stint in Druid school. In this way, I successfully bring myself to a peaceful state of conscious-ness and then ask the Universe for a merciful outcome while I quietly resign myself to its fate. At that very same moment, I hear the first sounds of gunfire.

In all the lost hours of silence, this sound catches me off guard and I jump, raising my heart rate right back up to panic mode. The space around me erupts into chaos with the sounds of automatic weapons, shouting, and the screams of men in obvious pain. I roll to my side and try to shrink myself down. I hear bullets pinging off metal all around me, and I smell a sulfuric odor not unlike fireworks being released. I try to refocus on my breathing techniques, but in the midst of the most negative type of energy caused by the violence, I find peace in my mind impossible. Instead, I just lay there and shake.

I think I hear someone calling my name, but with my mouth taped all I can do is squeal and moan. Then someone grabs at me and lifts me up under my knees and starts moving at a quick pace, all the time mumbling a series of incomprehensible words. It sounds like my Tax Man, but with all the noise and confusion I can't be sure. I try to squirm and break away, and then the person puts me down and pulls off the blindfold covering my eyes. I squint in the sudden brightness after being in the dark for so long. The man in front of me is dressed from head to toe in black tactical gear, an automatic weapon slung over his shoulder and a hood covering his entire head with only the barest eye slit cut out from which to see. I don't recognize him as my Declan, and still being in panic mode, I try to scoot away but he stops me. He tucks me into his lap and pulls off the Gaiter Hood, and I recognize his green eyes and the ginger stubble on his chin causing me to burst into tears.

"It's gonna be okay, Rosie, Love. It's over now. I promise ya. Let me get the tape off your mouth, Lass. It's gonna hurt a mite, so I'm gonna do it as fast as I ken. Count with me, 1...2..." Then he rips off the tape before he says 3.

It hurts like a sonofabitch, and I yelp. My hands are still tied behind my back; so my Tax Man, who now looks more like Spy Man, pulls a big, scary knife from his belt and cuts the zip ties and carefully eases my arms to the front of my body, all the while trying to rub sensation back into them. He notes the ring finger on my left hand and swears. "Those damn mathair feckers! They dislocated your knuckle trying to get the ring off. Glad to know the bastards are all dead."

It's then that I notice the blood splatter on the front of his vest, mixed in with some type of unidentified gray matter. His touching that knuckle sends shock waves of pain straight to my nervous system, and I feel my stomach roiling in reaction.

Declan pulls me in a little closer and whispers to me in a voice so layered with grief and regret I want to kiss him immediately, but my face is swollen and gooey from the tape and it probably would only make that cut on my lip worse. "Oh, Love, I am so very sorry this happened to you," Declan says. "'Tis my fault. I should never have left you. Not last night and not today. I do not know how I will ever make this up to you, *Mo Shiorghra*."

There are so many things I want to say to him, need to tell him, but my head is feeling strange and woozy, and the bile is rising up and burning the back of my throat. The only thing I possibly can do in this very special moment is to throw up in my Soul Mate's lap.

TOOTH 45

ROSIE MY LOVE

I WOULD BE TOTALLY MORTIFIED if I still weren't so absolutely out of it. Everything seems to be occurring in slow motion, and all of the words I attempt to speak chunk up in my mouth along with the remnants of my vomit. Puke drips off my Tax Man's body armor and pools on the ground between us. I can tell Declan bravely is trying not to take any deep breaths and gag while also calling out for help. "Dunc...come give me a hand here, will ya?"

Another man in tactical gear appears from somewhere behind me. He pulls off his Gaiter mask, and I recognize my Tax Man's cousin. "How does our Rosie fare, Fitz?" he asks.

"My Lady seems to be without major injury but is feeling quite ill from the drugs she was given," Declan states. "Can you please carry her over to Robyn so he can attend to her needs? I need to locate the Black Knight for further orders before we can leave."

"Aye, Sir. I will see that your Lady is safe with the Doc," Duncan replies.

D.P.'s cousin bends down and scoops me up under the knees, which is impressive because I'm guessing I weigh more than he does. Plus, even I can tell that I reek of sweat, urine, and vomit. I am wholly disgusting and not a pleasure to carry anywhere, especially across an entire parking lot to a waiting white van with its engine running. I try to apologize, but it comes out as "Sto slurry, Duncn'...I know I stin bad."

"Save your energy, Rosie. Ya ben through hell. Like I said this mornin', yar a courageous woman, ya are. Don' you be worryin' about being ill. Robyn will take good care of ya."

Duncan frees up a hand and bangs on the rear doors of the van. They swing open, and another man, obviously Fae as well, jumps out to help lift me up inside what is clearly a mobile medical unit. They slide me onto a stretcher, and the other man introduces himself. "Hello, Dr. Parker. I'm Dr. Brannigan. I'm going to make sure you haven't sustained any injuries that require hospitalization, okay?"

I nod my head in consent, and the doctor takes my vitals. It takes me a few minutes to realize just who this guy is; Dr. Robyn Brannigan is the leading specialist in Fae medicine and genetics in the Otherworld as well as a highly respected obstetrician here in the Mundane World. He's the head of obstetrics at the prestigious North Shore Medical Center here in Salem, and because he is here, treating me in an unmarked, high-tech ambulance, he's obviously part of the Black Knight's spy shet. These guys move in elite circles.

He does a thorough exam, draws blood, and takes x-rays of my dislocated finger. By the time my Tax Man joins me in the van, Dr. Brannigan pronounces me in good enough shape to skip the hospital and go straight home to recuperate. "You were given a powerful mix of drugs, Dr. Parker, and it will take at least another 24 to 36 hours before they wear off completely," the doctor explains, "but I don't believe you will suffer any long-term effects. I'm going to hold off straightening that finger until tomorrow, as I don't want to add any more narcotics into your system right now. I'll swing by tomorrow and take care of that finger then. Your face still is pretty bruised and swollen, but it doesn't appear to have any fractures, so time will be the best medicine for that. For now, I suggest plenty of rest and as much clear fluids and soft food as your stomach will allow you to hold down. The drugs in your system probably will make you queasy and a bit dizzy for another ten or twelve hours. I recommend that you have someone help you to get around, and until then, don't get up, take a shower, or wander around the house on your own. You don't want to add a serious fall to your existing problems right now."

The Tax Man jumps in before I can answer. "I will personally see that my Lady follows all your orders, Robyn. You have my promise on that."

The doctor smiles at my Tax Man and adds, "I have no doubt she's in the best of hands, Fitz."

I feel the van begin to move. Declan holds my good

hand all the way home but is unusually quiet. I doze off, but when the van stops, I awake with a start. The doors open, and I note we are parked in the back alley behind my house. The doctor helps Declan get me off the stretcher and out of the van. I can tell by the shadows on my garage roof that it is late afternoon or early evening. My neighbors are in the yard, but the two men don't seem concerned by their presence, so I figure that they're magically veiling our activity. At the back door, the Tax Man thanks the doctor for his help, then carries me through the kitchen and upstairs to my bedroom on his own.

By now I am beyond ripe, and all I want is a good, long, hot shower. I don't even need to ask. Declan runs the water in the shower and helps me undress. He sits me on the shower bench and angles the water so I can sit back and let it run over my aching body. He then undresses as well and steps into the shower to help me wash, even lathering up my hair and shampooing it for me. This has nothing to do with sexy time. This is all about simple, deep-felt care. I feel love and concern in his touch, but also angst about what happened during his absences. I know we need to talk about this, but I don't want to spoil the peace of this moment.

He dries me off and helps me put on a pair of pajamas he's dug out of my dresser drawer. They are faded and worn and have images of SpongeBob printed all over them along with a pale burgundy stain on one sleeve from the time I spilled wine on them while watching TV. It crosses my mind that this is so far from the stuff of which romance novels are made that I don't know whether to laugh or cry because it's happening to me.

Once I'm settled in bed and the Tax Man somehow has found himself a new set of clothes from God knows where, he sets about conjuring up some plain chicken broth and apple juice for me. Though I'm not a fan of either, I try to consume some of it in appreciation of his attempts at nursing me. I am neither hungry nor thirsty right now. What I really want is an honest conversation. I know we both have questions and things we want to say to each other. I literally can feel it, like a thick fog that has filled the space between us.

After a few moments of deathly silence Declan speaks first. "I am more sorry than I ever can express, my Love. What happened to ya' 'tis all my fault. For my very life, I ken not understand why I ever made those decisions to leave you as I did. I swear…it is not in my nature to make such grievous errors in judgment. I have always been a very logical and cautious man, but in these past few days, I do not know what has come over me. My *Mathair* truly is right. I have been cursed by the Universe for what happened to my brother at our birth. I waited 20 years for my *Mo Shiorghra* to come to me and then I almost lose her to death, not once, but twice in less than forty-eight hours because of my complete stupidity. I cannot inflict my life curse upon you or onto my service to *I Idir*. I have offered my resignation to the Black Knight, and though he did not accept it, it is only a matter of time until he realizes I am not the man for the job. Difficult as that was, it is nothing compared to having to ask you to walk away from me and my offer of handfasting. I care for ya' too much to allow ya' to join yourself to one that the Universe looks so unfavorably on. Feck! I would rather have taken

Duncan's brass bullet than watch you walk away, but I believe 'tis for the best, Rosie Lass."

As much as I want to be a calm, rational, adult woman, I'm too exhausted, too mentally weary, and too physically achy to have this discussion with the love of my life. So, I lean over and pinch him on the arm. Hard. He absolutely isn't expecting this. He jumps a bit in his chair. "Shet! Did you just pinch me, Lass?"

I roll over so that I'm looking Declan Phineas Fitzpatrick, Lord *Mac Nuada*, straight in the eye while I talk to him. "Listen up, Tax Man, and listen good. I've been twice threatened with a gun to my belly, slapped in the face, and had my finger dislocated. I've dug a bullet out of a strange man's groin, peed myself, and thrown up in my lover's lap. I do not have the energy or patience to have a few 'go-arounds' with someone who can argue the pants off of me...literally."

D.P. starts to open his mouth but I cut him off. "I'm not finished, Tax Man. Has it ever occurred to you that everything that has happened in the past few days was the exact way the Universe wanted it to happen?"

He makes a face. "I do not think the Universe works in such a crazy manner, Rosie."

"Bullshit, Declan! Nobody knows how the Universe works! That's why it's such a damn big mystery. Let me ask you this...how were you able to find me after the Chechens took me out of the clinic? No one saw us leave. There are no security cameras. You didn't even know how they escaped or in which direction. Yet, you were able to find and rescue me before anything really bad happened to me. How, Tax Man?"

He blinks a few times before answering, as if the same thoughts are now reaching him as well. "You called to me, Rosie…you opened a line of mental communication and you spoke to me. That mental connection stayed open the whole time, despite all the trauma and drugs you were experiencing. I was able to find where they were holding you."

"And just what was it I said to you during that mental communication, Declan?" I ask.

He gets a little choked up, and the words come out strangled. "Ya' declared that you loved me, Lass, and you didn't want ta pass on from this life without telling me. My heart almost stopped right there and then, Love. I drove like a mad man back to the clinic, but you'd already been taken. I was without reason. I contacted the Black Knight and my team, and we contrived a plan to retrieve you in the quickest and safest manner. There was never a man so happy to be vomited upon. I knew then that you were gonna be okay, Rosie, my Love." He pauses and then quietly asks, "It's true, then…you love me, *Mo Shiorghra?*"

"I do, Declan. It was the only thing I could think of when I realized I might never be able to tell you in person. It shoved away all my second thoughts, my doubts, my 'what-ifs,' and made it very real in the here and now. The Universe has made it all possible, Tax Man; it's made me face the facts about what is truly important to me."

D.P. takes my hands in his and kisses them, my lip being in no shape for intimate contact. "I have wanted to tell you that I've loved you as well on that vera night I showed up with your scone basket, but I was sure ya'd think me a crazy man, a psycho stalker. We hardly knew each other. I was lost as to how I could even get to know ya well enough to tell ya how I felt. When the Black Knight offered up the possibility of us spending more time together, I took it as a sign."

"Duh…because it probably was a sign. No coincidences…remember?"

"Aye. No coincidences, Love." Declan looks at me intently, and his face shows every feeling inside him. "Does this mean you agree to our handfasting, Rosie?"

"It does. Absolutely. But can we take a rain check on this conversation, Tax Man? I'm really in need of a good night's sleep."

Declan gets up from the chair to lean over and kiss the top of my head. "Of course, Love. You need to rest. We can finish this conversation tomorrow." He settles himself back down in the chair. "I will be right here if you need to get up."

I stare at him in utter disbelief. "You're not going to sleep in this bed next to me?"

He shakes his head in the negative. "I think you would rest better if…"

I don't let him finish. I pull the covers back from the other side of the bed and pat the mattress with my good hand. "Hell no, Tax Man! We're not playing that game again. Been there, done that. You come here and park that cute Fae ass next to me, or else I'm gonna insist on going to work tomorrow."

My Tax Man laughs, and it warms my heart. "Well, Lass, we certainly wouldn't want that." He undresses and slides in next to me. "I've parked my ass as requested," he whispers, "but only for sleeping this evening, Love.

Doctor's orders." He turns off the light and holds me close.

"That's ok. I'll take a raincheck for anything more," I tease.

"Agreed, Love. I do like those rainchecks of yours, Dr. Parker. Vera, vera much."

TOOTH 46

THE COTTAGE YOU LIVE IN

A GOOD NIGHT'S rest and the simple passage of time does wonders to clear the cobwebs in my head left by the Chechen drug cocktail. Rest does nothing, however, to relieve the overall damage done to my body. The side of my face is still painfully sore and covered in multiple, vibrant shades of blacks, blues and greens. My split lip is crusted over with an ugly scab resembling a large caterpillar trying to crawl into my mouth, and the glue from the duct tape has left me with a pimply rash under my nose and on my chin. The state of my face currently would scare the bejeezus out of every one of my young patients. Furthermore, even though Dr. Brannigan realigned my left ring finger, it is still swollen to twice its normal size and totally useless. On the good Doc's orders and much solicitous haranguing by my Tax Man, I reluctantly agree to take a short leave of absence from my practice, something I have never done during my entire career.

I call Mel to explain a little of what has happened, and I give her my word that she may visit me at home later tonight, at which time I will give her the whole juicy enchilada, as she so colorfully calls it. A retired dentist friend of mine is willing to fill-in for me for the next six weeks while I not only recuperate but also tie the knot with the Tax Man. (Yes, we literally will be tying a knot... that's where this wedding expression originated.) As for the cause of my injuries, the official story that we will tell people is that I fell off a ladder while hanging drapes. This isn't nearly as exciting as what really happened, but it is more acceptable in the Mundane world than declaring that I'm a tooth fairy who was taken hostage by foreign agents bent on dominating the Fae Otherworld.

During breakfast and amidst a lot of ass grabbing, Declan and I decide to formally handfast as quickly as possible. We agree that we've experienced more together during the past two weeks than some dating couples do over an entire year. And, considering that we are both intelligent, professional adults, we naively presume that we'll be able to overcome any potential relationship obstacles with logic and maturity despite being practically strangers. Many years from now, I'm sure we will reminisce about our nonchalant attitude and have a good, hearty laugh about it, but this morning at my kitchen table it seems like a damn good plan.

We also decide to tell our non-Fae friends and colleagues that we're engaged but have no firm wedding date in mind, and then sometime later in the not-too-distant future we'll announce that we ran off and eloped. We think this is the easiest way to handle everything with most of the people we know; but the Tax Man, always the numbers guy, determines that for practical business purposes we need to have a civil ceremony here in the Mundane world some time soon. This makes perfect sense to me so I agree, though I'm so bat-shit-crazy in love and lust that I'm pretty sure that if Declan asked me to ride an elephant bareback through *I Idir* wearing nothing but my birthday suit I'd probably agree, hosting the same stupid grin on my face that I'm wearing right now.

After my recent experiences, and in light of my brand, new future, I've decided to take the advice of one of my old Druid teachers. He had counseled that when faced with a fear of the unknown, one should put it in writing and then offer the words up to the Fate of the Universe. Thus, I've decided to keep a journal of my thoughts as I move into my new life phase. I still have a lot of important things to discuss with my *Mo Shiorghra*, including the very important question about whether to have children and when to start moving forward if we both agree we want them. Also, there's the question of where we'll live, both here and in *I Idir*. But the most important issue of all is how in the Universe will I ever make any headway in getting along with the Tax Man's hellacious, nasty-ass *Mathair*?

Right now, the rest of the important stuff can wait. The Doctor to the Fae Stars has given me the A-Okay to resume normal activities determined by my body's physical limits. After a hearty breakfast and a quick inventory,

I determine that I'm more than physically able to tackle collecting a few of the rain checks my Tax Man owes me. So for now, I leave you with this sincere blessing,

Beannachd leat fein agus leat,
A bharrachd air a' bhothan anns a bheil thu a' fuireach.
Gum biodh tughadh math air a' mhullach,
Agus tha an fheadhainn a-staigh air an deagh mhaidseadh.

Bless you and yours,
As well as the cottage you live in.
May the roof overhead be well thatched,
And those inside be well matched.

* * *

Find out what happens to Rosie and Declan in
Toothaches and Wedding Cakes

Also by Victoria Rocus

The Tooth Fairy Chronicles

Tooth Decay With A Side Of Fae

Toothaches And Wedding Cakes

Baby Tooth And Tangled Roots

More from Serenade Publishing

Brigadier Station Series

By Sarah Williams:

The Brothers of Brigadier Station

The Sky over Brigadier Station

The Legacies of Brigadier Station

Christmas at Brigadier Station (An Outback Christmas Novella)

The Outback Governess (A Sweet Outback Novella)

Heart of the Hinterland Series

By Sarah Williams:

The Dairy Farmer's Daughter

Their Perfect Blend

Beyond the Barre

Primrose Series

By Tanya Renee

Prairie Sky

Prairie Nights

Prairie Fire

Prairie Hearts

The Spring of Love Series

By Virginia Taylor

Forever Delighted

Forever Amused

Forever Heartfelt

A New Page

By Aimee MacRae

It Happened in Paris

By Michelle Beesley

Mim and Wiggy's Grand Adventure

By Jay McKenzie

Winner Winner Chicken Dinner

By Sarah Jackson

For more information visit:

www.serenadepublishing.com

ABOUT THE AUTHOR

Victoria Rocus is a retired educator, accomplished miniaturist, and full-time author living near the home of country music, Nashville, Tennessee, USA. When she's not writing new adventures for her imaginary friends, catering beach parties for mermaids, or finding homes for orphaned dragons, she's building and rehabbing one-of-a-kind dollhouses and accessories, just like her favorite character, Dr. Rosie Parker. Many of her multiple miniature buildings are 1/12 scale replicas of settings from her unique fantasy stories.

Victoria started her writing career as a weekly blogger while still teaching middle school language arts. Now retired from the educational field, she's been able to make writing a full-time adventure, penning several fantasy and romance stories she hopes readers will enjoy with both a sigh and a smile. *Tooth Decay With A Side Of Fae* is her debut novel and the fulfillment of a life-long dream.

Find out more at: victoriarocusauthor.com

instagram.com/victoriarocusauthor
tiktok.com/@victoriarocusauthor

Acknowledgments

Author Ernest Hemingway once said, "Writing, at its best, is a lonely life." With apologies to one of the twentieth century's literary geniuses, I heartily disagree. Sorry, Ernie…but my writing journey has been anything but solitary. In addition to the clan of lively and outspoken characters who live rent free in my head, I've been inspired, supported, and pushed along by a large number of very special people. I'd like to take this opportunity to thank the remarkable group behind this story.

First, I owe a deep sense of gratitude to Sarah Williams, CEO of Serenade Publishing, for taking a chance on an unknown author living in a completely different hemisphere, with additional thanks to the very patient and talented staff at Serenade that helped put Rose and Declan in the best light possible.

From the bottom of my heart, I also send a big hug and my deepest, heart-felt thanks to Marcia Joy Wurmbrand Crabtree, aka "The Lady of the Words," as well as the very best friend, coach, and draft editor any writer could ever possibly desire. You made me believe this writing dream was possible and never once complained about my obsessive love affair with unnecessary commas. I am blessed to share this crazy ride with you.

To Carol Peden Fuller, Donna Gentile Ruth, Michele

S. Kaspar, Shannon Greene, Daniel Caddigan, and Kaia Viney, along with talented fellow authors, Arla Jones and K.C. Nord; you are the most awesome Beta Reader and Gold Medal Cheer Team any author could ever have. Thank you for your undivided loyalty and support of each and every piece I've ever penned, including a crazy, serial cookbook that doesn't include a single image of food. You people are the absolute best and I am forever grateful for your friendship and guidance.

On a professional note, I'd also like to thank Mr. Mark W. Strama, Attorney at Law / Tax Accountant, for helping develop Declan Fitzpatrick as an IRS Enrolled Agent and certified "numbers guy," as well as Mr. James K. Kenny, Attorney at Law, who patiently answered my never-ending, and often ridiculous, legal questions.

To my beloved family…my husband, Victor, for supporting this second dream career that took the place of the retirement you originally had imagined, and my sons Steven and Michael, as well as my lovely daughter-in-law, Allison, for believing in me even when I couldn't. Love you all.

Lastly, to my dearest readers, *le mile buiochas* ("a thousand words of gratitude") for taking a chance on a debut novel about a formidable tooth fairy and her handsome Tax Man. I know you have lots of wonderful choices in book land, and I truly appreciate you picking this one up. Hugs to you all.

Made in the USA
Columbia, SC
29 April 2025

57319522R00163